D0427001

Mormama

TOR BOOKS BY KIT REED

@Expectations

Thinner Than Thou

Dogs of Truth

The Baby Merchant

The Night Children

Enclave

Where

Mormama

Mormama

KIT REED

A TOM DOHERTY ASSOCIATES BOOK
NEW YORK

This is a work of fiction. All of the characters, organizations, and events portrayed in this novel are either products of the author's imagination or are used fictitiously.

MORMAMA

A Tor Book
Published by Tom Doherty Associates
175 Fifth Avenue
New York, NY 10010

www.tor-forge.com

Tor® is a registered trademark of Macmillan Publishing Group, LLC.

The Library of Congress Cataloging-in-Publication Data is available upon request.

ISBN 978-0-7653-9044-8 (hardcover)
ISBN 978-0-7653-9046-2 (e-book)

Our books may be purchased in bulk for promotional, educational, or business use. Please contact your local bookseller or the Macmillan Corporate and Premium Sales Department at 1-800-221-7945, extension 5442, or by e-mail at MacmillanSpecialMarkets@macmillan.com.

First Edition: May 2017

Printed in the United States of America

0 9 8 7 6 5 4 3 2 1

For David

Mormama

CHAPTER 1

Dell

"I happened to be in the neighborhood, so I thought I'd drop by."

Not a line that gets you in the door no questions asked, Dell knows. Not on this street in this drab urban wasteland where the city swallowed the neighborhood whole and moved on, leaving a trail of ruined streets flanked by overgrown parking lots and tin sheds and mutilated houses—all but the one he is approaching.

He is here for a reason. When they returned his clothes the day the doctors cleared him, the pockets were empty except for this index card. It fell out of the sagging tweed jacket stuffed into the top of the plastic bag. It reads,

553 MAY STREET
JACKSONVILLE, FLORIDA

It's all he has of his past life. This and the flash drive. The thing slid out of his shoe while he was dressing, so sleek that his first instinct was to smash the object like a scorpion. Instead he shoved it into the jacket; he got dizzy looking at it, and it wasn't just the head injury. He couldn't throw it away; he couldn't have it in his life. By the time it ate its way through the lining, he'd collected so much stuff that he had a dozen places to stash it. He needs to bury the damn thing.

Maybe here, at this address.

Something about 553 shouts, *home,* although it looms like a dowager queen waiting for him to explain himself. With its fluted columns and French windows coated with grit, the once white house looks like Tara, all used up and kicked to the curb. The row of trees to the right does nothing to hide the dented metal shed on the seedy parking lot that replaced another big house. To its left, a brick veneer front with combination windows hangs like a mask on an ex-mansion, with external fire escapes clamped on the sides to bring it up to code. A sign sunk in the green cement signifying *lawn* reads: MARVISTA.

Apartments, boardinghouse or crack motel? He doesn't know. Is this even the right neighborhood? He rubs the grit off a brass plate bolted to the gate in front of Tara here. It reads: 553 May Street, and underneath, *Ellis.* Reflexively, he fingers the frayed index card he's carried ever since the doctors signed off on him and the cab company settled his bill. He left the hospital in clothes returned in the regulation plastic bag marked with his room number. The frayed tweed jacket, the shirt, the canvas boots looked strange to him. It's all strange. The taxi that hit him knocked everything out of his head.

Fretting, he went through the pockets: no wallet, no ID, no glasses, just an unmarked envelope stuffed with small bills— payoff, he supposes— and this index card with the address in black ballpoint. He's carried it for so long and studied it so closely that he doesn't need to look.

Yep. This is the place.

Dell can't tell you exactly why he's at the Ellis family's front gate. Unless he won't. He is either a godsend or a threat to the women living in the house, and. This is bad. He doesn't know which. The taxi knocked everything out of his head except the guilt.

Dell is not his real name. He grabbed this one off the wall like a hat off a hook. "Dell," he told the others holed up in the gulch below the overpass where he bedded down when he reached Jacksonville. You don't just walk in and put down your stuff without some kind of introduction. He liked the way it sounded. No last name. Dell was good enough for them. Look at it this way. Who, temporarily sleeping in a mess of cartons, wants to give up his particulars to guys who might give him up to the guys out looking for him.

"My name is Dell." Dell what? To be determined. It's past time to pick up a last name and put it on. No point scoring new ID until he can pay for that fake license, fake SSN, but still. He's highly qualified, but he hasn't had a real job since the accident. He used to be good at what he did. Tech, he thinks, but the details blurred somewhere between there and here. Situational amnesia?

Look. There are things a man needs to forget. He doesn't really want to talk about the psychic train wreck that spilled him out here in the shadow of the interstate, where he showers at the Y as often as he can and takes care of the rest whenever. Not yet. Maybe the rest will come back to him when he penetrates this old ark.

If he really wants to know who he is, and that's what bothers him.

Open the damn gate, stupid, go up on their fancy steamboat porch and knock on that door like a man, and when they ask you in, let them tell *you* what you're doing here. Check out the interior through that beveled glass and work on your damn smile while you wait for them to come. Smile. Whoever you used to be, people liked you. Talk your way in.

Then what? Not sure.

Dell may not know why he's here, but he spent weeks researching the occupants before he marched out today. The Ellis family owns 553. Have done ever since Dakin Ellis, the paterfamilias or whatever, broke ground in 1888 and built this heap for his new wife. It's in all the city directories between then and now, and he checked every one. It gave him a sense of purpose. He moved on to a library PC with greasy keys, searched every Web reference to the family and followed up with visits to local historical societies, museums, decaying files in the belly of the *Jacksonville Journal*.

Procrastinating? Pretty much.

Jacksonville pioneers, the Ellises, one of the city's first families, with too many men lost to notable accidents and untimely deaths. In its own way that's creepy, and the creepiest thing? Their old world shifted and the neighborhood went from seedy to dangerous, but there are three old women still in the house like clueless passengers wondering why all the deck chairs are sliding downhill. He needs to get in there and find out what brought him to this old ark.

And he can't get past the ornamental iron gate. It isn't locked. It's him.

Dell backs into the shade of their big live oak and considers. Scope the territory, he decides. Look for a way in and when you find it, leave. Let the rest come later.

It had damn well better!

He didn't expect to be in Jacksonville this long. He slouched into this overgrown city months ago, looking to locate the address on this card and figure out what comes next. Instead he retreated into research, the perfect paradigm for what he is right now: all movement, no action. In late summer it was like walking the ocean bottom with the whole Atlantic on his back. Fall here was easy but in northern Florida, even winter is harder than he thought. It never snows, at least he doesn't think it does, but it's too cold to sleep in the elbow of the overpass. The other guys moved out weeks ago but until last night, he temporized. It was the first frost.

Even his teeth got cold. Whatever he has to do inside this old heap, he'd better get started. He enters through a gap in the hedge and darts for the ornamental shrubs below the long front porch with its grimy rockers and dead plants overflowing cement urns. The jumble of hibiscus and bougainvillea is so thick that a person coming out the front door might or might not hear something, but she won't see him running along below. He rounds the corner and drops into a crouch, looking for a basement window. He won't know that the first Dakin Ellis built this place like a plantation house in flood country, with an unbroken foundation: proof against high tides on the St. Johns River— in sinkhole territory, which Dakin didn't know.

Safely behind the house, Dell steps away to study the back. A long porch runs the width of the house, with stairs coming down from the kitchen to ground level. The main business goes on above his head, on the sprawling first floor of the Ellis house. There are three rusty lawn chairs on the back porch, a weathered table and an old Kelvinator, leftover red wagon, ancient tricycle. Down here, lattice hides whatever goes on within.

Basement windows. Basement door, Dell supposes, with everything in him running ahead to winter. Openings just waiting to be cracked. He'll find one where he can come and go without being seen and stake out a place. Then he waits. Until. The thought drops off a cliff. He can't go there. Yet.

Feeling his way along the lattice, Dell moves into the long shadow of the back steps. Here. Hinges in the lattice at the point where the stairs intersect the porch. This part opens and shuts like a secret door. He raises the latch and ducks inside.

As he does, a scrap of Dante comes back to him: "Abandon hope, all ye who enter here." For one riveting second, his blood stops running. Words drop into his head like ice cubes, **Get out before it's too late.** *What?*

Hell with it! This new squat is everything he hoped. Big. He could roll in a Harley, if he had one. Furnish the place if he wanted, and they'd never know. Late afternoon sunlight slants in. He turns off his flash. He's a spy, safe behind enemy lines.

Then why is every hair on the back of his neck standing up?

The place is dead clean. The floor is bald, as though enemies torched the crops and salted the earth before they moved on. There's no door into the main basement that he can find; no damn windows! To his left, a cement rectangle spreads in front of cast-iron laundry sinks backed up to the brick foundation, with, yep, streaks of lime and rust. The faucets are still dripping, so, cool. His new squat may be cold but there's running water here. He can bundle newspapers for insulation, lug in an extension cord long enough to reach the garage and Dumpster-dive for a space heater. Soon, when the December sun drops before 5 P.M., he'll come back with his stuff and move in.

Stop temporizing, asshole.

Tonight.

Then he can take his time finding a guy who dupes driver's licenses to document his identity: license and a Social. He'll be Dell-Something. Maybe his real name will come back to him. Is that a good thing? Probably not, but he's sick of winging it. All he has is this index card. He forgets, but he can't leave off grieving over whatever came down back then. Worse, he can't bring back anything about it but this shit feeling of guilt that clings like tar that you rolled in on purpose. You can't get it off.

He was probably fucked up before the taxi hit him, but when his skull broke, everything he knew leaked out into the street. Dell doesn't know what he did or who he's hiding from. It's either selective amnesia or it isn't. Split personality, maybe, good Dell/bad Dell like the guy in that movie?

No. Dell is afraid of what he did. No. Of what he might do if they found out.

Whatever, here he is in Jacksonville, Florida, broke and temporarily homeless, with an uncertain welcome in the house above. At least he's come to the right address, but he doesn't know who wrote it on the card for him and stuffed it into the jacket. Or if it's really his jacket.

Ignorant but hopeful, he's here.

Dell squats in the gray Florida dirt, considering. He's a decent-looking guy, he keeps himself neat. For all he knows, he has every right to walk into this house. He can walk in and they'll know him. One of the old ladies will say. Will say . . .

OK, what? *Thank God you've come?* Hey, he could be the missing heir, a genuine Ellis whelp with a valid claim to some scrap of life here on May Street.

Unless, unlike Dell, they know what he did and they call the cops. They'll double back on the— and the word smashes into him like an eighteen-wheeler— atrocity.

Atrocity?

Don't go there. Think: prodigal son.

Unless you have . . . Dell snaps to, riveted. *Special powers.*

The lattice pops open. "Are you in there?"

He stands so fast that his head smacks a beam. "Holy crap!"

"Come out or I'll call the cops." It's a kid.

Dell picks a splinter out of his forehead. Barks. "Building inspector, there's an issue with the basement."

A sound comes out of the kid: *pfuh.* "They don't have fucking basements in Florida, I'm coming in."

Make up some story, do it fast. "Hazmat issue, stay out!"

"Give up, asshole, I live here." He's inside, the arrogant little pest. Twelve, maybe. Sweet face for a garbage-mouth, scuzzy wild hair. Confrontational. "Who the fuck are you?"

They are more or less face-to-face here; he has to answer. "Dell."

"Dell what?"

Think fast. "Duval," Dell says. It is an inspiration. He adds, "Of the Jacksonville Duvals. I think we may be related, but I don't want to bother them until I'm sure." Questions chase each other across the kid's face like an LED banner. *Think fast.* "Does your mom know you hang out down here?"

That face: yeah, she doesn't. "She says it's haunted."

"So you'd better beat it, right?"

"No shit. This ancestor Teddy got on fire down here back in the day. It took out half the porch before they got to him."

It is not safe.

What? "You'd better go."

No way. He has an audience. "Too late for this kid Teddy. Aunt Rosemary says he screamed forever but shiftless Vincent got to him too late."

"Who?"

"Vincent. He was Biggie's husband? She did all the wash. And the aunts are all, 'Biggie could have put that fire out but no, she was upstairs in the kitchen, boiling water. Why didn't the stupid girl run down and throw it on that fire?' Down here they always blame black people." He snorts. "But, shit! Berzillion years, and they still can't let it go!"

"Who can't?"

"The aunts."

That would be Ivy Ellis, eighty-five, Rosemary Ellis Deering, eighty-one and Iris E. Worzecka, eighty-one, according to the new City Directory, City of Jacksonville: same girly names as the ones listed in the 1908 directory at this same address. Generations of sentimental Southerners, he supposes, passing down names like the family jewels.

"It happened right here where they poured the cement."

"How do you know?"

"Aunt Ivy obsesses. She's all instant replay, plus moral. Like, don't play with matches, kids . . ."

Dell sighs. So they pass down stories too. "You should go."

"She can't help it, I guess."

Overhead, a screen door slams. Dell's gut clenches. "Hear that? They're looking for you."

There are no footsteps; just the sound of rubber wheels going back and forth on the boards above and a woman's anxious, hollow shout, "Who's down there?"

"I'm named for him. Is that creepy or what?"

"Teddy? Is that you?"

"Don't call me Teddy!" He goes all guttural, whispering, *"He was only three years old."*

"Better hurry." Dell opens the hatch, as though that will make him go.

But the kid hangs in place, gnawing his knuckles. "Teddy's fucking dead, lady. I'm Theo. Theo Hale."

"Come on up here right now, you hear?"

Dell plays on their being in his secret place. "Quick, before she catches you."

"No way, that's just Aunt Ivy. She can't."

Ivy Ware Ellis, eighty-five. "That's what you think."

"She'll never make it. Dakin Junior's racking horse reared up and fell over backward on her, like forever ago. She's a cripple, man."

Ivy's voice goes up a notch. "What are you doing down there, Teddy Hale?"

The kid gnaws his knuckles until he draws blood.

"Fooling around in the dark with God knows who."

Dell says, "Why are you so nervous?"

She cries, "It isn't safe!"

The answer comes up like phlegm. "It's a fucking trap!"

"This place?"

"The whole house. Look what happened to that kid!"

Dell nudges him toward the exit. "You should go."

"Theodore Hale, you answer me!" On the porch the sound of wheels stops. She's directly overhead.

"Beat it." Dell is surprised by the thud of a gravity knife in his palm— his knife, he supposes, no blade showing, just the big bone handle. Thump.

"No way."

"Really." She's so close that the base of Dell's spine twitches. One flick and the knife turns deadly. "Go."

"Fuck that." Theo whirls on him, all spit and fury. *"Your ancestor didn't burn up down here. **You** go."*

"Theodore Ellis Hale!!! Who's down there?"

Thump. "Now."

"Nobody, Aunt Ivy, OK?" Frantic, he repeats, *"Three years old."*

"Come out before I send Vincent down after you."

"They were all pissed at Vincent because he couldn't get close enough to put the fire out. Like he was fucking *stalling.*"

She doesn't exactly shriek. *"Did you hear me?"*

But the kid is in love with his recital. "And that's not the worst thing that happened in this house."

Go before I hurt you. Dell releases the blade with a snap. *"Tcha!"*

"OK, OK, but just so you know . . ." Shaken, the kid exits the hatch. After a two-second beat he sticks his head back in, all bloated and rasping like a demon in a bad movie. "This house is under a curse."

CHAPTER 2

Theo Hale

In the dark, in this awful house, Mormama speaks to me. She comes in the night. When she's in a good mood, she plants herself at the end of the bed and tells stories. *Three suitcases and a steamer trunk,* she says. Again. *That's all I had left in the world when I came to this house. Little Manette had all my grandchildren lined up on the porch to greet me. Dakin Junior and Randolph, Ivy and Everett, even the twins, everybody but the baby, and my daughter? She left Dakin to do the job, and do you know what my handsome son-in-law said to me?*

I never ask. I don't have to, she can't stop telling it.

He said, children, this is your Mormama. One more Mama than we need.

She can't stop telling it and I can't get her to go away.

When she's in a bad mood, she hangs in the air so close that it creeps me out and says shitty things. *Boys are not welcome in this house. It isn't safe!*

And Mom thinks this tight little room is, like, sealed against whatever. She said so on our first night in this creaky old ark. At bedtime she took me up the big front stairs, all hahaha, like a tour guide. "Look at the panels, Theo. Solid mahogany. Your great-great-great Grandy spared no expense."

"My *what*?"

"The first Dakin Ellis. That's him on the landing in the big gold frame. Wait'll you see your room!" It was just sad, her going, "Aren't you excited?

Not really. Poor Lane, ever since Dad bailed you've been a mess, nailing hopes to the wall like circus posters, or pasting on fucking smileys that everyone hates because it's so fake. *Give it a rest, Mom. Just give it a rest. I know you're bummed about moving in here with **them**.*

But she doesn't know that I know, so I make that belch where they think you answered, and they're too embarrassed to go, "What?"

She, like, skipped on upstairs to the first landing, where the grandfather clock that the aunts fight over looms like a funny uncle, *mwa haaaa.* It bongs every fifteen minutes, obnoxious much? "Look!"

She was waiting for me to say I loved it. I said what you say. "OK."

So she turned me around and pointed. From here it's a straight shot down past the newel post with the shitty brass goddess of wisdom on top holding her light-up torch and on out that front door.

She said, "You can see everything from here," like we're in a museum and the exit is Exhibit A, and, me?

I studied it. Thick glass in the top half with a crap curtain hanging over it so you can't see out the door, but above that there's a wide glass transom, so you can. "Oh."

Mom is all *ta-daaa.* "You can see who's out there without them knowing. Theo, look!" Then, shit! She pushed the panel next to the clock. Booya. Secret door. "My room, after Mom got so sick that we had to move in here."

That would be Poor Elena, according to the aunts, who talked about Poor Elena and all the other Elenas hanging from the family tree for, like, *forever* before Aunt Rosemary, who is either the Good Twin or the Bad Twin, depending on what she makes for dinner, said grace so we could eat.

"We were leaving as soon as she got well."

Poor Mom. Shit happens to Lane, it just does. Her mother died upstairs in Sister's room which is where they put Mom the night we moved in, and when I went, Who's Sister, Aunt Rosemary was all, Don't ask. They've been calling Mom Little Elena ever since we walked in even though she corrects them every time: as in, Elena was her mother. My mom is Lane.

Lane, trying to make me glad. "You get the best room in the house!"

Oh, Mom. Don't try so hard! I went, "Great," because it was so fucking sad.

It was this extra-big closet, pine paneled with brass fittings and a round window that opened and shut so I could pretend that I was on a boat. She stood there waiting for me to say, "cool," but I couldn't so she said, "The captain's cabin. So you're in charge."

As if.

"Look!" She opened the porthole and made me hang out. Right, it's too high for junkies to reach and too small to fit anybody but me, and Mom was prompting, like, "Repel all boarders, get it?"

Oh Mom, just leave.

"For when they fight."

I just wanted her to stop talking.

"They're all cute and excited because we just got here, but they've been in here together for too long. They fight, and when it gets really bad, watch out, they don't care who they hurt." I guess she couldn't stop talking and I couldn't stop her either, not the

way she was. "This is the one safe place." Then she sort of crashed.
"Besides. She won't come in here, she promised."

I was supposed to ask her who. There was us and there was
that clock ticking. Like everything else in the house had stopped.
I thought, one of us has got to say something, but it won't be me.

She said, "I was an orphan."

Poor Lane. "You win." I hugged her and she left.

See, her dad's car crashed and exploded before she was old
enough to know. She and poor Elena made it alone OK until cancer got her and they ended up here. After that it was just Lane and
these fucking aunts, what are they, a thousand years old?

The ones that can still walk are the twins. Aunt Rosemary is the
warden, quartermaster, whatever, kitchen police; don't piss her off
if you expect to eat. Aunt Iris is the general. I don't know what her
hair used to look like, but it's gone all scouring pad on her, this
extreme not-blond, with long black hairs that she doesn't know
about sticking out of her chin. Aunt Ivy is the crippled one. Excuse
me. Disabled. She used to be an OK person, but everything changed
after that horse rolled on her. She can go anywhere the scooter goes,
she can even roll out on the back porch and make trouble for me,
but tip that thing over and she'd flop around like a fish.

And my mom? She had to stay here after her mom died, and they
never called her Lane. It was Little Elena, come here. Do this, do
that, until she found the will. Turns out her dad was rich before
he pissed it all away, how cool is that? After they had Mom, he did
two things. So, did he have a premonition or what? See, he bought
these bonds in her name. They're in the bank down town. As soon
she collects, we're done with this creepy place.

The other thing her dad did was sign her up for boarding school,
four years bought and paid for up front. So Mom escaped when
she was fourteen. No more Little Elena. Get it? She took the train
to Virginia all by herself and met the great big, scary headmistress
of Chatham Hall with a great big grin. "Call me Lane." She's that
smart. Done deal.

They helped her get a scholarship to FSU but she didn't finish; she had me instead. She says she got so starved for family that she quit and married my dad so she could have one of her own. They were in love, but she swears I'm the only good thing that came out of it. So fuck you, Barry Hale, for wrecking the only real family we ever had, and fuck us ending up in this ginormous dump, stuck with the same old ladies going all "Little Elena" on her and, like Mom says, us fucking beholden to them.

That night she told me it's just until she gets a job; she told me it wouldn't take long and it will be a million miles from Jacksonville. She told me that this was my safe room. Look how that turned out.

That first night I turned the latch and put the pillow over my head but it didn't shut them out, nothing does. I heard her and the aunts bonking around upstairs and after Mom stopped trying and went to bed I heard them yelling downstairs in Aunt Ivy's room, which they did until the clock on the landing choked out eleven bongs and they all went to bed. On the eleventh bong the whole house shut down. By that time I had to pee, but it was dark out there and I was afraid to go upstairs to the bathroom, so I didn't what you would call sleep.

It's the house. It's *too old,* like, nothing's where you thought it would be, and it makes all these weird noises. Plus it smells bad, e.g. the blanket and this bedspread smell like mothballs and the sheets smell like feet and mildew and bad perfume, like ghost sheets ironed and put away by people that got old and died a hundred years ago, and on my first night in this room I lay there wide awake and blinking for, like, years.

Who could sleep?

I'd swear I didn't sleep at all, except the next time I heard the clock was when it happened. It was dark as fuck inside my room, and I only counted three bongs.

The clock didn't wake me up and it wasn't having to pee, either. Around 1 A.M. I peed in my canteen because I wasn't sleeping and

I could hardly stand it and I guess I went unconscious, because then. Oh, fuck. Then.

It was the cold. With the furnace going and the blankets and the window closed, there was a *difference*. This weird chunk of air was in my room. I could feel this dense shaft of nothing by the bed, like a column of ice or an ice *person*. It wasn't a draft, it wasn't something breathing, either. It was like nothing you can imagine. It didn't speak and it didn't touch me. It didn't come through the door or blow in on the wind. Nothing to see. It was just *there*.

I guess it was her, but I didn't know it at the time.

But that was before Mom and me drove out to the Publix and we had The Talk.

About whatever it was. It wasn't a thing, like, Thing. You know, from the movies. It was an object. I just lay there and waited for it to go away, although it didn't blow out the door when I realized there was a *presence*. It didn't speak either. It just stayed. It wasn't like I went to sleep after that. It was more that I quit counting bongs and forgot time. Next time I heard the clock, I counted. It bonged eight times. It was light in the room and the cold, cold chunk of nothing was gone. I told myself, OK, it was a stupid dream. It had to be, because otherwise I was batshit crazy, and on top of everything that's come down since Dad blew us off, crazy was one fucking thing too much.

Tuesday she was there again, but at the time I didn't know it was her. I didn't even know it was a person. I just knew it was way creepy, and this time made twice. I didn't make it up or imagine it.

This happened.

The *cold* didn't do anything, it didn't say anything, it was just *there* for as long as it took to, like, make an impression? You'd think I'd freak with a chunk of black ice standing over me but it was OK. I thought I knew what the drill was. The sun would come up like it did yesterday and it would go away. *Thing* or not, I peed into my canteen like I do every night now, because no matter what's in your room with you, you don't want to go out there, ever, all by yourself in the dark.

I wash it out in the downstairs bathroom before anybody gets up. They fixed up the second-class sitting room for Aunt Ivy because of the scooter, but she has to wait for Aunt Iris to come downstairs and get her up.

It went on like that. Some nights she came. Others, I slept through, which was a relief. I didn't tell anybody, because certain things aren't real until you name them. Couldn't see her, didn't hear her, but I knew she would keep coming. I just felt it. Chunk of cold by the bed, solid as a post, but then it spoke to me.

Some of us are trapped here, blood of my blood.

At least I think it spoke.

Get out while you still can.

I didn't know what it was, not then, and I wasn't about to tell Mom, either. She has enough going on right now, between the aunts and snarky phone calls from Dad's lawyers, plus, as long as I didn't pin words to the wuddiyou say, *presence,* I could pretend it wasn't happening. Maybe it would give up and go away. When that didn't work I shook my fist at it and went, **get out,** and it didn't say or do anything but THIS came into my head: *I can't,* and that creeped me out, but I would die before I would bother Mom with it. Yeah, right.

This: *Get out while you still can.*

CHAPTER 3

Dell

His first night in the belly of the house was harder than he expected, filled with extreme silence broken by sudden cracking sounds
as the footprint of the old house sank deeper into the earth. He
unrolled his sleeping bag on the cement apron by the old washtubs,
but it felt wrong. He moved on to the area under the back steps,
but the insect life in the dirt and hanging in the air drove him out.
After a series of uneasy moves and restless nights in different spots,
he settled on the space behind a partition at the far end of the enclosure. He thinks they used it to keep firewood or coal, or whatever the house ran on before that kid— he was a *baby*— before
Teddy caught fire, back when this was new, the floor scrubbed
clean, all traces removed.

No telling how the women heat their house these days— not
much, Dell knows. Yes, he's been inside. It's how he learns these
things.

Accidentally or not, the old lady in the wheelchair taught him how to come and go without their knowing. He was on his way around the house with his head down when he caught her on a bad day. He heard her up there on the porch, spitting with frustration. She was scolding that scooter thing she drives, desperate to get it aimed directly at the sun. Then her voice filled up with tears, so he had to swarm up and over the rail and help her, how could he not? She blinked up at him without seeing, frustrated and resentful. "Vincent, we've been waiting for you!"

"Ma'am?"

"Miss Ivy, *please*!"

He studied her, wondering. *How old are you, anyway?* Older than the City Directory says, he's sure. This once-lovely woman looks as old as God. Poor old thing; she's waiting. "Yes, Miss Ivy," he said. Carefully, he turned her scooter. Her eyelids snapped shut; sunlight deepened every one of the thousand wrinkles in her face. "Yes Ma'am."

"You're late! Get in there and start the fires, boy. It's freezing inside!" She'd plunged into deep past and stayed. Giving orders to long-dead servants, he supposed. With her eyes still closed, she continued. "Start in the dining room, Vincent, and for heaven's sake, use the hatch. You can't be tearing up Mama's Persian runners like you do, dragging your logs through the house every whichway."

"Yes Ma'am."

"*Miss Ivy!*" Then her eyes popped open. "Oh! I'm sorry, it isn't you!"

"Sorry, Miss Ivy. I'm not him." Dell flashed his best grin.

She drew herself up. "Hello, Mr."

"Dell. And if there's anything I can do."

"Not right now, thank you. You were sweet to bring me out into this beautiful sun."

"Glad to help, and now I have to." *Don't even try.* Smiling, smiling, he backed away.

Hatch, she said. Under the dining room bay window, he

discovered when he dropped off the edge of the porch to inspect. He went into the shadows on his hands and knees. Right. Like the sprawling porches, the bay juts over the foundation but in a small way, like an overbite. Duly noted. Now leave before Miss Ivy remembers what she just told you. Yes, that's "Miss." She looks like she was born at least a hundred years before they even thought of Ms.

God he feels sorry for her.

CHAPTER 4

Charlotte Robichaux:
Mormama

I never thought I'd be a mother for so long. The son I loved so much is lost to me, and the daughter? The evil is in the details.

I never wanted to be a mother at all.

It happens to girls in my situation. I was born in the Ware house on Tradd Street in Charleston. For girls born into society in my time, there was no other choice. I was brought up to be a lady, and ladies, Mother told me before I was old enough to resent it, do not work, it is beneath them. A lady may embroider or dabble with watercolors to occupy her hands but the rest will be done for her, unless a bad wind comes in and blows the servants away, and that must never happen; it would be too terrible, never mind that it does happen, has happened, will happen, and ladies end up doing things that ladies never do.

This is what ladies do. They marry gentlemen who want to do certain things to them, and it's best if they marry well. When I was small I lived my life as though none of this mattered, but my body changed. Mother saw. One day she pulled me into the sitting room. For a tea party, she said. Margaret came in with a tray with macaroons, a pot of tea and three cups. I thought, How nice, a party! Mother poured. I handed mine to Margaret. "You first!"

And didn't Mother slap my fingers then! "Charlotte, *hush*! Thank you, Margaret. That will be all."

"Yes, Miss Manette."

When she was gone Mother said, "Ladies don't sit down with servants, Charlotte. Maids leave the tray and go. Ladies pour." The third cup was for her china baby doll that I hated and I had to practice pouring over and over again.

My brother came in with a clatter. I thought, Here's Jared. Please God, make her ask him about school.

"Now. For a lady, position is everything in life." Without missing a beat she waved him away. "Not now, dear."

Jared turned red and his face broke into pieces. He dropped his books and ran out before Mother saw him laughing, but I could hear the snorts exploding with every step as he pounded down the hall and out the door. I love my brother but I hated him, with his bright and shiny future spelled out in gold braid and boots polished to a shine. All the best boys from Porter go on to the Citadel. They are Charleston's finest, who finish as commissioned officers and gentlemen, best boys for life.

Best boys threw themselves on horses, bicycles. They ran and shouted, they got drunk and rowdy, they did bad things in the strangest places and walked away scot-free, but I was expected to do what ladies do.

Mother lectured as though their willful freedom was none of my concern, when all I wanted was . . . Whatever I thought I wanted went up in flames that day. Mother saw, and poured words on the fire until it went out. The coral necklace she gave me *snapped* off my neck just then. Beads rolled everywhere. I dropped to my knees as if to retrieve them. Like Jared, I didn't want her to see my face.

Oh, she was furious. She wished she could stamp me down and make me go along on my belly to look for them, I heard it in her tone. She wanted to see me writhing across the carpet finding every single bead, but ladies don't.

"Get up." She stood over me, rigid with spite. I hated Mother, and Mother hated me. She rang for Margaret and made me watch as Margaret scrambled for the beads. "Look what you made poor Margaret do!"

I started to cry.

"Pretty is as pretty does, Charlotte. Remember, pretty is as pretty does."

If she could see what time has done to me and to my daughter her simulacrum, oh, oh, my! I wanted her to die. She lived on. Then Little Manette fell into her hands. She was my daughter, but Mother named her little instrument of revenge.

Given family resources and her station, Mother was presented at St. James's in London, but that was before the war. The house on Tradd Street was the same when it ended, but everything else had changed. At the end of the coming season, I would be presented at the St. Cecilia Society Ball. Douglas Revenaugh would be my escort. He was the most highly placed of Jared's friends, and if it went well enough . . . Damn you Mother, with your expectations. I could never measure up.

She saw to it that I had a pretty dress for every luncheon, every tea dance, every musicale because, Mother explained, this was my introduction to society. She took over my life in an orgy of preparation. Walk this way, practice modesty of the eyes, men avoid girls who are too direct. Unless they're too attractive for their own good, and then. Just guard yourself Missy, guard yourself! Don't do this, never say that, what would people think? Dress for the occasion, and in the name of our Savior, do not embarrass me.

I changed costumes twice, sometimes three times in a day. It was exhausting. There were more than a dozen parties. I was expected to be charming but not too charming at these events, I must play the part life wrote for me at every one of them and do all this smiling, smiling, whereas Jared slipped into the Citadel like a sword into a sheath.

I let William Robichaux find me at the St. Cecilia Ball; it wasn't hard, and nature did the rest. He was a nice man. Older, clumsy and heavy-handed, but he kept his place. We had a girl, he was very sweet about it but I knew it was a disappointment. To be honest, I was disappointed too, and so was she. My daughter tore me apart in her rush to separate from me. I bled for months. The minute they put that child into my arms, she went rigid and hatred poured out of her in a long, unbroken screech. Then her tiny fists knotted and the battle began.

Mother never liked me. That day she grew fangs. In her extreme vanity, when the midwife came out into the hall for William, Mother pushed him aside like a chair that was in her way. I heard her: "My girl needs me!"

That woman rushed into the room where I lay sobbing, exhausted by the raging fury I could not contain. She descended on my child like the bad fairy and stole her soul before I knew, and before I could stop her, she stamped and sealed the vile transaction with her own name.

"Oh, my sweet baby," she said; I knew she didn't mean me. Then she seized the writhing bundle, and in naming her, Manette Patricia Millard Ware of the Charleston Wares claimed my frantic first child for her own. The baby's body unclenched to the tune of Mother crooning, "My very own Little Manette."

I was too ravaged by the shock to stop this transaction, and it was a transaction. Something dark passed between them when Mother breathed her given name into my daughter's open mouth. "Hush-hush, my darling, hush-hush, sweet Little Manette."

In an instant the baby fell silent, and giddy with relief, I thought, *Thank God.*

I didn't know!

William was happy that our second child was a boy, and I was relieved because my darling Billy curled up in my arms. At last, a baby I could love! I thought well, that's that, but with men it never is. Never mind, he was a banker, and he was well fixed. We were invited to all the best places and as for the physical particulars between us, William was a gentleman in all things, even that. Then he died of the Spanish flu. Little Manette was three years old and my sweet little Billy was two.

Never mind, William was a banker. Of course he'd have put away enough to see us through. By that time Margaret was coming around to take my daughter over to Tradd Street on most afternoons— to ease my lot, Mother said after William died, but that was not what she meant. I was too distracted to notice, or too blind to see what she was doing, my mother, the consummate lady.

What she had already done.

Thank God Jared's death sent her into a decline. An explosion, wherever the army sent him in that awful war. It was simple enough to send Little Manette to Tradd Street to comfort Mother after her terrible loss. It was my way of pretending that I cared for her, when I didn't care at all. In fact, I was happy to let my daughter sit in my mother's parlor drinking cambric tea while I cuddled my son. Sweet Billy was my favorite, and they both knew. He settled into my arms like a ball into a socket, a hand into a glove.

I loved Little Manette but I never liked her. Mother did. My daughter was her beautiful doll. She was happy too. She came home from these visits with chocolate smears on her smug little face and some trinket from Mother's jewel box— her cameo necklace, her jade bracelet, the ruby brooch I always wanted, my grandfather's signet ring.

Despite my best efforts, Little Manette was everything my mother had wasted a hundred thousand words trying to make of me. A perfect lady. She wore a size four and a half shoe and her bare foot never touched the ground. Could I have stopped the process if I'd known? To be honest, if I did know what was going on in the parlor at Tradd Street, I didn't care. I was happy to have the girl safely occupied. I thought: one less thing to worry about, and I had Billy. He was my sunny, sweet, beautiful boy. His path led to Porter and the Citadel, a happy future ensured, and I thought it was, until. Until!

I can't. Not now.

William's brothers took care of the money. After the funeral they sat me down and warned me to be frugal and I was, I know I was, and in spite of Little Manette and her incessant demands, I believed I had enough to send her to Ashley Hall which I did, and on the days when I left her at school all the air rushed out of me and my heart eased.

When Mother invited her to stay on Tradd Street on schooldays because it was that much closer I said, "Of course!" and everything went smoothly for a time. Then William's brothers let me know that they had been carrying most of my expenses ever since his death and what little we had left was almost gone.

I left the William Robichaux house in the hands of his brothers, the banker and the lawyer, in exchange for what seemed at the time like a fair amount. By that time Mother had taken to her bed. With Jared gone and Mother in a decline, I assumed the house on Tradd Street would be mine to rule.

Until Little Manette met me at the door with Margaret behind her; she was sixteen, with her head high and her hair caught up with not a single stray curl. So mannered. So beautifully groomed. My daughter showed me into the house with a sweep of her hand. Quite the lady, with Mother's garnet pendant swinging between her breasts: Little Manette, looking down her elegant nose. "Well, *Mother*. It's about time!" Then I understood all at once and exactly how the Manettes had become what they were. My child treated Margaret like a slave. "A set tea for company, Margaret. On the veranda, with proper linens. Lapsang souchong and those biscuits from London. Raspberries and clotted cream."

I'd never seen Margaret angry. "Yes, Miss Manette."

My daughter called after her. "Oh, and Margaret, set the table for three. Your mistress is coming down. The Clayton family damask and the Minton tonight, and Great Grandmother Ware's crystal, of course. Tell cook." I wanted to turn on the girl and snatch her bald-headed, but she was too old to discipline. Too much of a lady, every line in her body a warning: *ladies don't*.

Then Mother's mannered puppet showed me around the house!

"And that," she said as we came to the sitting room. She gestured at the mahogany overmantel with the French prisoner's painting of Fort Sumter set into the wood, "Well, the gold is behind one of those panels, Mama just never found out where."

"Mama?"

She raked me with a look that I knew at once. So condescending. So careless of everything but herself. "I suppose she was 'Mother' to you, *Mother*."

Our futures were set in stone. I wonder if my mother knew what she had unleashed.

CHAPTER 5

Ivy

Such a sweet boy. Sweet man, I suppose, a little bit older than our Randolph when he ran away; poor boy, we all knew he left because of Father. New Little Elena and that boy were off somewhere and I fought with Iris until she sighed and aimed me at the head of the little ramp outside the great door. She opened it with that nasty snarl of hers and gave me an extra push. "You want to go outside? OK, *go outside* and stay there until the cows come home!"

As though I had a choice. When I woke up crippled I wanted to die, but I haven't. I've been not dying for so long now that I don't think I can. None of us can. I don't know about the others, but I *know* we've been around for too long, way too long.

Never mind, I have a friend! He came at just the right time the other day, when Iris got mad at me, so she pushed me outside too hard. Scooter and I shot down that ramp so fast that we lost our equilibrium. We tried to turn but our steering wheel seized up and we kept rolling until we ran smack into the cement urn with Rose's dying hydrangea at the top of our front steps. We were hanging by the left rear wheel of my poor Scooter, another inch and we'd have rolled straight down those stairs to our death on the flagstone walk, and what a liberation that would be!

Why, I could just hear Iris wailing, "Ivy Marie Ellis, look what you've done to yourself!" but I knew what she would be thinking while she and Rosemary waited for 911, which they would take their own sweet time getting around to calling.

Finally.

I could almost hear them celebrating after the ambulance took me away.

You want me dead, you bitch? Well, so do I! Do you think I like having to depend on you and Rosemary for every little thing? I was this close to turning my front wheel so we could clear the urn and make the plunge, but of course I didn't. You don't. You tell yourself, *They have a new armature that you put on like an overall, and even quadriplegics walk! I saw it on TV.*

Why, one day they'll bring one of those gadgets to our house, and I'll put it on like a coverall and for the first time since I took off on Dakie's palomino, I will walk! Then I can say goodbye to Scooter and march away to a real life in the real world!

Soon, make it soon.

But I didn't say any of that out loud, even though Little Elena and the boy had run off somewhere in her dinky car and my sisters were inside and wouldn't hear. I said, "Or let's us just rock a little bit, Scoot. It isn't too hard, we'll just keep rocking until this thing jolts free and we get it over with." It would be easy, poor Scooter could die of its own weight.

I took a deep breath and thought, *All right, get on with it,* and I would have, but I heard the nicest voice. It came out of nowhere, like a sign from God. "Oh lady, wait! We don't want to do that."

And like an angel my friend was here, that sweet, sweet boy, same sandy hair as Randolph's, I miss him so much! In fact he reminded me of our long-lost big brother. Ran escaped Mama's greedy house when he was seventeen and that night the house, or something deep inside it, let out a great big sigh. That sigh is still backed up inside my hateful sisters, more like relief than grief: *At least we're done with him.*

Randolph left a long time ago, and here was this sweet young man, only a little older than my beloved best brother the night he sat me down on the back porch and we hugged goodbye.

Lovely man, this new one, tall, easy-talking and gentle. He put us to rights before we could stop him, Scooter and me. He parked us in the safest place on the veranda, by the rail overlooking the porte cochère. He lined us up right next to the very last rocker, a lovely place to sit and talk, although nobody ever comes to talk to us. He parked us there with our brakes secured and left before I could say thank you, and what's your name.

But he came back, we were so glad! I could swear he was gone less than a minute, and, good Lord, he put a nice cold Coca-Cola in my hands! Then he saw the way I was, I mean my hands, and he took my drink away from me long enough to put his finger into the ring and open it and take away the tab, he was the perfect gentleman, "Wouldn't want to hurt your mouth on that," and instead of throwing the tab into the urn along with the twins' Coke tabs and cigarette butts, he folded it and slipped it into the watch pocket of his jeans and gave me the nicest smile. Then we heard Iris open the front doors with a crash and he went, "Shhh," and slipped over the rail like a pirate leaving a treasure ship.

By the time Iris stomped across the porch to roll me back inside, by the time Rose came out to stare over the rail, my private Galahad wasn't anywhere. If it hadn't been for that Coke, which my sisters thought little Teddy had stolen behind their backs and given me to spite them, you wouldn't know he'd ever been.

CHAPTER 6

Lane

God damn these *skinny* women poking their thin, Southern-lady noses into my luggage, my personal affairs, my everything, Rosemary inspecting my makeup bag, as in, "You look so tired, honey. Here, I'll do that," all because I can't bring myself to unpack. I caught Iris sniffing my underwear as she rifled my suitcase— looking for drugs, the pill or a six-pack of condoms, whatever vices she could root out. "You haven't even unpacked! Let's put some of these things away."

"Don't!"

She gave me that swimmy, wounded look they all have, these old, old aunts. It hits like a sock full of sand, so what I have to say comes out: *ooof*. "I'm not staying long."

"You know, this is Sister's room; we don't let just anybody sleep in Sister's room, but Little Elena, you—"

"Stop that. It's Lane!" *To keep away the Big Bad.* Yeah, there is one. I personally think it's the house.

Iris took off the smile and went back to being herself. "Oh Elena, you're just tired."

"Elena was my mother." It breaks my heart, just hearing her name. I loved her so much! "Goddammit, I'm Lane!"

Rosemary snapped, "Language!" As if I'm still fourteen. When I left for Chatham Hall I thought, Well, that's that, but it never is. It never fucking is. Eight years of freedom— boarding school, in Gainesville at FSU— correction, two years of freedom in college before I met Barry, the charming, shitty, deceitful jerk, and fourteen years of what-you-might-call-freedom as that bastard's deluded, as in, thinks *this-is-forever* wife; after fourteen years of deception and stealth financing to preserve that delusion, of impending misery warded off by the arrival of Theo, with his spiky hair and that wonderful grin; after all that, I don't want my life back, I want MY LIFE.

Mine and Theo's. I promised him we'd start over in some great place just as soon as I cashed in our bonds, but the aunts temporized for days. By Sunday, I'd had enough. We faced off in Sister's bedroom— Sister was the youngest of the first generation born in this old house and she ended badly, Iris reminded me, to head off what was coming.

We were there for the big confrontation, but Rosemary didn't know it. She was fooling with my suitcase. "Oh honey, let's hang up these pretty things."

I said, "Look, y'all are sweet, but don't unpack me just yet. I'll be out by the end of the week." Translation, and Iris knew it: I'm only here until I march you down to the bank to countersign for me.

She thrust her jaw at me; the bitch was loaded for bear. "As if any girl who's been off the job market for as long as you have can get a job in just five days."

They went on fussing with my clothes to spite me, hanging this up, tsk-tsking over that, picking out items for Ivy to mend. "I'm not a girl!"

Rosemary stopped shuffling my lacy bras and went all there-there on me, "Don't worry, sweetheart. It won't matter how old you are, you're still an Ellis girl, and that means something in this town. Our name opens the very best doors in Jacksonville."

Iris started. "Be practical. Think of the money you'll save, living here! Rose is a wonderful cook, and you won't have to worry about rent or shopping or anything, there's a 7-Eleven around here somewhere for emergencies, and the Publix delivers anything you want! The playground's gone, but we've put little Teddy's name in at Jacksonville Country Day, and besides . . ."

"His name is Theo, Iris."

Rosemary finished. "Papa founded a Teddy Ellis scholarship to protect his children and their children's children, so that splendid private school won't cost you a thing."

"Oh, we're not staying in Jacksonville."

"Of course you are!"

"We're going north as soon as we cash in my birthday bonds."

"The bonds?" Rosemary blinked as though I'd said "fuck" in her presence. Or smacked her in the face with a dead fish.

So odd: I could swear I saw their tongues flick around their lips like lizards' tongues in the seconds before Iris went all angry commandant. "If that's what you're counting on, don't count on it!"

Rosemary wailed, "You're leaving so *soon*?" In another minute she'd cry, and that's never been a good thing.

Downstairs in the hall that night, when I went to kiss Ivy good night before coming up for the confrontation, my desperate Aunt Ivy pressed a bill into my hand and whispered into the dark, "Go, little bird. Fly."

It was a ten.

Iris and I were at a standoff. I looked my tough, exacting aunt in the eye and repeated. "My bonds. Government bonds that my father put away when I was born. First National. Safe-deposit box."

Blink blink blink.

"You know the ones. It's my money, Iris. I need it now!"

Her face went through a bunch of changes, as though figures scrolled nonstop behind her eyes. After too long, she looked down that thin, sharp nose at me and said like a reproachful accountant, "Your little trust fund took care of the tuition, dear, but there were other expenses. Roofing. Your uniforms. We never complained, but we had to cash them in," and I could swear I saw a flicker of triumph cross her face like a raptor trailing its scrap of torn flesh.

Bottom line? They know I'm screwed. Me. "Fuck that shit," I told Iris, and she can flinch all she wants, she knows it's a direct challenge and she knows I mean it. "Let's us go down to that bank and open that safe-deposit box and you can damn well pull out the paperwork and show me what went where."

Iris started a long, complex explanation designed to confuse; I tuned out some time around "We live in a landmark house, Elena. It's an honor."

I think: *Millstone dragging you down into this ocean of heirloom furniture and worthless junk, and you don't even know which of these things is which.*

"Our legacy and yours, Elena." Rosemary's eyes glistened. Tears? "And the least we can do is keep it up!"

Iris was saying, "You're a lucky girl, Elena."

Yes I would not respond. I stared her down.

The day after Mom's funeral, I dreamed I heard Mormama, warning me. *Get out now, or you'll never get out.*

I was eight years old and I was grieving. I think I yelled, "You get out. Go away!"

I could swear I heard, *If God would let me, I would!*

By that time I was bawling. "I don't want you, I don't want anything, go away!"

I can't! God, she was sad. *I have to stay and take care.*

I snorted tears. "Take care of what?" I heard, or comprehended her wail in the seconds before I crashed into sleep.

All of you.

When I walked back into 553 last week I could swear I heard our Mormama groan. *Not again.*

Look, lady, Barry left me with no money and no place to go and yeah, I take your warning, and it scares the crap out of me. Something inside this house keeps its women close. Three old, old women who never change. It gnaws people to bits, and sooner or later, it will swallow them whole.

Well, not me, Mormama. Understand? Not me! I'm out of here!

While I confronted the unthinkable, the twins talked on. The bonds. The exigencies. "This beautiful, beautiful house . . . it's an honor and a responsibility . . ."

"Fuck that shit," I told Iris, although I know I'm screwed. "You can't just say I'm broke and get away with it."

"Language!" With that ladylike shudder.

Go ahead. Shudder and flinch. This is a challenge. Deal with it. "That was my money. Let's us go down to that bank and open that safe-deposit box and you can damn well pull out the paperwork and show me exactly where it went."

CHAPTER 7

Mormama

Bad things happen in the bowels of this house. There was trouble in this house before I entered it, but I lost my dear Teddy to **undercroft** before I met or comprehended the horror that lies below. He was only three! The sweetest of Little Manette's four boys, my darling Teddy reduced to ash and chunks of bone in the dawn of his life in this miserable heap of dreams, *and I could not take care of him*.

I blame Little Manette. I blame the vein of evil in her that prompted this pretentious, monstrous house, and to this day I cannot tell you whether it sprang to life in the murky **undercroft** when my daughter commanded it built or entered the building in Dakin's arms the day he carried the new Mrs. Dakin Ellis in the front door.

I only know that there is evil in this house.

I loved my daughter but I never liked her, and she despised me. It was unnatural. She was her grandmother's beautiful, precious doll, much, much too special for the likes of me. She was demanding and given to tantrums. When I denied her anything she battered me, howling, "So much for you, Mother, my Mama— *Mama* loves me, yes she does." I begged Mother not to indulge her, for all the good that it did. Greed burned inside my daughter all her adult life and when she was thwarted, anger flared up and scorched the earth.

Understand, this is on her soul. In her overwhelming greed, my daughter made Dakin Ellis build this overblown shrine to vanity before she would consent to him, and Mother urged her on.

By that time they were so close that when Mother said "Smile," my daughter smiled. You see, with me, Mother had always been harsh and judgmental, but she was "dearest Mama" to Little Manette. Saccharine and indulgent, winning the child's love with a parade of gifts so rich that when Mother said "Dance," my dainty daughter danced, and an ugly dance it was, because given things men did to them, true ladies must have everything done their way.

They colluded over blueprints for Manette's new home in Jacksonville, ordering this addition to the floor plan and then demanding that— stained glass in the stairwell— and on and on before she would accept Dakin's ring. Things the poor boy had to do to get what he took from her. Dakin's bride saw to it that he set their eighteen rooms on an unbroken foundation so the house rode high, like a great plantation house, proof against floods, vermin, Yankees, I suppose, and she insisted that uncertain ground or not, Dakin must build on this particular plot on the best street.

He did warn her: too close to the river, with one too many flood tides, the complex limestone layers might shift, but Little Manette, she of the small mind and tiny feet, demanded this spot in this fine neighborhood because in those days, all the best people built along the river.

We didn't know that he had it built over a— what? Vortex? Void? I call it **undercroft**, but when I first came into my daughter's house, I had no idea what lay below. I only know that I was uneasy from the day I walked in, and it wasn't only Dakin's condescension when he lined up seven children on the porch and introduced me. *Mormama. One more Mama than we need.*

The big boys were grinning: Dakin Junior and Randolph. Little Teddy covered his giggle with tiny hands, but I loved those eyes. Puny Everett lifted his arms to his father, whining to be coddled, and the little girls? A maid came and whisked them away, leaving me with Dakin Senior, hampered by the family weakling's skinny, thrashing legs. He handed me off to Tillie in the entryway with its rich décor, and carried Little Manette's darling Everett upstairs.

Tillie was a sweet colored girl in a gray gown with a starched white collar and a white apron. Neither of us knew what to say to the other. I took her to be a nurse. "Is Mrs. Ellis ill?"

"No Ma'am. She said, 'See to her,' so I does. She down with the wet cloths on her eyes."

"I see. And you?"

"I feeds her babies. I done the twins, but this girlbaby . . . She took this one hard."

Oh. The wet nurse. "I see."

By the time I came to Jacksonville Manette had named her three girls for flowers: Ivy, Iris and Rose. "So you're feeding little Violet, Magnolia, Daisy or Hyacinth? What is it this time, Hydrangea?"

Tillie tried to cover her smile. We both smiled. "No Ma'am. This girlbaby name Leah."

"Pretty!"

"She say it come from a cow." Even though everyone else had vanished, she covered her mouth so nobody could hear. "This the one that broke the camel's back."

CHAPTER 8

Theo

I woke up feeling bad. Like Mormama sneaked in and planted words in my head when I was out cold, so I couldn't stop her.

Mom got that there was a problem; she got whatever stink was coming off me and today around five when I was just about to die of it she said, "Let's us go out to the Publix. I need Advil and some Tapatío sauce, Rosemary's a no-onions, no-spices kind of cook. Come on, we can get your Aunt Ivy a quart of her favorite ice cream on the way home. Double chocolate in sugar cones for us. Plus I can get these job apps printed at Staples while we're out. I've posted their forms, plus photo, but they all want my signature on hard copy."

She was so bright and grinny that it scared me, like she was on to me, because this is how Lane gets when she's fixing to back me into a corner so tight that I freak and yack up the truth.

We got in the car and all the breath came out of me. I thought, *OK,* and waited for Mom to start, but she just drove. We didn't stop at the Publix on Riverside, she drove right past, like we might keep going until we ended up in Boston and maybe Dad would come out of that girl's house and beg us to hook up with him.

Mom took the bridge to San Marco and I rode along waiting for her to pry the lid off and start on me, but she didn't. We talked about pretty much nothing, you know, riding along with the radio on, both of us all happy and lalala, with her saying, this is where I used to, when she wanted to know what was the matter and me saying, Mom, is that a real flamingo or one of those plastic things when all I wanted to say was, This *scary thing* keeps showing up in my room.

In the bottom of my soul I was thinking, *don't ask,* and she didn't, so I didn't say. We stopped under a big tree at the far end of the parking lot of the big Publix over on Atlantic Boulevard, they had free samples and that was cool. When we came out with her Advil plus Twizzlers I thought, whew. Maybe we really are running away and I won't have to tell her after all.

Stupid not to get that she'd parked us in this big patch of shade for a reason. So we had the showdown or whatever you want to call it in the parking lot at the Publix on Atlantic, and it wasn't her prying until I gave up and told her what was the matter so she could say that's crazy, honey. Chill.

Except. Son of a bitch, she brought it up!

"It's. Uh. I don't want to weird you out or anything, but. Uh." She was trying for casual, and it wasn't working. "It's about May Street, I mean the house."

I pulled off a pretty good shrug: *you don't scare me.* "It's old, it's creepy, what else is new?"

For a minute I thought she'd choked on a Twizzler. It took her that long to get it out. "There's something in the house."

Lady, I've fucking seen it.

I've played it so cool that she still thinks that I, at least, have escaped the . . . Word! Is there even a word for this? I don't know what the fuck it is or how it got into my life. The visitations. That shaft of *cold* in my tight little room, talking, talking, talking. I tried for cool and managed. "Oh-kaaay."

"That's one reason I put you in the wet nurse's room; she wouldn't be caught dead."

"What's a wet nurse?"

Boy, was she embarrassed. "See, your great-great— oh never mind. Little Manette got married when she was eighteen and they had too many babies so fast that she brought in a wet nurse to feed them."

Ewww. I had to say something, so I said, "Little?"

"OK. She was your great-great-great-great whatever, you have so many greats in this place there's no keeping track, Theo. Shut up and listen, OK?"

OK.

"It was too much. Little Manette and her mother didn't get along, but when the last baby came, old Charlotte got on a train and came down to help. Like, *surprise*. She just showed up on their front porch with three suitcases in the carriage and a steamer trunk coming in a van. It was everything she had, and do you know what she told them? She said, 'I'm here to take care,' and she . . . It . . . All I can say is . . . Look. If you run into anything weird in the upstairs hall . . ."

Don't ask, T. Just wait.

"Don't worry, it's nothing to be afraid of, it . . ."

It's embarrassing. I go, "Ice cream," like, if she doesn't say it, I won't have to deal. "We have to go get Aunt Ivy's marshmallow fudge whatever at Baskin-Robbins, right?"

Too late. She's all gritted and clenched and bound to tell me. "It's not a ghost, exactly, and it isn't your neighborhood predator sneaking in to rob us blind, but there's, oh, gack! She's kind of living here. If you call that living."

We're in it now.

"So if you see anything in the night, like, oh, a moving shadow in the hall, like, *lurking*, don't freak. It's just . . ."

If I don't ask, we can pretend she isn't real, OK? "OK Mom. We have to go print your letters and this resume before they close."

"Shut up, Theo. She won't hurt you, I don't think. And don't mention it to the aunts, they're too busy pretending everything is fine." Then in case I didn't get it she fed me the setup line. "So if she turns up, don't worry, it's just . . ."

She was waiting for me to ask so she could finish. My mouth fell open and words popped out. "The fuck!"

Auto-snap. "Language!" She put the car in reverse and hit the gas so fast that my head jerked and we left the parking lot. She drove with her jaw so tight that I knew as far as I was concerned, she was done.

Yeah, I caved. "It's just what?" *Say it, lady. Go ahead and say it.*

"It's just Mormama, trying to help."

This is how you get your mom to tell you more than she wants. "No way. She'd be a thousand years old by now."

"Or dead."

So we're up against it. "Right."

Then Lane gives me what all our greats and great-greats passed down to her, pretty much word for word. "The trouble was, she wasn't welcome here.

"One woman alone," Mom said. Then her voice broke a little bit, "See, her mother spent more money than they had. The bank took the house the day she buried her mother. She didn't have anywhere else to go."

Better not say, *like us.* When Dad bailed on us he canceled Mom's credit cards and defaulted on the mortgage, don't ask.

About the question period. There was no question period.

Mom said in a flat voice, "OK, we're home." We parked between the garbage truck in front of the truckers' parking lot and the exterminator's van outside the Marvista, and do you want to know what I thought? I thought, *fuck!*

CHAPTER 9

Mormama

When our Teddy died, instead of grieving, Manette raged.

She was furious! Like Mother, she expected her children's lives to march in line. She gave Dakin Ellis eight children, but Everett was the only one she really cared about.

Dakin Junior was independent, and she never forgave him. Randolph had a temper and my sweet Teddy was happy but too quick and too wiry to hug, dear God, I think he knew her for what she was. Teddy was my favorite, and Everett? He was the weakling, and he whined. Tractable and pretty as a porcelain shepherd boy around his mother, and Manette loved him more than all the rest. She and Tillie carried that child around on a pillow until he was four years old.

He was docile— that is, as long as they were fussing over him, and when they weren't, he made everybody miserable. It was hell, watching her coddle Everett while her other boys ran wild. Long after his big brothers grew up and left the house, Everett endured because no matter where he went or what he tried or what went wrong, there were always women in this house happy to take him back. He was born puny but he outlived all his brothers. He tried a few things here, there, but he lacked moral fiber. He tried, he failed, and he came back every time. He came home and his sisters kept care of that boy all his mortal life. He died in this house at eighty-five.

On the day Teddy died, Tillie and I were out with the babies in the pony cart. My daughter was dressing Everett in his little organdie sailor suit. She had him standing up on a chair so she could tie his neckerchief when Biggie ran upstairs bawling, *Fire, fire!* All Manette heard was the racket, and she flew off at Biggie and took her time brushing Everett's yellow curls before she carried him downstairs and saw Dakin in the front hall with his face smeared with soot and streaked with tears. Tillie and I came in the front door with the babies just then.

And Little Manette dropped Everett and ran to him. It was the only time I ever saw them hug, and he was grieving. That man grieved for the rest of his life; every one of us on May Street grieved.

And Little Manette? She didn't grieve, she raged!

She was that spoiled.

Oh, how she raged. *Three years old. That stupid, disobedient boy.* She blamed poor Teddy. She blamed his big brothers for not minding him. They were miles away at the time but she berated them until they ran away. Dakin Junior enlisted in the army. He said it was the war but we knew. He couldn't wait to get shut of her because in all these things, the boys were always blamed, and dear Randolph?

She had it in for Randolph because of something we didn't know about, and she railed at him until the day she died, long after he vanished from our lives. She blamed Vincent because the flames were so high that he couldn't reach the child and she blamed Biggie for being in the kitchen, boiling water for Manette's precious white wash; she was busy doing what her mistress wanted when Teddy sneaked out behind her back. She even blamed little Ivy; I never knew why. The child loved horses, she was helping Vincent in the carriage house. She blamed Tillie for taking us out in the pony cart. Of course she blamed me.

My daughter would never blame Dakin. After all, he organized, ordered, supervised, bought and paid for every item on her growing list of wants, but I know he feels guilty all the same. I know I do, for not being there. We all do, and Manette?

She blamed everything and everybody but herself.

And Vincent and Tillie and Biggie and every living soul in this great big house? We grieved. Dakin grieved, but never where the rest of us could see, although he and the big boys rolled the empty white coffin into the church. Naturally Little Manette had taken to her bed.

Dakin had workmen come in as soon as the Hewell brothers took what we had of our Teddy away, but I know: like me, the essential part of him is trapped in the belly of this house.

They poured cement on the spot and leveled it, although Biggie would never again do laundry in the iron washtubs. He had carpenters wall off the area below the porch, as though lattice would make us safe from **undercroft,** or keep the animus or the terror— whatever seethes below— out of the body of the house.

The fool didn't know what I knew in all my secret places— that there is no safe place. Oh, he endured, but he endured in grief for the rest of his mortal life. And every year he went downstairs to inspect the lattice.

As though cheap lattice and cold cement would trap the evil in the belly of the house.

As though it would prevent his youngest daughter from going down there to meet that boy; they never thought to warn Leah because she was just a baby when Teddy died. Lovely girl, she was Dakin's favorite, although her mother wouldn't let him in to see her after the doctor came back and they found out the worst.

The day it happened nobody missed Leah until supper when we sat down, all but that sweet girl. Dakin was frantic; he searched, her brothers searched. They found her sobbing her heart out in **undercroft**, too shattered and distracted to make sense, even after Dr. Woods came and gave her laudanum to calm her down. She wouldn't tell us how or why she went down there or what happened to her or who did it, she just cried and cried. It was a man, we discovered soon enough, and Little Manette despised Leah for what it made of her. She was so bent on protecting her family's reputation in Jacksonville that she put Leah to bed and kept her there until it was time for Dr. Woods— she was just sixteen!

Manette cared more for her position in society than she did for that poor child. Nobody was allowed into Leah's room, not even her father, Manette told us when she locked that door and slipped the key into a velvet pouch she wore around her neck. She told the children that Leah had contracted a wasting disease. Who was I to tell them it was a lie?

"She's contagious, darlings." No visitors, just Little Manette, when she happened to think of it, and Tillie, our sweet little wet nurse who stayed on for years after she went dry, looking after the Ellis children until she got too old to work and Little Manette sent her away.

Poor Leah stayed in that bedroom until it was time to call Dr. Woods. He and the midwife came, and Little Manette took to her bed. I heard the child screaming, but they wouldn't let me go to her! After two awful days, the doctor opened Leah up and pulled her baby out. Another girl, healthy and perfectly formed. He waited too long! There was too much blood, and we lost Leah that day.

When the Hewell brothers came to take her away, Dakin ordered them to report it as a death from dengue fever, Manette's orders. It was right there in the death notice printed in the *Jacksonville Times-Union* along with Leah's sixteenth-birthday photograph, so as far as the family was concerned, incurable fever put Leah Ellis in the grave.

And her baby? My vain, greedy daughter named that child Elena after some dead saint, and as she had before, at the one time none of them will talk about, she claimed Leah's motherless baby as her own and all Jacksonville believed her because by that time there was something growing in her belly that even the cleverest dressmakers and finest silks could not exactly hide.

There was a party, so all Jacksonville could see Manette Robichaux Ellis cuddling her nice new baby in the christening dress my vain mother had bought for my daughter's christening—the sheerest silk organza, with a thousand flounces trimmed in Belgian lace.

So much for Leah's poor orphan child. Manette put Tillie in charge and went on about her business, trotting Poor Elena out to curtsy to every guest who came into the house. It's a mercy that God took a hand and put my daughter in her grave before she could do anything worse.

By the time my daughter died and Poor Elena escaped this house, the girl was almost too old to find an acceptable man. Little Manette kept the girl home by taking to her bed: she was Poor Elena's bounden duty and her anchor, forever demanding, never satisfied. Leah's mean, conceited twin sisters had been married and divorced by the time their mother died. The tumor had stopped growing but it turned to stone.

The twins were back and they ruled the roost, as strict and demanding as Little Manette at her worst. I saw Cinderella played out on this very hearth. Poor Elena managed to meet that nice boy in spite of her jealous aunts. She and Edwin Parkson were in love. I helped the child elope, never mind how, for by that time I was just a shadow in this world. They honeymooned downtown at the Windsor Hotel, but only for a night. Poor Elena brought her sweet young husband home to May Street the very next day— "Just until we find a house," she said. Of course it dragged on and on. Foolish girl. I tried to warn her, but I was long dead. In a way.

I was . . .

Never mind what I am.

What could I do to protect the sweet boy our Poor Elena married, what could I possibly do? He died in a terrible accident on the back stairs. It happened the week before Elena had their little girl. Edwin was dead by the time the doctor came, and he was only the newest in this strange, long line of sad lives and untimely deaths brought on by Ellis women who dared to bring new men into this terrible house. And they?

Every man jack of them died. And what shall I do about this new, angry, disorderly boy who is bound to defy me?

Take care of him!

CHAPTER 10

Dell

So far, he's moved his stuff from the overpass to May Street in stages, but not into his shelter under 553. He's stashed everything but the sleeping bag behind the last truck in the truckers' shed at the back of the ruined parking lot next door, where the old ladies never go. The bedroll's the only thing he keeps in his new quarters. He won't move the rest until it's time, but that's not the whole reason. It's an issue of incompleteness that he's not ready to address.

These nights, he waits until the house goes dark to enter. Then he slips through the gap between the shed and cyclone fence behind the poplars the old ladies planted to hide the obscenity next door. When he's satisfied that they're done for the night, he enters. He unrolls his sleeping bag and lies here in the dark, pondering.

Crucial parts of him are missing. A whole chunk of his life, for one. That part is so huge and so fucked up that he's fixed on a problem he thinks he can solve. He thinks it's the flash drive. It was the only leftover from his ex-life that he recognized when the hospital returned his stuff the day he was discharged. High-tops that felt like they were his, the jeans were close enough, jacket was too big. Then the object slithered out and bit his hand.

Dell doesn't know why he had the flash drive or what's on it, and unless he scores a computer, he can't find out. Forget the library computers, they're all connected. Insert that thing long enough to open it and you're yelling, Look, everybody, it's me. Connect and any fool can track him down.

Any fool could sneak up from behind and hit him with a sock full of shit.

He needs to destroy this record of things he doesn't want to know about. Drop the flash drive in the river or smash it with a rock, he thinks, although he has no idea why thinking about it makes his mouth dry up and his belly clench. Bury it. No. Stupid. Throw it under a bus.

Or open it.

Guilt rolls in and smashes him flat. OK then. Get it. Open it and find out, so you can get over it.

The problem is, it's lost. He was so close to done moving that he got careless on his last run on the squat. Creeping out with his flashlight, he examines every carton and garbage bag in the truckers' shed and comes up empty.

He'd have heard it drop on the road between here and the last rise. He would have heard a clink, scrape, something. It must have fallen out of a hole in one of his cartons or a rip in the garbage bags when he dragged them uphill from the squat. Crap! His fault, he was so crazy to get in out of the cold.

It's worse not knowing where the flash is than it was carrying it. He'll go back and find it tomorrow at first light.

Sleep. Get up. Get your shit together. Get coffee. Retrace your steps.

He's up and out before dawn, fanning the road between here and there with his Maglite, just in case. Nothing. He gets more coffee and goes to the head of the path that leads downhill through sandy rubble studded with patches of sandspurs. Cradling his extra-large coffee, he waits for the sun to get high enough. Then he'll scour the path downhill to the abandoned squat. The terrain has changed, but at this distance, he can't figure out what happened down there. It just looks different. It . . .

"Yo, Dell!"

Tensed for confrontation, he turns so fast that coffee flies. After months of this life, any surprise is a threat. Oh. It's just one of the guys he more or less hung with before winter moved in and they all left. Bland, nameless itinerant guys. Like Dell: Peaceable. Past history, don't ask. This bulky, easygoing squatter has a name. "Oh, Duane. Hey."

Duane wipes coffee off his front. "What the fuck?"

"Sorry about that. What are you . . . Like, why . . ."

"Come to see the renovations. You?"

Easy, Dell, this Duane is a kind-of friend. "Dropped a . . ." *Flash drive!* He stops. *Don't say it. Don't.* Right, "Phone, came back to hunt for it."

"Good luck with that. You seen what they're uptuh?"

"Not really."

"City cleaned the damn place out. Reamed it with a backhoe, so by this time, your phone's toast. Landmarks people or whatever. Making it so we never come back. You know. Cement, probably. Cut some grooves to kill your butt, plant spikes so you can't lay down."

Dell isn't exactly listening. *What phone?* He used to have a phone, he guesses. Normal people do. His portable brain or his office or both. It probably got trashed when the cab hit him, unless they're after him and he axed it to shut down the GPS.

So, did he actually lose a smartphone too, another one of those things that even normal people do? He no longer knows what happened and what didn't. He hates being like this.

Duane sighs. "Means we won't be back next year. Sucks."

What else have I lost? Dell says what you say. "Sucks."

Then out of nowhere, Duane blindsides him. "I wouldn't be coming back to dig for it if I was you."

"Say what?"

"Guys come around a couple weeks ago, sat down with us and a fifth of Jack, all nicey-nicey, but with money changing hands if we told them anything they didn't know."

Dell's life comes to a full stop. "Guys?"

"Suits, white shirts, the whole nine, with a fifth and paper cups instead of passing around the bottle like normal people do. Stupid as hell in this neighborhood, them suits, but the whiskey was good."

"DEA?"

"Not the way they was with us."

"Fuck did they want?" Reflexively, he fingers the objects in his jeans pocket; loose bill, no change, so they'll never hear you coming. Gravity knife, one flick and he's armed.

"Not like they said."

"And you said . . ." His hand closes on the knife.

Duane's cracked lips split in a grin. "I don't know nothing. I make a point of it. But they was looking for you."

"Me?"

"Think so." Nice guy, Duane, standing easy in his shoes. Lingering, kind of. Does not have to say, *or something you've got.*

Shit! If your sort-of friend here sees you scuffing around in the neatly turned dirt down there, if he follows, then the suits got to him. Go, "Phone's probably toast, might get a rebate, so. Uh." Casual, like it makes no never-mind.

"Need help?"

Worse: *Duane cuts to the chase and tells the suits who I am and where I am.* One false move and you'll have to— *Don't go there.* Dell takes his hand off the knife but his jaws clamp tight and his gut clenches. *You don't know what that place is.* "Not really."

"OK then."

CHAPTER 11

Theo

We've been on May Street for three weeks now. Like she was waiting for my mom to bring her onstage for her hours of standup, Mormama got all up close and personal every time she came, yacking up old, old stories, like her and me were tight.

She won't stop coming, drops in whenever she feels like it. Three A.M. Her favorite time. Sometimes she's in a good mood and other times she's awful. Like now.

You know boys are not welcome in this house.

Fuck I hate when that happens. Fuck I wonder what she'd do if she was alive right now and I said fuck. They didn't have these words back when she was a real person. Probably she'd just blink like that creepy china baby doll Mormama brought for this Leah's baby, but the twins took it away. They keep it in a glass box on the bottom shelf of the pier table, this great big marble-topped thing in the front room, and dead center on top is great-great-great Grandy's watch under glass along with a brooch with one of fucking Teddy's curls that I guess Mormama cut off before it happened, and here she is, all up in my face.

You have brought trouble into this place, and you know it. Scat, while you still can!

I try, "Go away. I'm not scared of you."

I'm trying to help you.

"Don't yell!"

Bad things happen to boys in this house. It isn't safe.

"You don't scare me."

You don't belong.

"Well, neither do you!" Dead forever ago, but here she is. Not again. I mean, still. She'd be about 160 years old by now. Nothing you can catch with your phone and so you can show your I-guess-it's-a-Mormie to the cops or your exorcist priest and go, See! Not like I didn't try. Nothing to see here; she is just that cold, cold presence in the room. In the portrait tucked into the downstairs bathroom she looks teeny, but what's left of her is huge.

Be quiet, child.

When Mormama is pissed at you it's like barbwire twisting in your gut.

I saw you down there. You brought trouble down on us, and trouble moved into **undercroft**.

"The what?"

I saw the two of you, you and that guttersnipe fouling my baby's tomb.

"I did not!" That first time creeped me out. A couple of times I sneaked back down to her stupid undercroft and went inside just to check, but Dell was gone and I couldn't be down there all by myself. I told her, but she wouldn't quit!

The two of you, trampling poor Teddy's bones.

"No way! He's out there in Dakin Ellis Park with all the rest of them, I saw it! Aunt Iris left me and Aunt Rosemary off at the graveyard the day Mom and her went down to the bank. She made me climb up on the stone thing."

Sarcophagus, dear.

"She made me pat the angel's head!"

We were supposed to go to a movie that day when they went downtown to parlay with the banker, but Aunt Iris made Mom drop us at the graveyard instead, me and Aunt Rose, she said it was important for me to get in touch with my roots. We walked to the family plot with its very own spiked fence and at the end Aunt Rose broke the rusty lock and made me promise not to tell. Then I had to go up the marble steps to the marble coffin thing and hold on to the baby marble angel kneeling on top while she gave this stupid lecture.

I had to read the words out loud to her before she let me get down: TAKEN FROM US TOO SOON, and when I was done my old aunt went, "That's your baby great-uncle, don't ever play with matches, you hear?" And she put a crumpled flower on his grave.

Tonight I go, "No shit, Mormama. I saw him."

But something put Mormama in an ugly mood. *You only think you did.*

"Really! He's out there, under all that stone."

She let me have it right in the gut. *Just the parts they could find.*

She went from tiny to tremendous. She *loomed.* **Understand, I am here to protect him. Poor little soul. We're trapped here until there's nothing left of him.**

I put up both hands, like I could push her out of my life. I heard me gargling, "Don't!"

Now, go down there and tell that intruder he has to go.

"What makes you think there's a . . ." Shit!

He's trouble. Terrible trouble, he has to go!

"He's gone." Um. I *think.*

I saw you colluding down there, you and that stranger, defiling poor Teddy's grave.

Shit, she knows! "No way."

I saw the both of you.

"I have to *go!*" Like there's anyplace safer than bed right now.

All right, go, if you think you're brave enough, but understand this, Theodore Dakin Ellis-whatever-your-last-name-is, you go anywhere you want in this house as long as it tolerates you, but **you do not go back to undercroft.** *You can* NOT *be there, understand?*

"Yes, Ma'am."

It isn't safe! Now, promise.

"Yes Ma'am." *Anything, if you'll just go.*

Truth? She so weirded me out that I only went back that one time, just to check but man, she is suspicious. It's not like I've found Dell there either, lady, so chill.

You know I can hear your thoughts.

"That's bull!" What can she do if I say bullshit? Face it, lady, you can't hurt me. You're dead. Still, I close my eyes and make the sign of the cross like this is a vampire and that will get rid of her, but she doesn't go. She isn't done. Her cold shape hangs over the bed. And she begins.

Things happen down there in the dark. Terrible things.

"I know!"

You only think you do. Then she surprises me. *Biggie dropped a pot of boiling water on herself, we didn't know that was the beginning. Dakin should have moved those sinks out to the carriage house that very day, but lazy Little Manette wanted her white things boiled. Bedding. Double damask dinner napkins. Everything, so the tubs stayed where they were.*

And then my poor Teddy. Oh, oh!

"Aunt Rosemary told all about it, so don't." If only she would stop!

Be quiet, boy, and let me make my point. *Nine children, eight live births, and boys were a mystery to that vain, dainty, self-centered fool I spawned! Boys. Trouble simmering, just fixing to boil over and explode. Boys love secret places, going where they can't be seen. Bad things happen then. You should know.*

Why does this make me feel guilty?

I know what you've been up to, child. Be still. If my Teddy had been playing out in the open where we could see him, oh, oh!

A great big groan comes out of her.

You and your secret places. I lost my darling boy! Dakin Junior was born haughty, and Randolph, well, he had itchy feet, and my Teddy was so easy that his mother didn't care a fig for him. He was my favorite, born sweet. But Everett was born sickly, and sickly was perfect for Little Manette. That child sucked up all the love in her the minute they cut the cord.

While my poor Teddy was abandoned, and then he . . . nobody knew until they heard the screams . . . the baby burned bright down there in his own little hell, and we didn't know, we didn't know! He died in the shadows under the porch where you and that heathen stranger . . .

"Don't!"

But she finishes anyway. *I'm not telling you this because I enjoy it. I'm telling you to keep you safe! You can't be there, you two with your heads together, you and that dirty boy.*

"He's not a boy!"

Right, Mormama. Diss the man and vanish. She lays this down inside my head, like a flower on a fresh grave. *They're all boys to me.*

"Besides," I tell her. "He hasn't been back, so shut up," I said and I was begging because I needed at least one other guy around here, but he wasn't anywhere.

The old bitch strikes back.

Oh, yes he has.

CHAPTER 12

Lane

Nice-looking man comes ambling along May Street at just the right time, the first good thing that's happened since I moved back into the kingdom of the aunts. Their clocks rewound the second I walked in. I'm ten years old again, poor little orphan girl, beholden. Which I am, since they cashed in my escape fund to feed this monstrous house. And will be, until I grapple my new Ikea workstation out of the car and in the front door.

He stops to watch. OK, I am a spectacle. Buff woman failing to budge the box, which the guys at Ikea slipped into my hatchback slicker than a greased manatee. He's not staring, exactly. He's just waiting to see what happens.

Dude, would you please go away so I can do this? It's a matter of pride. This shouldn't be a problem, but it is.

My next move— call it my hope for the future— is wedged into my car tighter than a cork in a wine bottle. It'll take six winged monkeys to assemble the thing after I get it in the house, which is another problem. I can't afford the yard man, who comes back to do certain things for the aunts, and I'm damned if I'll ask them to front for it. I'll manage. I'm getting used to managing on my own. And the new desk I can't afford for the refurbished laptop and bottom-of-the-line printer I bought on credit?

Cheap at the price. Equipment for Operation Job Search. Anything to spring us from the ancestral roach motel, where nobody and nothing has changed since I was fourteen. This is essential equipment. If I can get it out of the damn car.

"Wait, let me."

My hands freeze on the carton. "I've got this, OK?"

I drove the hell down the coast and inland to Orlando to get the impressively oversized workstation, accent on *work*. Yep, ladies, I'm making a statement.

The drive was easy. The hard part was getting out of the house before they cut me off at the pass. Rosemary and Iris intersected me in the front hall, a classic pincer maneuver, with Ivy shuttling back and forth behind them on Scooter, afraid I'd never come back. The twins closed in on me with dripping coffee mugs: where was I going, I was buying a *what?* Why would I want to drag a piece of junk like that into a beautiful place like this. The Preservation Society comes every year because this is a fine old family home and all the best people in Jacksonville come flocking every tenth of June. We keep everything just the way Little Manette had it, it's our sacred duty, Little Elena.

Like the flock of overflowing ashtrays and flat-screen TVs in every sacred room have been here ever since Dakin carried Manette over the mahogany threshold in 1893. Elena, you hear?

"Don't call me that."

They never learn. "Elena Ellis Upchurch Hale, do you hear?"

"It's not my name!"

"Honor your mother, Elena."

"Lane!"

"After everything we've done for you!"

The fight with the great-aunts took twelve years off my life because? Because this is my first stab at pretending I have one in this house. Life, I mean, now that I'm temporarily shackled here, and without the bonds they'd mysteriously cashed without my signature, beholden.

I need the machine so I can follow up leads from here and the workstation to make it official: Don't bother me, I'm working.

They had a hissy fit when I explained. Warden Rosemary: "Elena, you can't."

"I am."

General Iris: "In the room where our beloved Sister died? Sweetie, it's a sacrilege."

I grabbed my son. "Come on, Theo. Let's go."

In the end I had to leave Theo with them, my son the living hostage, promissory note, whatever it took. He glared at me like a trapped groundhog. Poor kid!

Finally I dangled the idea Haircut Needed, and Iris snapped at the bait. Poor Theo, with his face clenched in that I-will-never-forgive-you glare. Oh, dude! Sorry, but this is the only way out. I made it to Orlando, I made it back, and I will damn well make it up to you, but now that I'm out here on May Street in broad daylight, struggling with our Get Out of Jail Free card, why are you not out here with me, wrangling it into the house?

Nice voice: "Please, let me."

"What!" It comes out more like *eek*. God this is embarrassing. "It's OK, I've got this, thanks." Yeah, I don't, but I have to look as if I do.

It's Pavlovian. If the great-aunts saw this tall, easygoing stranger coming up the front walk with me, they'd freak. *He can't come in!* They reek of fear, all three of them. After Mom died they ramped up the lectures, like I was their job. They said, *Never talk to strangers,* but they meant *strange men.* Unless, and I can't get to the bottom of it, they just meant *men.* But the twins meant what they said when they told me, *You don't know where they came from or what they're up to or what they want.* They've kept at it year-round since I was eight. Do it this way. Wear that. Watch out for this, for that, and in the name of God don't embarrass us. And don't think you can go out wearing *that*.

You'd think I was a rhesus monkey they could imprint.

Well, nobody imprints me.

Meanwhile this nice guy hangs in place like a cursor on my screen, waiting for me to decide. He looks OK, great face, with just enough things wrong with it— scar through the eyebrow, nose off-kilter— to keep it real. Besides, this carton is fighting to win. I stand back. God, I am embarrassed. In seconds he has it upended on the walk. Blush. Gasp. "Thanks so much!"

"No problem."

Great smile, too. Faded T-shirt. Tech logo I don't recognize. Black jeans worn silver at the knees. This new man is easy in his body, but. What. Tentative. "Let me get it up those steps for you, OK? And if you want, I'll help you get it into the house." Another great, hesitant smile. "If that's OK."

"Thanks, but I'd better take it from here." The bleached eyes, the bemused look make me add, "Ordinarily I'd." Put your shoulder to it, bitch. "Um." Shove. Pause for breath. Return his smile. "See, the relatives are . . ." How can I explain the part that I know but won't tell anyone? Apologetic shrug. "A little weird."

"No prob." He aims the box at the gate for me and slides it through.

Just then I hear Iris shrilling from inside. "Elena, who's out there?"

I did what I had to. I put my shoulder to the box. Born xenophobes, those bitches. They never change. Nobody calls me Elena, but they can't be taught. No, won't.

Warden Rosemary barks, "Elena."

General Iris: "Elena Ellis Upchurch Hale, get in here!"

Even poor old Ivy is on my case, but I can't make out what she just said.

For Ivy's sake, I call. "In a minute, OK?" Bunch your muscles, lady, lean into that box. God damn you, Barry Hale, for getting me pregnant in the middle of senior year. I thought you were forever and this was true love. OK, I thought it was the great escape. Freedom from May Street with all that this implies. A life.

For twelve years I coped with the baby, the chores, the half-dozen moves, the suits you needed for the next big thing, the side trips, because your business was too important to explain. Well damn you and damn your online stock market trades and God damn you to hell for taking charge of the finances, you were all, "Sweetheart, I've got this."

As if.

Shove. Six inches.

Asshole! You said you knew what you were doing, you and your night-school MBA, but you didn't know shit, how could I not see that? I didn't find out that you'd defaulted on the mortgage until the bank foreclosed— split seconds after you took off for North Wherever just beyond Out of Here some time between midnight and 5 A.M., while Theo and I were dead asleep.

"Drop that thing and come on up here." All three of them are out front watching. Hoik. Shove!

Iris shrills, "Right now, you hear!"

Shove. Another foot.

It was tough after Barry left but I thought Theo and I could make it. After all, the house was paid off. I could get something, temp agency, sell houses, work in Walmart or bag groceries at the Publix, scrub floors if I had to, anything to make enough to keep the two of us afloat, I could . . .

"Elena!"

Faster, Lane. Woman, put your back into it. You don't want them coming out here, all cranked up to call 911.

Then the bank sent someone to nail their FOR SALE sign on the front of what I thought was our house.

What difference did it make, by that time trucks had come for all the cool furniture you bought on credit when we moved to Daytona, "Perfect for our new love nest, honey," charges deferred for up to a year. Apologetic, the repo men, tsk-tsking around their cigars. The only thing they left was the car.

Thoughtful, asshole! So, what. Did you think Theo and I could live out of the trunk, wash in the park fountain and sleep in a different parking lot every night?

The screen door opens. "Elena, stop dawdling!"

Oh, shit.

"You sure you don't need a hand?"

"Who is that bum?"

Snap!

Twenty years of instant replay on fast-forward, and I'm only halfway up the walk. Now, handsome stranger back there is offering to help, but from a distance. Nice guy, it's just a little weird, him standing outside the gate like a vampire waiting to be invited in.

"I'm fine," I tell him because they're on the sill, rolling Ivy out on the porch. Move fast, or they'll come down here, level cannon, all, "Fire in the hold." I lean into the carton and move it two feet, living proof that I'm *FINE*. "I just needed a minute to catch my breath."

General Iris chugs out the door with Warden Rosemary at her side, both of them glowering and loaded for bear. If our general had an Uzi she'd aim it at my midsection and cut me in half. "Elena, *who is that man*?" She lifts her chin and throws her voice over my head, to make certain he hears. "Whoever you are, we don't want any, go away!"

Humiliated, I turn to apologize, but the walk is empty except for me and the carton. It's as if he was never there.

CHAPTER 13

Mormama

I was never welcome in this house. Odd, how long it's been since I walked through those front doors into my daughter's overblown temple to material things. Odd that of all of those who died here but remain trapped here, only I endure.

Mother took Little Manette's wedding out of my hands. I was necessary but not welcome, even then. I wanted to give Manette's wedding party in Mother's house on Tradd Street, but they would have none of it. I warned that our finances were precarious, but they didn't care. Mother borrowed all over Charleston to please the girl and when it was done, she invited me to lunch. She commanded creamed chicken on toast points, frilly linens and the second-best silver on the long porch, and she glared at Margaret until she went back inside.

Then she leaned across the table, all perfumed and smiling, and said, "Honey, Little Manette and I went ahead with the arrangements, so you don't have to worry about a thing." She did it without a care, because she knew who they would come to when it was time to collect. "Don't look at me like that! You know we couldn't count on you to *do* like *ladies* do."

So my daughter married Dakin Ellis at St. Michael's Church, where all the best weddings took place, full choir, altar banked with gardenias and white orchids, with, at the Carolina Yacht Club, set luncheons and champagne for a hundred guests. Dainty Manette used the silver Millard family cake knife to cut into a cake the size of Fort Sumter, and she cut a piece of wedding cake for me to sleep on, slipping it into my purse with a spiteful grin.

Then my only living child bestowed a cold, mock hug and a pretend-kiss and she and handsome young Dakin walked out of my life and into her grand new house near the St. Johns River in Jacksonville without so much as a thank-you or a come-down-and-see-us-sometime. Dakin gave her too many babies too fast. I knew, although I wasn't told.

I'd sent violet-sprigged notepaper for her birthday, but she never wrote. Oh, she did offer to bring "dearest Mama" down to see her first great-grandchild, but they both knew that was out of the question. Mother had taken to her bed, it was too hard a trip; by that time Margaret was gone and I was taking care of Mother in the Ware house on Tradd Street. It was all we had left. I offered to come, but Manette tsk-tsked, "We couldn't possibly tear you away from dearest Mama."

When she had Randolph I wrote, but Little Manette sent a polite note: "Oh no, the trip would be too much for you," the only time I saw those violets on an envelope. After Everett, they had Teddy, and next, oopsy-daisy, the twins. Twins! When the twins came I offered again. This time, Dakin wrote. The letter was typewritten on office stationery— by his secretary, I suppose, although he did sign it in sepia ink to confirm his intentions. Never mind what he wrote. He meant, don't bother, I'd only be in the way.

Then Little Manette had Leah. Too soon! Nobody bothered to tell me; I came upon the card among Mother's things months after she died. All of Manette Senior's bad debts had come home to roost, and to satisfy them, the bank foreclosed on the house.

This time, I didn't offer to help with the children. I went. I sent a telegram the day I hired a carriage to take me and my things to the train station. It said, ENROUTE FROM CHARLESTON. COMING TO HELP.

By the time Western Union rang the bell, I was halfway to Jacksonville, with the last of my money and my diamonds in the tapestry bag, and the rest in the baggage car, a steamer trunk and three suitcases, one woman alone, with nowhere else to go. It was a hard trip, longer than any trip should be. I was weeping with exhaustion by the time I arrived at the house. At first sight it was gorgeous, white as a wedding cake and decorated like one, and, Lord, Dakin had lined his children up on the porch to welcome me!

Well, you know how that went. He groaned as he watched the men unloading my suitcases from the carriage, and I did not have the heart to tell him about the steamer trunk.

Then Dakin drove the first nail in the coffin, although we did not know it at the time, repeating under his breath as he opened the great front door for me, ". . . One more Mama than we need," making clear that Little Manette was "Mama" now, and I cannot tell you why my heart clenched, only that I was afraid of the great house I was entering and what it might contain. I teetered on the sill. I couldn't go in; I couldn't flee. Ever the gentleman, heedless Dakin grasped my elbow and ushered me into the maw. In all the winters of my life, in all these years in my daughter's house, I've never been so cold.

He looked down at me, concerned. "You're trembling."

"It's nothing," I said, and Mother rushed into my head, triumphant. *Now, say what ladies say.*

"You must be tired."

Now. "What a lovely house!"

"Oh, please." He waved me into the slipper chair. "Here."

"I'm sorry, I'm." I don't know what I was.

"I'll fetch Tillie to see to you." Dakin tugged on a fringed bell-pull and a sweet little colored girl came. "Please show Mrs. Robichaux to her room."

My heart went out. I tried, "Thank you."

Dakin's face was a revelation. Pride fought with pleasure and pain as he said, "Well, I guess you're here to stay."

Now they're gone and I'm still here, whether as victim or mistress, I don't know, shuttling back and forth, up and down in this ghastly house. I am either subject to **undercroft** or fixed in place to oppose it, but there is nobody living or dead who can tell me which.

Whether from the pressure of responsibility or by the power of love, I am in this house for a reason. That, at least, I know. An essential part of my poor, dear Teddy is still here, trapped down there, under the cement they poured to cover the spot where he died, and I *can not go* until God frees us both. We can't go. I am here for Teddy's soul and all the others trapped here, living and dead.

I'm here to defend them all from the forces stirring in **undercroft** because knowingly or not, creator or carrier, my vain, thoughtless daughter designed this temple to greed and when she entered, the evil sprang to life. Damn it. Damn this house and damn each ornament and every stick of furniture my daughter fed into its maw. Damn Little Manette and her voracious will, damn Dakin for his folly. Damn me.

CHAPTER 14

Dell

Who am I now that she's seen me? He doesn't know. He was an unknown quantity here, and as far as the people in the house were concerned, more or less invisible. Until today. Stupid, stupid, jumping in to help Lane Hale, but that carton probably out-weighed her. She'd never get it out of the car single-handed. He couldn't just hang back and watch her wrestle a box bigger than she is.

But they've all seen him now: this pretty woman and her kid and needy old Ivy, who seems to depend on him for something he has zero power to provide, and to complete the set, scooter lady's mean-looking sisters, who had no idea he lived under the porch. The evil— twins, he decides— just spilled out the front door, pissed off and sputtering. They can't see past the porch rail but they're fixed on him like star witnesses scrutinizing mug shots, bent on making the ID that sends him up the river for whatever the hell he did.

He and the kid have an understanding, and Lane? *She likes me.* Yes. He knows her name. He knows a lot about the women in this house, stealing information without their knowing it. She'd know him anywhere, not by name, because names can morph in seconds and in that instant, change lives. It's the vibe. Kindred outsiders, at war with the ethos, the static, congested nature of the house. They were shoving the box along when the matched set came out on the porch, one barking, "What's that?" "Who's out there?" "No strangers on this property!" and the other squawking, "Elena, what were you thinking?" and "I'm warning you!" while at their backs poor scooter lady shuttled, begging them to get out of her way.

Lane went all whites of the eyes at the first shout, and turned to him with her face filling up with things unspoken. She said over her shoulder, "I've got this." She threw her whole weight against the carton and it slid through the front gate, at least a little bit. It took everything Dell had to stay back and let her do it.

Nice that she turned back to him with that desperate, apologetic grin.

Like she was protecting both of us.

He took the warning and faded, leaving her to hump that carton up the long walk alone. Given the givens, he had to, even though he'd come out today thinking to move the last of his cartons out of the shed and into his quarters. He's been sleeping under the sprawling back porch for long enough to think of it as safe.

More.

At night, he roams the great house overhead. Accidentally or not, sweet old Ivy told him how to come and go because, he supposes, she took to him the morning he helped her turn that scooter. He enters and leaves the body of the house through the long-dead Vincent's hatch.

Since then he's prowled the double parlors during the darkest hours, inspected the flaking ancestral portraits and tried his breath on the beveled mirror above the heavy marble-topped pier table that stands like a little altar in the big front room, covered with sacred objects exactly where the first lady of the house had the help put them. It looks like one of those museum model rooms, cordoned off by velvet ropes so strangers can't trample the carpets or make off with personal treasures. He wonders if they closed the sliding doors between this and the second parlor to keep the children off the rococo chairs and the plum velvet sofa with its mahogany claws and scrolled mahogany trim.

Probably. It's a shrine to whatever the grand lady of the house thought she was.

Look at her, hanging above the sofa in her golden oval frame: flaking gold leaf, to match the golden chains around her delicate throat. Triangular face, with hair combed high off the white, white forehead to accentuate her widow's peak. Tight little mouth. Beautiful jewelry. Dead eyes. Planted where visitors could see it from the hall. Romanticized portrait, with plaque:

MANETTE WARE ELLIS

So dainty and so . . . *something*. Whatever that something is, it makes him sick. Well, fuck you.

The marble-topped pier table dominates the room. It stands between windows covered by fringed velvet drapes so dense that daylight never touches her precious things. With his Maglite, he's studied the objects enshrined there. A heavy gold watch in its ornamental case is centered under the gigantic mirror, like a little tabernacle. To its left a glass dome covers a lock of the dead child's hair; he doesn't have to read the plaque. It's Teddy's hair, flanked by a pair of five-branched candelabra that don't look right no matter which way they're turned. Dell points them in different directions every time he goes into the room, trying for symmetry, and he's done it as freely as Theo would if the old women weren't around to stop him, the difference being that Dell always waits until everybody has gone silent to come up from his quarters, into the body of the house.

And they are his quarters now.

He's made the move from his squat at the overpass via the shed next door cautiously, over time, putting down whatever fit in his backpack or under his arm in the far corner of the truck storage shed, stowing his gear behind a rusting semi. Last night he transferred all but the last few items from the shed, rifling each carton as he brought it inside. Face it, Dell. You're finding that fucking flash drive today.

He searched the last of his cartons before the sun came up rifling them with anxiety running up his heels: the missing USB stick. Guys on his trail, according to Duane. Is it something he did? Walk it off, he told himself. Go out and come back with some Dumpster furniture to make this place a home.

Then he blew it all by helping the girl.

Now he has to stay off the premises until well after midnight. Let the old ladies think he just happened by today, helpful working man on his way to the job. He can't come back until the last one awake up there, the last old woman shuffling around inside turns out the last light in the Ellis house. Then he'll have to wait that extra hour before he enters, just to be sure.

Walking, he has the rest of the day to plan.

Use up the day window-shopping for stuff you need that you can get free. Get coffee and browse Dumpsters, wander through box stores looking at things you don't have the money to buy, and as the day winds down you do what any normal person would do. Go back to the last place and wait until it's time to come home. Tent one of their abandoned cartons, if you can find one, and if you can't, grab a couple behind the Publix and drag them into the elbow of the overpass. Hey, it was home for a while. Wrong. What passes for home. You have a real place now, you just can't go back there until it's safe.

Sleep if you can. Treat yourself to a MacSomething-or-other before you even think about going back to 553. Coffee, for sure, he tells himself, walking until he forgets that he's still walking. You need to be sharp to divine next steps.

Divine. *Like I'm good enough to have foreknowledge delivered in a flash.*

As though whatever this is, this is fated.

As if he's expected here. Does he not have the index card that brought him all this way? In ways he doesn't understand, he is expected. Expected to what? He is expected to do something big with this life or something terrible, and Dell has spent more than one night under that back porch in lotus position, reflecting, in hopes of finding out which.

As though the mystery that hounds him will reveal itself if he can do the right things in the right order. Sit without moving for long enough. Think hard enough and it will come to him in a flash. Yeah, flash, and this is what keeps him walking.

He's up against it now. When the USB stick slithered out of his shoe at the hospital, he recoiled. He buried it every time he moved because he can't bear the sight of it. He should have pitched it into Narragansett Bay back then, or thrown it into a sewer after the thaw. Now he shores up his anxiety with reasons:

One. It could be loaded with information that incriminates him, or worse.

Two. There are guys out looking for him. Or it. Either way, it's bad.

Three. He needs to search and destroy. It's not like the thing holds the secrets of life in the universe.

Four. Unless it does.

He has to know.

Never mind that your last run on the defunct colony was a wash. Go back and search while the sun is high. If they see you, bring it. Stupid or dangerous or not, he steps off the street and slides down into the hollow.

Hell with it. Maybe I want to get caught.

Nick of time, so there's that. Stakes and string mark the area where road crews will pour cement over the footprint of the lost colony, burying the leftovers of their lives.

At the foot of the hill he drops to his knees and advances on all fours, sifting the sandy gray Florida dirt with his hands. He'll do it until his fingers are raw, working his way through the arch. If that's what it takes.

But, shit! Planted on a flat rock centered in the space that belonged to Dell real-last-name-still-pending, the missing flash drive sits like a tribal offering.

Or a warning.

Forget what you thought you were going to do with the rest of this wasted day, idiot. Either you open the thing, back up the contents and act accordingly or pitch it into the St. Johns River after all, but which? Find out. Forget the public library. Nobody plugs a flash drive that they don't know what's on it into a networked computer, hell, into anything that's connected. That's spilling your guts to the world. Get your own machine and disable wifi before you boot up.

Score a laptop and get this over with. There's enough furniture in Dumpsters to furnish half of Jacksonville, but with electronics, you have to know a guy. Given the few bucks you have in hand, it's either do crap jobs off the books for as long as it takes to scrape together the cash or, shit. You're not stupid.

You know what to do.

CHAPTER 15

Theo

So my mom is tied up most days and every night, all pointing and tapping on her cheap little— one step up from a PlayStation, although she gets pissed off when I call it that. She says it was expensive, and she passworded it so the screen dares me to guess what new string she entered before she left the house, and you know what? I've tried everything and I still can't crack it, I hate my life.

It's not like I want to troll porn sites, unless porn is running and rerunning your one video of that one day back when you used to be happy. See, my ex-Dad posted last year's Christmas video, which includes me shooting him striking funny poses on every ride we took so I could see how much fun we had together the day he took me to Disney World. We even stayed for the parade and the fireworks. He was making memories for us he said, and I thought there would be plenty.

He took his damn computer and Mom's laptop with him the night he left.

You bet I'm pissed at him, but I need to check that link, in case he posted something new. Like, a message to me. He could be thinking I had access and there's something big he wants to tell me. Like, he loves me but he had to go in a hurry because, and he wants me to know he loves me and that he's OK. Like, he's figuring out how to get us all back together, and he hopes it will be soon. Unless he's posted a new video signifying his whereabouts, you know, a secret message to me because he really did leave Mom forever, but he wants me to come with.

No way I can tell Mom what I want, so when she goes downstairs for more coffee, I go, "Let me see your PlayStation for a minute? I need to check out the movies."

"PlayStation! Stop that! What do you think I'm doing up there, checking out cute guys on Tinder or . . ." She shouts, just to piss them off, the great-whatevers who are almost always listening, "watching kiddie porn?"

OK, er*hem*. My mother is working hard on her new laptop, honing MS Office skills while she grinds out letters to print along with the resume she keeps rewriting because she has to get a fucking job so we can put together enough money to get out of this miserable haunted house.

What did you think it was?

E.g., crazy or not, Mormama's still here. Plus, there's something going on down underneath this place that I don't know about, I only know that it's bad. The old ladies are all up in my face about how lucky I am to be living in this beautiful home, which totally sucks. Are they too snotty to know it's a big old broken-down junk shop loaded with creaky furniture and moth-eaten curtains and crap that nobody wants? But they take on like we aren't all five of us, like, wading around under the weight of gajillion years and berzillion broken things, like everything is fine here at the

tippy bottom of the ocean where the past is so thick that you can't
wade through it and dust or time or something is so dense in here
that it's getting hard to breathe.

Fuck yes it's heavy, and I spend most of the time trying to break
out, because the old ladies don't want me to go outside. Their eyes
get all watery and their mouths shrivel when they catch me heading for the door. "Teddy, don't! You know the neighborhood has
gone downhill since we were girls."

"This isn't . . ."

Pffft, they cut that one off. "Don't!"

"This is *not* Teddy! I'm Theo." Fuck, I sound like Mom.

They go, "Teddy, it isn't safe!" That's Aunt Iris, talking through
her nose.

Aunt Rosemary shrieks, "You have no idea what it's like out
there!"

"Theo, get it?"

Yes they are afraid. "Teddy, it isn't safe!"

Which, if I was Teddy, it sure as hell wasn't safe. Stupid little
kid. Burned to a crisp underneath the back porch. Safe is bullshit
in this place, and they're so dim that they don't get it. They take
on like it happened right in front of them. But I'm almost thirteen,
ladies, get a grip. I work out every day here, getting fit so I can
fight. I'm no baby, too little to be left alone with kitchen matches
and too dumb to walk away, I'm me.

So when they're not looking, I sneak. That means figuring out
when the aunts are gone, or as they say, tied up. Aunt Ivy's no
problem, she's stuck on the first floor, and it's not like she'll be
running out to stop me. I wait for the right times. When the twins
start bitching about how bad their hair looks and making lists,
that's one. They're generally gone for hours getting their hair done,
and you know they'll come back bitching about how it looks, all
that time and our good money for *this*. Plus picking up their freaking medications at the CVS and buying new makeup to make

them look better next time they go to the Ebb Tide Beauty Salon. Like that'll work.

Then there's weekdays at two, when *General Hospital* comes on. They get in so deep that they don't even hear the door close, but I can't go far because I have to be back in here before it's over, or I'm screwed.

The aunts are all, don't go out there honey, it isn't safe! In a way, I see what they mean. Hang a right when you go outside and it's like, alien surface of the moon, nothing but vacant lots and three more dumps like Marvista, except the other houses have cyclone fences to like, protect them from us, unless they're scared you'll get chomped up by their pit bull or Rottweiler or whatever crazy mixed-up savage dog that they found to keep out people like me, and they'll get sued.

All of those ex-houses have bars on the windows and once or twice I caught sad, cobwebby old people with their glasses pushed way down on their noses, trying to see what's going on out here. Nothing, OK? There's jagged shit in the bushes in most places and stuck in the weeds in all the vacant lots, smushed beer cans and busted whiskey bottles and crack pipes and all, plus I keep finding used rubbers and bent needles in the parking lot next door, step on one bare foot and you'll get AIDS— hey, I watch TV— and in the gravel in front of Marvista? Stuff that you don't want to know *what* it is.

The Marvista is gross. These skeezy guys live there, and they aren't always the same ones, plus gangs of temporary type ladies that either sleep over or get pissed off and come down the back steps or the fire escape ranting in the middle of the night. Maybe they really are dangerous like Aunt Iris says, although there's one old, old woman on the ground floor that I think she owns the building and a big lady with a baby on the top floor, either she's some guy's fat wife or a girlfriend that he left behind. She yells all the time and her baby just cries and cries.

Cop cars pull up in front of Marvista a couple times a week to drag people out because the party got too loud or somebody got hurt in the fight or it woke up Aunt Iris and she called 911. They're at it most nights. Even though I close the porthole, noise comes in. Sometimes it sounds like they're Doing It or fighting or whatever right here on the rug at the end of my bunk, and Mormama? You don't want to know.

Oh, OK. She comes and goes like she owns the place.

I can't stay here!

It's awful going out, but it's not as bad as coming in. So I go around the block and around the block when I can, thinking maybe I'll run into at least one other kid like me and we can talk. Mom's upstairs right now, working on her typing speed and the aunts are sitting in front of *General,* they call it *General*! And you know what? I don't care if I don't make it back before the end. I just need to speak to another living human being or, um, an imaginary one that doesn't think she's related to me.

Pardon me if the creaky front stairs scream *traitor* at each step.

This time, I have a, like, objective? So I turn left. I'm heading for the cross street down at the end where May Street meets the four-lane street that goes down to the overpass. This way you go past the storage shed with its parking lot. There are snakes and sharp things in the mess of sandspurs in the vacant lot just beyond. I'm heading for the creepy corner store with messed-up whitewash covering the front windows, like they don't want you seeing what they're doing in the back.

It's the kind of store that you don't want to go into, you know, all dark and stuffy, with smooshed roaches stuck to the steps and a sticky floor inside. It's run by a creepy old guy that really doesn't want you there so instead of buying one of his crap candy bars you stick your change back in your pocket and turn around and go, except, today, at least he'll have to tell me he's fresh out of whatever-it-is, all I need to do is go in and ask.

Face it, I'm going in that store to have a conversation. I just need to talk to somebody that isn't an old lady, you know?

It's pretty yuck inside, starting with creepy old guy. Most of the hair on creepy old guy's head is on his face, and there's food stuck in it. He won't smile and he's not about to start a conversation. I stand around, trying to figure out what product to ask for so we can start, but the stuff behind the glass front on the counter looks so old that I don't want to think about touching it, much less asking the guy to break my five bucks and pull thousand-year-old Junior Mints out of the case. I check out the magazine stand thinking maybe, but it's the same deal. There are Souvenir of Jacksonville postcards left over from I don't know when. The edges are all yellow and the palm trees look sick. There's a really old pay phone on the wall next to the door with a sign next to it: CUSTOMERS ONLY, and a really big sign above the counter. NO LOITERING, which is what I am. A centipede is humping from the bottom of the counter to the door. If something doesn't happen before that thing makes it to the door frame, I'm done.

"See that sign?"

NO LOITERING

"Right." I beat the centipede, no prob. The other side of May Street looked better, the one they warned me about. There are always guys hanging out under the banyan tree.

The aunts are scared of it because shadows. Plus, certain people in cars slow down to pick certain things up from these guys, handing off whatever they have to pay to get what they want, and I don't know if it's mollies or heroin or what. I don't need any, at least I don't think I do, but I could start a conversation by asking if they had weed and if my five would get me a joint that I could take to Dell, like, if I came to his place under the porch with a present, he'd have to let me in.

It's not like any of these guys even notice me, so I hang around and hang around trying to figure out how to start. After a while, I just stand there pretending to bond with them thinking just maybe they'll decide I'm OK and it can start. It doesn't, but it beats the hell out of going home. Then another car comes along May Street and it's way too familiar, that little red . . . *Noooo!* And, shit! My mom slows down and rolls down the street-side window and leans across the seat. One of the guys starts over to the car to, like, hand her something and I think, *Oh no, Mom. Not you!*

Then she shouts, and that shout sends all those guys back into the shadows under the banyan, "OK for you, Theodore Upchurch Hale. Get in."

"I'm sorry!" I'm sweating-hot and shaky after I get in, trying too hard to explain. "I just couldn't stand another . . ."

"Shut up," she said, "We're going to Staples," and that's all she said.

Staples again. In this big ugly, empty town going to Staples is like coming home. Everything pretty much like they had it when we lived in Deland. Ever since she found out about the no money, Mom has been here a lot. After the workstation and the laptop, we had to go back for a printer and a big pack of paper, with Mom praying that she gets some job before the bill comes in. She brought home the printer, all right, and it works fine. The trouble is, after, like, a hundred copies of her resume, the demo cartridge that came with the printer ran out, one of those things they don't tell you before you leave the store. Either that, or she thought she'd get a job and we could come back and buy a whole box of them.

Staples is an extremely cool place. If I could do it without up-setting Lane, I'd find an unoccupied corner and move in for good. Part of me wants to grab one of the shiny new phones off the display so I can get the Internet in my room, but no. Your mom would freak. Look at her, popping that printer cartridge into her cart. String it out, Lane. This is a hell of a lot homier than 553.

It's like she knows what I am thinking. When we head for the checkout counter, there's a line; she looks at me. "This is taking too long. Maybe we should go to Baskin-Robbins and come back afterward. What do you think?"

I pretend to be looking at Moleskine books, we could afford a small one, or I could, with a little help. I give her The Smile. "I'm cool. Take your time."

She looks so little standing there, with her one small item in that big red cart. "OK then." Then she gets to browsing, just like me.

I think she's looking for something in particular, I don't know what, so I wander off into the computer section thinking maybe one of the demo models is hooked up to the Internet and I can check out Barry's YouTube channel, so I go along trying keyboards one at a time, on down the aisle to the back of the store and, weird. Down at the tippy end, hunched over so I can't see what he's doing, it's Dell Duval.

I'm like, "Yo," and Dell looks up at me with this confusing smile.

He looks different out here in the daylight. I've only ever seen him back there underneath the porch, where it's so dark that you can't really tell what a person's like. My mom only saw him that one time, the day she got the new workstation, so it's not like she knows him like I do. Workstation Day he was gone before I came outside to help and the aunts made Vincent come over and help us get the thing into the house. Vincent is nice, but he's a little weird. He turns up whenever there's heavy lifting, but in an odd way, it's like he was never there.

Now, Dell, Dell is something else. In the daytime, he looks a lot nicer than I thought he was when I found him under our back porch. When he sees that it's me, he turns halfway and gives me this big you-can-trust-me smile. As it turns out he has equally trust-me color eyes, but he doesn't exactly straighten up right away. First, he finishes buttoning up his flannel shirt, like it's important to do this before I get too close. And hey, the part where his abs should be looks straight up and down and flat like he's hiding something. Which he is.

Then he grins for real, and says, like he's really glad to see me, "Theo. This is cool."

"OK . . ."

"Really. You're just in time."

I'm not going to ask him, in time for what. I'll make him tell me.

"I need you to do something for me," he says finally. We are laying out the terms for an agreement. "OK?"

"OK."

"OK." Now we are talking man to man, like, with respect. He jerks his head at an old guy in the store T-shirt, the only one in this section. "Could you tell him you want to check out the new Apple watch?"

"Like . . ." Weird. I would do anything for him. I don't want another father, I had one, and he turned out to be a pisser. I just want him to be my friend.

"It won't take long."

And I don't want him to spell it out for me. I go, "Right." Create a diversion. "OK, cool."

He goes, "Thanks, I owe you," and if Dell is gone by the time me and the clerk are done inspecting the new gadget that we don't want and if I did, the gadget that we have no way of paying for, that's cool too.

So Mom finds me talking to the clerk and she's so happy that I've found someone to talk to that we pretty much marvel over the demo and when he's done we thank him nicely and quit the store. Then it's a hop, skip and a jump to Baskin-Robbins, and the next time I go out the back porch steps way and Dell is home, even without the house present, he and I are tight now. He owes me, we both know it, I just need to give him time to set up. Then I can go down to his place and check in on his Internet *or else*. It won't take long and as soon as that's over, I'll bring out the

Ghirardelli bar Mom got me when she paid for the printer cartridge, and we can hang out.

As soon as I get in the house she pounces. Cold breath on the back of my neck. *You and that dirty boy.*

There are no boys here, lady. Just men, and we are in this together.

Take that, Mormama. All right for you.

CHAPTER 16

Lane

We were driving home from Baskin-Robbins in San Marco when my boy Theo dropped this odd, off-beat sentence in the air. The kind that makes mothers worry. It was so nice hanging out with him that when we left Staples, I drove over to San Marco instead of going to the one down town. We were on our way back over the river to May Street when the afternoon turned into rush hour and we ended up stuck on the bridge.

Theo just started. "She said look underneath the mattress in Sister's room."

"Who did?"

He wouldn't answer. I knew that look.

The car in front of us moved a half-yard. We moved a half-yard. We were going to be here a while, so I leaned on him. I knew what he was trying to tell me, and I needed him to know it too. "I said, *who was it?*"

Then he got all congested and weird. "Not sure."

"OK then, where did you hear this? Were you spying on the three witches?"

"What?"

"You know, *Macbeth*. The aunts!"

"Not really."

"Then who?"

Egregious shrug. "It's not important."

If the traffic hadn't de-clogged just then I would have pulled over and shaken it out of him. Then we could get down to it. Mormama. One more reason to leave that miserable house for good. "Dammit, Theo, where do you get this stuff?"

His face went eight ways to Sunday and he yelled, "I overheard it!"

We were close to the end of another long day in Jacksonville, forgive me, I snapped. "Just say it, Theo. Don't jerk me around."

I was working when the twins came banging on the bedroom door this afternoon, semi-hysterical. Their "Teddy" was missing. Missing! A thousand horror movies flashed through my head while I searched the house and the dilapidated garage-cum-servants' quarters out back, followed by worse scenarios as I got into the car: death by coral snake in one of the vacant lots on May Street, kidnap by sex offender, violation, certain death and no, that was not the worst.

Kidnap by estranged dad with the time and the money to take our boy anywhere and keep him there, and I might never get him back. That was the worst. I took off after my kid, planning to comb the neighborhood before I called the police; I was crazy with worry and ready to kill Barry, if it came to that.

Silly me. My boy Theo was out there on the corner playing like he was just one of the guys hanging out under the banyan tree across from the dinky corner store. When he saw me he flashed a big grin. As if he'd been waiting for me. He wasn't hurt, he wasn't anything, in spite of the aunts' hysteria, so I kept it all in and made up this trip to Staples to keep from embarrassing him. All that plus a chocolate chip cookie dough shake in San Marco, and he came at me with this cryptic *thing*.

His hair stood up in peaks the way it does when he can't let go. "Just go look under the fucking mattress, Mom."

Yes I yelled. "Where is this coming from??"

My only son yelled back. "It's not like you'd believe me. She did, OK? Just look under the mattress in Sister's room."

"Why should I do that?"

Then his voice went cold and still. He set down the words like cement blocks, evenly spaced, with careful attention to each one. "Because she said so."

No need to ask him who. We both knew. "Oh, shit."

"Yeah, shit." He looked relieved. "She says it's about us."

"You know this is a lot of nothing, right?"

"That's what she told me, Mom."

"OK, I promise." In the morning, show him the empty spot and forget it. "Now let it go."

"Just do it, OK?"

That night, after the aunts went to bed and Theo was stashed in his stairway cabin, unlikely to show up and say *I told you so,* I looked. I lifted the mattress in the sacred Sister's room, unleashing the dust of the ages. First I thought I was right: ancient ticking, leaking stuffing, nothing to see here, Theo. There is no Mormama, just let it go. I looked and there's nothing to see.

Then there was. The notebook had a leather cover, with heavy rag paper in eight- or ten-page signatures sewn in by hand long before machines did these things. Instead of lines, the pages were scored like pages in a ledger, at least half of them filled with neat, self-conscious schoolgirl script: that finishing-school flourish that girls made before Theo and I were even imagined, with the tails on each *y* and *g* in the text truncated, as though the writer had taken special care, steadying her hand with a wooden ruler as she wrote, word by word, with careful attention to making them march in line.

At my back, something stirred. I turned on her. "All right for you, Mormama. I found the damn book. Now, beat it."

And so she spoke to me directly. *You know I can't.*

CHAPTER 17

THIS BOOK BELONGS TO LEAH ELLIS

July 18, 1919

I am tired of bed.

Tillie says I was half dead and sobbing when they brought me upstairs, honey, you were in no condition, you was all torn up and crying like to die.

When I ask her why I'm still here she says, Miss Leah, you had a terrible horrible awful time down there in the old laundry room! When they carried you inside after, your mama took one look and she called me in from the kitchen and she say "Tillie, you take this child upstairs and put her right straight to bed." Child, you was sobbing so hard!

"Poor girl, I can't bear it," Miss Manette said, but I think she couldn't bear to think about it. She tell me, "After a thing like that, you need to rest your soul!"

As if Mama thinks I really have a soul, when she treats me like something that the cat dragged in. Mama didn't put me to bed because it happened, she did it because she thinks it serves me right.

She thinks I went down there all fluffy-ruffle and excited in spite of all her warnings about terrible things that happen inside your body, that I went down in the undercroft looking for trouble, and that is how I brought it on myself. On her way in here to see me, she scolds in case they're listening: "You did this, Miss Girl, taking to your bed with the shades down and no visitors," but I know different and so does she.

At first she said, "Don't cry, sweetheart, it's only 'til you get well," but after Dr. Woods came, that changed. Mama told them that I had scarlet fever; she said I was in quarantine and no one was allowed, she said she had to protect her darlings, so I guess I wasn't her darling any more, although she says it's for my own good. I thought it was just 'til I got over it. What Happened. She never let on that I was locked in here for good.

Mama was in the kitchen that night when Vincent carried me inside; when I was late for dinner and they couldn't find me, Mama sent Vincent to search the house and the yard. He came hunting in the bushes between our house and the Dawsons when he heard the faintest sound, I was hurt and trying not to sob; I tried so hard to hold still, so we wouldn't be found. Then Vincent would leave and we could stay together, but the first time hurt so much I just couldn't hold it in, so Vincent heard.

He came crashing in on us when all I wanted was to be left alone while I got used to the terrible first pain of real love.

Mama was furious! She made Vincent carry me up the back stairs with a blanket over my head so nobody could see because I was ruined; she didn't look at me, she just decided. "Ruined," she said, and glowered until Vincent put me down in the guest bedroom. "In the undercroft. Defy the Lord and the Lord punishes you! This is our secret," she said to me, grinding her mouth into my ear, whispering through those teeth. "As far as they know you fell down the back steps and hurt yourself, so foolish! You are broken in several places, foolish girl," she said, although I was torn in only the one, "and you will stay in bed until there is no trace." She glared and Vincent and Tillie faded away. "This is the devil's work. Nobody must ever know."

Mama says she's keeping me close so she can take care of me, when Tillie and I know that Tillie does all the taking care. Breakfast, lunch and supper on a nice tray, all the sponge baths and the chamber pot and clean underthings and a clean nightgown every mortal day. Mama hardly ever comes. She told me that I have to stay in bed because I'm an hysteric, but that's a lie. I haven't cried out loud since it happened, Mama, and I know you ordered Tillie to spy on me.

Why am I still here?

I am tired of bed.

* * *

I was sobbing because it hurt, he loved me, but it hurt so much! He was gone and I knew he wouldn't be back because he jumped up the minute I cried out. He didn't mean to hurt me, but, Lord, there was blood. I couldn't help it, I screamed! Oh hush, he said, sweet darling, please hush, but I couldn't. Then we heard them stamping down the back steps from the kitchen and before I knew it my dearest Laury was gone, kicking out the lattice between us and the yard next door and Vincent found me alone in the wood room at the bottom of Mama's sacred perfect house, crying to break my heart. I was sobbing so hard that I couldn't speak, so it's my fault that they thought the worst.

They thought I was forcibly defiled, but it was love! We were in love, and when I lay down with Laurence Archambault that night I just knew we would run away and get married; I thought my sweet boy would take me away with him that very night. He'd carry me off to some beautiful place far away from Jacksonville

*Florida and we'd live like prince and princess until our wedding
day; I thought Papa loves me, he'll understand, I thought he would
mollify Mama and she would give us their blessing, and I thought
they'd rejoice to see Mama's disappointing* one girl too many, *her
very last baby, all settled down in a nice new place with her handsome prince.*

*All that was before Laury and I lay down together in the beau-
tiful, soft night. He brought a quilt to make us comfortable, and
before the time in our love when he stopped running his fingers
through my hair and whispering into the soft skin above my ear,
before he slid those sweet fingers down my neck and on down into
my unmentionables and on down— at first it felt so good but even
then, in the mean, inner soul of me, the guilty part that I can't get
shut of, I knew that what we were doing was bad.*

*Evening prayers from the cradle into my seventeenth year, and
now this. I said Laury I love you forever, but we have to stop. We
had to stop, we did! But he didn't hear. Then I shouted, Stop! But
my Laury went on nuzzling and stroking, he kept on even after I
began to scream because he was doing things to me that made me
want to do them back to him and keep on doing it even though
good-bad Leah knew that part of me was about to tear, I was too
caught up in what we were doing to care that upstairs they were
calling me; then it tore; we were still moving, I needed it, but forgive me, I screamed that scream and seconds before Vincent came
into the undercroft calling, my Laury jumped up. He crashed out
through the latticework between our wood room and the Dawsons' carriage house before I could cry, don't stop! I was gasping
so hard that no words came out when Vincent picked me up and
carried me out through the hole that my dear, lost Laury had made
in the trellis wall, and we were cold, standing there in the Dawsons' side yard.*

*Mama thought I was sobbing because I was violated and torn,
but I wasn't, although that secret part of me hurt so bad. I was
wailing because my Laury was gone and before I could try to*

explain or say anything that would stop it, Vincent carried me up the back stairs quickly, bump bump bump, while there was nobody around but Mama to see.

Vincent told her something terrible had happened, even though next to Papa, she was the last one I wanted to know.

After Dr. Wood came, Mama turned her back on me and spoke to him in a voice so low that only he could hear.

"No," he said, and I did not understand it. "Only until she gets her period."

Then Mama said, as though she wanted me to hear, "And when she doesn't?"

He tried to make it sound as though he was joking, "Now now, Mrs. Ellis, let's not trouble trouble until trouble troubles us."

I heard her hiss at him and thank God I couldn't make out what she said.

He scowled at Mama, or was he scowling at me? She put her head close to his, whispering buzz-buzz-buzz until he said, "Not in front of the girl!" and she nodded and thanked him and they left.

After Dr. Wood went away, Vincent came upstairs with a hammer and nails and a special lock and Mama brought in Bella the seamstress to make Roman shades of white organdie to cover every window in the front bedroom. As though it was all right for light to come in, but nothing that goes on in here could go out. Like the thing that was starting to happen inside me was catching and it would poison the world.

• • •

Mama says I'm in here for my own good, but I know. I'm in this bed in the nicest bedroom because she never wants to see me again. Last night I asked, "At least let Papa come visit," and she turned on me.

"Dear Lord, Leah, you don't want your father to see you like this."

For a while, my sisters slipped notes under the door for me, or one of them did, but Dakie died in the war and Randolph ran away and Papa never comes, and I don't know if they hate what happened to me or they just hate me because they always did, and Mama doesn't say. Tillie says Mama told them that visitors would upset me and it's due respect, but I know better.

· · ·

Last night Everett came up and pestered Tillie when she brought my supper tray. I heard that mean, weedy voice of his, "What are Leah's symptoms, is she going to die, will I catch it, what if she infects us all?" Everett was too sickly for the army, too sickly to go to college, too sickly to go to work in Papa's office down town. Even here in our very own house, he puts toilet paper down on the seat, he's that worried about germs. He's Mama's precious, so she followed him upstairs that night although she seldom comes. She caught him outside my room. I heard her out there, playing on his fears to keep him close.

"Everett Robichaux Ellis, you go back down to that dinner table and don't come up here again. You're in delicate health, darling, and your sister has a disease. It isn't safe!"

She cares about him so much that she caught him right outside my door but she never bothered to come in.

This is how bad it is. Mama hates Mormama, but she won't even let her come, even though she wants Mormama to catch something awful and die. If I really did have scarlet fever or the pox, that would kill an old lady, Mama would have said oh yes mother, you go right on in.

The one time I asked she said, "Your Mormama is much too frail to be in here with you," but then she couldn't stop herself, she said, "She'd just be in the way," and I thought: like me. One girl too many, she called me when I made her cross. No matter what bad things my sisters said or did, Mama always punished me.

She would shake me hard, with her mouth all tight and her eyes all squinched up and her face too close, so only I could hear her hiss. "I swear, Leah Ellis, you are the last straw!" Then she'd smile for Everett and my spiteful big sisters who know I am the prettiest, "And don't you forget it!"

She didn't want Mormama in this house any more than she wanted me and Mormama knew it, so we've always been close. The night after I got hurt down there, Tillie brought in my supper with a different smile, and she tilted her head and tapped the tray in a certain spot before she put it down on my lap. I lifted the napkin and found this very notebook, with my name inked inside the front cover in Mormama's shaky handwriting, along with the date, so I know that at least one other person in this house loves me, and whatever happens, I have this to show.

* * *

These days Mama comes to my room only when Tillie pleads, and on these visits she makes it her business to say, "You are living like a princess in the finest room in the house," but she is wrong. I am in prison here and Mama is bitter, bitter, as though this change in my body is happening to her, and when we're alone she says awful things to me. Last night she said, "Stop complaining, idiot child. You brought this on yourself!" Then she left.

I can't help it, I cried. Tillie came in and put down the tray and sat down on the bed and hugged me until it stopped. "Honey, save your tears for better things. You were the very last baby, and it made her mean." That's what Tillie says, and I did, because Mama's always angry.

* * *

When she comes to see me Mama wears a mask, although it's clear now that my ailment isn't catching. For the first few months I knew that in addition to the tearing, I was different, but she claimed I was contagious until my body stopped doing what it used to every month, so even I know exactly what I have.

I have part of Laury growing inside me like a tumor that will change everything about my life. I started checking myself in the long mirror every night when the lines began to change. Then I stopped looking because I love Laury, and I don't want him to see me like this!

I will be beautiful.

If he came tonight, good Lord, if he came tonight I would tear up these lavender sheets and make a ladder to let down to him; I would run out on the roof in my bare feet to join my only love, and then, and then . . .

We met last June at Sallie Priddy's summer tea dance, the first dance Mama allowed me to attend because Brucie Patterson invited me. She said, after all, the Pattersons are one of Jacksonville's first families, you may want to . . . I don't want to write about what she whispered to me then.

The last time I begged her to let me go downstairs and live my life, she said, "Oh Leah, Leah, look at yourself! No decent man will want you now!"

Oh, but that afternoon at the yacht club, they did want to look at me; I saw their heads come up. I saw them trying to get my attention as soon as we came in. I had on my yellow organdie, and this handsome boy was heading my way as Brucie Patterson trundled me onto the dance floor, he was trying so hard, that suitable, fat old thing. My handsome boy pushed Brucie aside so fast that my head rattled!

And I knew. This one was important to me. He pulled me to him with that smile, and with such force that I fell in love. We danced and danced until Papa cut in all of a sudden, which is not done, and right in front of everyone Papa whirled me out the door and to the far rail of the veranda, harshing into my ear. "He's a bad lot, Leah. You're well away."

Then he rushed me through the garden and bundled me into the Nash.

But I saw Laury again, I knew I would. When you are in love, you find your ways. Notes, tucked in the second urn under the porte cochère. Necessary visits to the archaeology section of the library. Accidental meetings at the next party and the next, and the next, and whispered promises; our one sweet night in the wood room underneath the big back porch. I know he loves me and I know his baby will be beautiful, and if he doesn't come for me soon, I will take the note I've written on the last page of this gift from Mormama, I call it my book of sighs, and I'll make Tillie take my note to Vincent to carry to the cigar store that Mama so disapproves of because Mr. Archambault Senior is the proprietor. Tillie loves me and she and Vincent understand too well that it's a private, personal matter, specific to Laury and to me.

Then my beautiful Laury will know that it's nothing he did, and I'm so terribly, terribly sorry that I screamed. Then he'll come to 553 May Street and take me away and I'll never have to think about it again. Oh Laury, then you'll come back and sneak up to the frilly guest room and pick me up and take me out of this ugly life in this terrible house; please come get me, Laurence DuBois Archambault. Come back, my dearest love. Come back to Mama's house and find your way in over the front porch roof, for I am her prisoner up here, and you, and you alone can save my life!

Then I'll get shut of this miserable bedroom and run free with the man I love. We'll get married in Valdosta tonight and go on up the coast as far as we can, go house-hunting in Savannah or get the money to buy back Mormama's old house in Charleston, where we can be happy, the three of us all alone.

Oh, Lord it's time. It's way past time. I'll ask Tillie to take it to Vincent tomorrow. I don't have anything to give her but she loves me, so she will. I don't know how long it will be until Vincent gets his day off and he can deliver it, all I can do is hope that it reaches Laury soon.

Until then, all I can do is write in my book and wait for this part to end.

. . .

Oh Miss Leah, Tillie says, and she's been crying. Bad news for the city of Jacksonville. They're burying that nice Mr. Archambault today, Miss Manette threw away the newspaper so you wouldn't know. She done made Vincent burn all the letters so's you think he ran away.

Then Tillie cries out for all of us.

Honey, a car mashed him into the railing on the downtown bridge!

. . .

So if this thing inside me isn't Laury's, if it's a malignant tumor and not the last, dear part of Laury Archambault that I have left in this world, I hope it gets big enough to split me wide open and kill me dead.

Mama and I will both be glad.

CHAPTER 18

Lane

"Poor Leah!" She's back. She was here from the second I put down the book. I won't see her, but I know.

She is your great-great grandmother.

Mormama, in my personal space. No point telling her to go away, Lane. Say the obvious. "Terrible story, but. What does it have to do with me?"

You are the last girl in the family line. As though she knew we were coming before we did. As though she engineered this to destroy me, she says, *Get out while you still can.*

"I'm trying!" Yes I am pissed off at her.

This rips into my brain like a bolt of ice: *I'm not the only soul trapped here.*

CHAPTER 19

Mormama

I tell them and I tell them, but they won't listen to me—unless they can't hear me at all.

Children, the house smells new blood.

The last of dear Leah's descendents, but she won't give me the time of day. The girl turned on me in her fury of denial. "Go away!"

Yes you are still a girl, at least in this dimension. So much for you.

Now, *you . . .*

Boy, wake up. Wake up or I'll snatch you bald-headed, you hear? I'm not the talking scarecrow that you think I am. I'm warning you!

Go ahead, fool. Put your head under that pillow and pretend that you don't hear.

I'm telling you.

Little Manette was born with a greedy spirit. Get. Take. Keep.

I can't swear that my daughter embodied, or was, or became the element that keeps us here, but it grieves me to tell you that it entered the house with her on that first day, and it entered my daughter on her first day in the world.

Now, here we are.

In the matter of Little Manette, I have been less than forthcoming. Yes, she emerged from me in a rage. She tore out of me with a vindictive screech. Yes I thought the racket would never end, and until Mother swanned in with her velvet cloak and that ridiculous golden reticule, it did not. She swooped down on the child and took possession.

That baby stopped howling the second my mother picked her up, mesmerized by her perfumed charm, and I thought My God, my God. Then Mother, who never had a soft word for me, rocked her, crooning, "Manette, my Little Manette." She stamped my daughter with her given name. Passing it down like a gypsy curse, and I could swear the evil passed between them, dark and visible, like smoke.

Little Manette was never mine. She was just something I had.

I knew it and she knew it too.

Mother sealed it with the locket. It was a little gold heart. Little Manette was born with her grandmother's lust for luxury. Mother took over, bringing out the worst in her. Together they had the power, but it was in the matter of sweet Billy, my adorable little boy, who loved me *so much,* that the monstrous emerged in Little Manette. Then.

Oh, dear God, I am not ready to tell you that.

Hush, boy. I was never here. Now, go about your business.

I am not ready to talk about it. Yet.

CHAPTER 20

Dell

Now that he has everything he wants, he doesn't want it. He wants all the electronics to go away. The toxic flash drive. The laptop he scored. It's charging via a network of extension cords he ran from a socket behind the ancient glider on the back porch tonight, snaking it through the floorboards to here via openings he made at the crack of 1 A.M., when even Ivy was asleep. Hey, he did all that and brought it this far with nothing but a Maglite and a multipurpose tool. He took his time pulling cards out of the motherboard, carefully cutting his new machine off from the world before he plugged it in.

Belt plus suspenders, he thought when he switched it on. Disable wifi in Settings. Laptop, you will never know the Internets. Do this one job and then you die.

Then habit kicked in. He needs to teach the new machine all the tricks he's taught every PC, laptop, tablet, smartphone he ever owned as soon as he opened the box. Dude, you know a lot of shit you forgot you knew. Take your time. Never mind that as soon as you're done doing what you have to do, your new toy is junk. This is who you are. He dinks until he gets everything just exactly how he wants it. Wait. There's more. He messes with this, tries that— until there's nothing left to do but start.

He stretches, temporizing.

OK then. Stick this flash drive you never asked for and do not want into the USB port and find out what . . .

Stick it in. Retrieve memory. His mouth floods, the way it does before he has to heave.

Long night, getting everything the way he wants it. He probably needs coffee first. The screen glares at him in the dark. *You're showing too much light.* "Shh," he says, and shuts it down.

It sits there on his upended carton like a live grenade.

Not today, man. It's probably too late to start. Do this when you're fresh. The bitches shuffle out at first light and you need silence to do what you have to do. As in, nothing going on to break your concentration, no chance of the kid busting in or some unknown element . . . What? Head injury last winter, remember? Everything in your head blurred. You need to be sharp when. OK then. Tomorrow.

Conscience needles him.

Today, after you get coffee? No way. Too many distractions out there. Truckers bring their rigs into the lot next door whenever. All that backing and filling. Air brakes. Plus yard men and garbage guys come into the neighborhood early, people all up in your face. Big racket. Leaf blowers: sandstorm and flying weeds. Shut your new toy down and wrap it in plastic, secure it until.

For crap's sake, get coffee, you're too fucked up to think. It makes no sense to do it in the Ellis kitchen, either, but he's too scattered to go out. He skins up through the hatch outside the dining room and enters the house, transits via the pantry, scopes the silent kitchen: no problem, it's cool.

Dell is standing over the big gas stove just before dawn, willing the water to boil when, oh, shit!

A dry *a-HEM* rivets him: the sound of an old lady hocking up gobs. The spoon he's holding flips before he can drop it into the folded paper towel he'd fixed to filter his coffee, and the family's stale Maxwell House flies. Stale, but, hey, any port in a— never mind.

She hocks up words. "Who's there?"

Oh, holy crap. No need to ask, it's Ivy, he can tell by the hum and the double thud as her scooter noses over the sill. Too late to douse the stove. If she screams, he'll have to— he doesn't know what he'll have to do. He says, "Hey. It's me."

"What are you doing here in the dark?"

He counters. "It's four o'clock in the morning. What are you doing here?"

This time she hocks until gunk comes up. Then she says through her fingers, "They forgot."

He doesn't want to know what that was. Busying himself with the coffee, he says, "How could that happen?"

"I'm sad to say they forgot about me."

He turns; it's OK, she's folding it into a handkerchief and shoving it up her sleeve. "Are you all right?"

"It happens all the time."

"That's terrible."

"What are you doing in here, puttering in the dark?"

"Making coffee."

She brightens. "Well, let's have a little light on the subject."

"Don't!" Can she reach the switch from that scooter? He doesn't know. Think fast. "Want some?"

Ivy scoots into the kitchen. "That would be lovely." Old. She repeats these things because she's old. "Let's have a little light on the subject!"

"Shh!" He flicks on his Maglite. "We don't want to wake them up. This is our secret."

She giggles. "Our secret! And the Russian tea biscuits would be lovely too. Right there on the counter, in the tin! And when we're done, you need to wheel me back where you found me and clean up as though this never was, and we were never here."

CHAPTER 21

Theo

Mormama is getting weirder and weirder, wow. You don't rightly see her face, you probably won't ever, but she's definitely real, and now that we're getting used to each other, she talks to me. Usually it's like lunchroom gossip, except with relatives instead of other kids. She's been around forever so she's full of stories, which. It's almost fun.

Some of them, I don't even want to know.

She shows up in my room and just starts telling them, and you never know which kind you're going to get.

It started the night Mom and me got back from Staples and the skinny old great-whatevers pounced before we got in the door. They were all, "Where were you Little Elena, where did you take our Teddy, we were worried to death about him!" and, "You leave without telling us *one more time* and we'll put you out on the street," while Ivy ran her scooter back and forth in front of them with her face all up in a twist, like she was protecting us from death or dismembering, and it didn't matter what my mother said, it just got worse and worse.

So after that terrible cold dinner we had to eat afterward and subsequent bitching and Mom holding her ground, i.e., no apologies, she gave me The Look and said, "T., you don't need to hear this," translated, *go to your room*, so I did. That block of stone-cold air showed up the second I turned out the light and it hung there at the end of my bed, like, waiting for me to notice and be glad.

Not me. I was *over* family. I went, "You can leave now," but she didn't. Mormama was all up in my face that night, all puffed up and ranting until I threw my Chuckie at her to make it stop. She didn't even duck.

Shit, it went right through her, and I was like, *OK, Mormama, fuck you*. Never mind the dense and cold, there's no *real* to this thing, so what the hell can she do to me anyway? Plus, I thought she was boring. Yeah, right.

She came back the next night anyway, like a kid trying to make up after a fight, and the stories. I mean! She's definitely this dense, cold *thing* that you don't exactly see and can't quite name, but, scary? Not so much. In fact, I'm kind of getting used to her.

Not counting looming, once you know that Mormama can't, like, open holes in the floor that you could fall down into? Or start throwing books or rocks or broken jars or heavy shit that could kill you like in *Poltergeist,* it's OK. She's more like a transparent person, as in, not scary at all.

Now that she's faced the fact that I'm not scared of her either, she comes around a lot. She starts.

Did you see my portrait in the hall?

How am I supposed to know?

Tiny watercolor. In my maroon dress.

Truth is, I didn't, but in case she reads thoughts I think, loud: Um, you look great.

You'll find it in the back hall. Disgusted snort. *Behind the kitchen door.*

That makes me sit up straight in the bed.

False piety, that woman hanging it at all!

Who?

My selfish daughter. The high-and-mighty lady of the house.

Are we really having a conversation? No way!

She says, *You're not supposed to hate a child but I despised Everett on sight.*

Who?

Her favorite. That prissy little whiner with his flimsy bones and those runny eyes clung to Manette like a little incubus and I blame that child for bringing down great grief on all our lives.

Only crazy people talk to ghosts but Mormama answers questions I don't ask, like she knows that me talking out loud to something that isn't really there would be too weird. So I'm like, thinking at her. Incubus?

Incubus is the devil that attaches itself to a woman and sucks the mortal soul out of her breast and that was Everett to a T. Not that Little Manette had a soul that I know of. She was always narrow and mean. When the midwife cleaned her up and thrust her on me, evil came alive. For a second, she stared up at me with those black eyes, and in that second, I saw straight into her heart and I knew that it was just as black.

Then she screamed.

So forgive me, I glared into those slate-black eyes and I thought, **I wish you were a boy.**

And?

Then Billy came. How I loved that child! When he came, Little Manette wanted him gone. Gone! That sweet little baby, and he was only the first.

To my daughter, Dakin was a necessity, but the others?

There were issues with men. I never knew why or how, but

Manette's sons and her daughters' husbands didn't last long. Unfortunate things and terrible things happened to them, every single one.

All but her precious weakling, but eventually, even weaklings die.

Now it's only women in this house.

What about me?

She groaned. *I told you I was here to help.*

And.

Child, I'm warning you!

Before I can think anything back at her, she starts. *Teddy was the first. Everett was the only one she cared about; she took him into the bed with her— dear Lord, he was four years old! And Teddy? He was a cipher to her. She didn't care where he went or what he did, as long as he stayed out of her way.*

The big boys took care of themselves and Ivy played outdoors, but, the littles? Tillie took Leah away— Manette couldn't stand the sight of her. Usually, Vincent walked Tillie and the little girls over to the park, or he did until they bought the pony cart.

It's like she's a singer, and the song grabbed her up and it won't let go.

On those days the nursery was ours, and Teddy and I sat on the little nursery chairs and played, he was happy, like my darling Billy boy. We talked and laughed and had the best time! So handsome, with angel curls like my Billy's and a beautiful smile, I loved him so much!

But Little Manette was all wrapped up in puny Everett, and Dakin was in the office every day but Saturday, so nobody had time for that dear boy. And as you know, nobody else in the house had time for me. I loved him so much!

One day he fell down outside his mother's bedroom, he banged his head on the floor and didn't we hear him bawl? I ran out and saw to him and the whole time we sat on the hall rug with me rocking him, outside Little Manette's open door, we heard her crooning to Everett as though there was no Teddy, and it broke his heart. We hugged while he sobbed into my neck and when he could breathe, I said, Don't worry, Teddy, Mormama loves you.

I love you and I will always take care of you.

And then, and then . . .

Cold air came out of her; I guess it was a sepulchral sob.

She changes the subject, like she knows I'm creeped out. *Little Manette had no time for her boys. Dakin Junior was too much like his father to have any time for me at all. Poor boy, he died in the war. And, Randolph? A handsome, reckless one, our Randolph, he ran wild. I loved him, although I wonder what Little Manette's stillborn son Bruce would have been like . . .*

Who?

Where would Randolph be now, if Brucie had been born alive?

Like, dead, OK?

Ran infuriated his father by taking off on his bicycle every whipstitch, he didn't ask, he never explained, but he was always sweet with me. Then the fool stayed out all night, into the next day. Dakin sent Vincent out to bring him back. Dakin took off his belt right there in the front hall that day, and he whaled the tar out of Randolph up on the first-floor landing, where everyone could see. I think he felt bad, not about whipping the boy, but about losing control of himself in the stairwell with the whole family looking on.

Randolph would be gone for hours, but after that he always came home before dark, until the house went dark and he slipped out again. He brought us little presents. Trinkets, really, sneaked to the people who cared. Fancy cigarette lighters for Dakin Junior, baubles for the little girls, a cameo for me . . .

Did she just giggle?

Another secret for you and me to keep. You could do worse than rummage in the attic.

Me? Go up there?

It holds all the secrets, child.

Like I care.

And other things. Dakin kept a journal, you know. It explains a lot.

Lady, there are rats and cockroaches and monsters up there.

Don't be frightened, chickabiddy. This is important.

Then you go.

Big sigh comes out of Mormama. Hurt feelings, I guess. *I'm trying to help you!*

Well, don't!

Another sigh, like: OK then. She changes the subject, all Southern and polite. *Randolph was a lovely man, but his father never knew. The bad feeling between the two built up, and I do believe it was Manette's fault. It grew until one night Ran got tipsy on brandy from Dakin's carafe, the brilliant cut-crystal one with the ugly nick in the lip.*

It was a terrible scene; he ran out, and we didn't see him for a calendar week. That boy bicycled five miles down the St. Johns River to the **HMS Manette.** *Dakin's precious houseboat was his pride and joy, and Randolph knew it. He sneaked home in the middle of the night and stole food from the pantry and bottles from Dakin's wine rack, and he and three friends set up housekeeping on the boat. Vincent found them— upholstery ruined, campfires on the deck. Next morning Dakin took Randolph back to the scene in the Studebaker to regard what he had done.*

Something ugly went on between them then. When they came in afterward, we knew not to ask. Randolph wouldn't look at us, but his face was stained by grief. Dakin? Turned to stone. They never exchanged words. He was done with punishing that boy. In fact, he was done with Randolph in every respect. He took back poor Ran's tuition for his last year at Jacksonville Country Day, and then he . . .

Dear God, I think Dakin invited what happened next. Too bad the final misadventure ended so badly. It's his fault that Randolph vanished for the last time; he was only seventeen, but in a way?

Don't just hang in the air like that, old lady— you know, portending.

Oh dear, I just lost my place in time.

Say it!

Given what happened to the other men and boys in this house, I think it saved his life.

CHAPTER 22

Iris

They're *on our front porch*. Teetering on the landing, Iris adjusts her bifocals. Two men!

It doesn't happen that often.

This is not the season for visitors and besides. Nobody the Ellis girls used to know comes to visit now; there are no calling cards in the tarnished card receiver downstairs, no pretty boys waiting in the first sitting room. When they were girls, she and Rosemary were popular. Now they might as well be dead.

Strange men at the door. Who? She goes downstairs numbering the possibilities, one on each step.

The old people going door to door for all those charities have already been and gone. She remembers writing checks to the United Fund and the heart people and the cancer people, ten dollars for each, because the Ellis family has always been generous, and their reputation is hers to protect. Realtors stopped coming around last month, and good riddance. Insulting, those visits. Let's us get you out of this old firetrap, ladies, once we've unloaded your white elephant, we'll put you in a nice new condo near the waterfront, at no extra cost. Well! Didn't Iris burn their ears! They ran like scorched rabbits, and they won't be back until September, when the new realtors hatch.

They can't be politicians. That season is over too, and the years in which sons of their friends were candidates are past. She and Rosemary voted last month just like they always do, ever the good citizens. They filled in their absentee ballots and Ivy's too, dutifully checking off all the right names, just like they always do. Then they sealed and stamped the envelopes and left them in the brass mailbox for the mailman to take. It's what ladies do so they won't have to go out and stand in line like just anybody.

The Girl Scouts' fathers won't be around again until next year, either. Rosemary ate all her Tagalongs before Iris found out they were in the house; she should have ordered two boxes, the selfish bitch.

No visitors here at 553, really, and none expected, unless Little Elena had the nerve to invite intruders into *our home* without her permission. Well, Iris will send them away before they get the first word out— she's a master at chilly good manners, but if that girl expects to stay with us in this magnificent setting, she'd better watch herself.

Coming down the last steps to the Persian runner, Iris pauses in front of the mirror above the regency hall table before she and pats her hair goes to the door.

Knowing two strangers have come calling doesn't scare her, it worries her.

Iris Ellis Worzecka is not the kind of person who lets just anybody into her house. She hates that name, Worzecka sounds so *foreign,* but Stan forced his surname down your throat the day you walked down the aisle, and Mama held her nose and ordered calling cards with my new name engraved on cream laid stock: Mrs. Stanislaus Worzecka, although there was no occasion to use them.

—I still have them.

Poised behind Mama's lacy glass curtain that Rosemary keeps so nice, Iris broods, rummaging for first causes. Ivy would never, although we know she thinks about boys all the time. Fortunately, Ivy can't, and given her condition, not even these strangers would.

Who are they, and what do they want from us? All I have to do is wait, and they'll give up and stop bothering me. Squinting through the glass curtain, she grinds her teeth: *Go away!*

Behind this, she tells herself, I'm as good as invisible. After a time she moves the ruffles with the long nail on her pinkie and peeks.

They're still here.

Nicely dressed, both of them, she can see that much. White shirts and black ties on them, black suit jackets, maybe they're this year's Jehovah's Witnesses, but didn't the Watchtower people just come? She told them a few things; she always does, she's honed that speech down to a fine point. *No thank you. Our beliefs are our business, and we do not want to talk about it. We are High Church Episcopalians, go away.*

No briefcases in these men's hands, no tote bags, no religious tracts that she can see. Just two nice-looking boys, spreading their palms as if to say, nothing to see here, nothing to harm you, nothing hidden.

She drops the curtain. *My God! They know I'm here!*

Two strange men. They're settling in to wait! After a time, they exchange nods. The tall one lifts the big brass door knocker and bangs it down hard enough to raise the dead.

Unless she opens the front door right now, greedy Rosemary will hear and beat her to it. Now, in her long life as a twin, from the dawn of their lives in Mama's big bed right here on May Street to this moment, Iris has always come first.

She may have been brought up to be a lady, but in the course of her unfortunate marriage to Stan Worzecka, who carried her away over Mama's dead body, well, so to speak, Iris Ware Ellis learned a few things, like how to deal with strangers, first rule being, don't speak until you've been introduced, except in extreme circumstances, and this is one.

Of course the wedding had to wait until Mama was in the ground and Stan turned out to be a rat, but Iris doesn't dwell. She's a mover. Clearing her throat to settle the phlegm, she takes off her glasses.

She opens the door and confronts them. Stern. Chilly. "Yes?"

The tall one gives her a showroom-perfect smile. "Good morning, Ma'am."

Attractive pair, but Iris is not the gracious hostess. Not today. One does not smile for just anybody. "And?"

Young, so young! Handsome, in a sort of Dick Tracy way, the both of them. The shorter one says, "Good morning, Ms. . . ."

Cheer up, Iris. They look nice. We may have friends in common. She lifts her chin. "Miss."

"Good morning, Miss . . ."

"Ellis." So much for you, Stan Worzecka.

"Sorry to trouble you, Ms. Ellis. We're from." The tall one opens his wallet to flash a badge— at least she thinks it's a badge, so hard to tell without your glasses. It looks official.

Such a nice smile! The tension flows right out of her. "I see." Her voice gets lighter. As though it's floating.

"Do you mind if we ask you a few questions?"

She releases the chain and steps into the doorway— framed, she thinks, by everything she is. What is it they say on TV? "How can I help you?"

"We're looking for a . . ." He rephrases. "Have you had any visitors in the last few days?"

"Well, my daughter's here." Iris! "I mean, my niece. My niece and her son are visiting."

"Her son?" His ears snap forward, like a starving puppy's. "How old is he?"

"Ten, I think."

"Not twenty or so?" He sets the words down so carefully that it's insulting. "Or . . ."

"Maybe twelve."

He goes on as though she hasn't spoken, ". . . even thirty."

"I'm old, but I'm not blind!"

"And no other men on the premises?"

"Just Vincent, our yard man." She adds reflexively, "He's colored."

The two men exchange looks. The shorter one says, "Then we need to ask you whether you've had any other visitors, Ma'am. Not family, just someone else in the house."

She draws herself up. "Certainly not!"

"We don't mean to alarm you, but we're looking for a . . ."

The tall one shows her a flash of light and color. "This man."

He has a picture on his telephone! Everybody on TV has one of these gadgets, but Iris has never seen this kind of telephone up close, although she suspects Little Elena has sneaked one in. She squints. "Who's this?"

His partner says, "The. Uh. Person we're looking for. Have you seen him? He's . . ."

The tall man cuts him off, saying smoothly, "Wait, I can make this photo bigger, so you can be sure."

Iris leans closer, narrowing her eyes, but to tell the truth her glasses are in there on the hall table and she's not about to go back inside and get them. For the first time, she smiles. Charm. Mama taught her girls the uses of charm in certain situations. Blink blink with your pretty eyelashes, *faux naïve*. "Why, I'm not sure."

"Then you have seen him."

This is too interesting to let it go by, Iris. Temporize. "I may have seen him."

"Do you recognize him?"

She would do anything to please them. "Why, yes. Yes I do."

"Is he still on the premises?"

"Here? In our house? Good heavens, no. I wouldn't let him back in the house!" Never mind that she is making this up. Well, making it up on the basis of certain suspicions. It plays well.

But this little party is ending too fast. You'll have a lot to tell Rose and Ivy, but think of something, girl, or they'll go. Make it last, or it will be over before you have a chance to ask them in. She volunteers, "But I know his name!"

Both heads click in her direction. The tall one says flatly, reminding her, "His name."

"Yes," Iris says brightly. "He was here, but we told him to go away or we'd make the police come and get him out of the house." She sees the tall one messing with his telephone. She won't know that he is recording.

"When?"

"In the night."

"Last night?"

She nods.

"Do you know where he went?"

"No. He just deserted us." Yes, she is still bitter. In her heart, it's as close as yesterday. "I don't know where he went, but I can tell you who he is."

"Ma'am?"

"His name is Stan Worzecka." She adds— sadly, because the two nice young men are done with this interview and fixing to desert her. They'll be gone before she can offer her special Russian tea biscuits, and that's just sad. She calls after them. "If you're looking for Stan Worzecka, he's gone and he won't be back, so don't bother. He ran off into the wild blue with that Yankee trollop."

CHAPTER 23

Theo

I don't know what it is with this Mormama. She said her piece last night and I am damn well over her. After she bailed I thought OK, you're a ghost, you have to do these things, but I don't, lady, not just because you said to.

I thought we were done, but, holy crap.

Not again!

Child, it would behoove you to explore the attic.

You said that.

Then do it.

I already told you, no way!

That doesn't mean you won't.

Get off my back!

Don't be rude.

You're all up in my face.

I wouldn't think of touching you.

That's not what I mean!

I keep my distance.

I mean, go away.

I can't.

Then for crap's sake, stop looming!

Then, Theodore Upchurch Ellis, listen!

It's Hale. Theo Hale.

You're still an Ellis, and you can't be here.

This pisses me off. You think I like it here? I hate it!

It isn't safe.

That's not why I hate it. They're awful, and everything sucks.

Then go, idiot child. Leave this house and take your mother with you.

On what fortune?

It would behoove you to look in the attic.

Not again!

Look in the attic, or I'll . . .

You'll what? It's not like you can *do* anything.

There's something in it for you!

Like, there's money up there?

That sigh gives me the cold shivers. No.

Then, what am I looking for?

Just look in the attic. Weary. She sounds so weary.

If it's not money, what's the point? They spent Mom's bonds, and we can't go anywhere.

I know, I know.

I go, So beat it, you're just a ghost.

I'm not a ghost!

Then what are you, anyway?

The air shifts. *I am a presence.*

She's bigger.

Now, do as I say. Go up there and arm yourself.

Stall. OK, why? Did they used to keep, like, shotguns up there? Buried treasure?

Never mind what they keep. Go up now and find out.

I do what I have to. I F-bomb her. Fuck no, lady. I'm fucking sick of you!

It's your funeral.

Yeah I'm up all night over it, feeling shitty and guilty and a whole bunch of other things, like, you don't diss a poor old lady or whatever the hell this calls-herself-a-presence is; it just makes you feel bad. She guilted me and I can't let it go. Either that or it won't let me go. Her with the, *It would behoove you to look in the attic.* In hell!

OK, I can't because I'm scared of going up there in the dark. There's Florida critters up there, roaches and scorpions and worse. Hell, I'm scared of going up there in the daytime, when you might get light coming in through the holes in the roof, and a guy could see what the dangers are in this giant, broken-down shack. Busted stairsteps that trip you up. Gaps in the slats that trap your foot so you starve to death standing there.

I keep turning it over in my mind, looking at it this way, looking at it that way, but me, go up into that creepy place all alone and unarmed, with rats running across my feet and bats or worse, dead babies and what else, a zombie village? No way. I wouldn't go up there if I was Special Ops and I had my main man Dell Duval fully armed and walking point.

I don't care what Mormana wants, you hear?

I am not going up there. Ever.

I hate that it's 3 A.M. before I actually get the nerve to face up to her and say so, and now that I'm sending out thought waves, that fucking all-up-in-my-face lady isn't anywhere.

Do you read me? Not going up there!

. . .

No way, not me. Not ever. Not so much. Not really. Think harder: **OK?**

. . .

Well, not yet, OK?

Louder, she didn't hear you. **OK?**

CHAPTER 24

Dell

When Theo finally makes it— which won't be until push comes to shove, he will bite the bullet and climb fourteen creaky back steps to the formidable Ellis attic— he won't be the first.

Wild in his head and stupid with hope, the future of the sprawling house is already here, traveling on the only solid piece of information he had the day he got out of the hospital. The index card.

Poised at the top of the attic stairs, Dell is at a dead stop. The door opens on a dark, cavernous maw. He teeters on the sill, poleaxed. Can't go in, won't go back. So, what? Will his whole life flash before his eyes if he takes the plunge?

Stop thinking.

"OK." He steps out on the raw pine planks and into the Ellis family past which, he is beginning to believe, is his past too. Why, he wonders. Why not?

He wasted Day Two and half of last night in procrastination

and dithering, failed attempts and fits of nausea brought on by the flash drive. He used to stash it and forget it. Then he lost it, and guilt and responsibility kicked in. Now the thing is toxic. He doesn't really want to know what's on the drive or why he has it. Or why his body revolts every time he touches it.

He woke up today with his mind empty, but this scrap of dialog surfaced: *Get in and get on with it. Get it over with and get out.* Old movie, great scene.

Get it? Got it. Good.

Where is that thing? He picked it up. This time it didn't burn his hand. Instead, dry heaves shook him. Bent double, he dropped it like a scorpion and scrambled outside. Nobody wants to puke where he sleeps. His mouth flooded, but the retching stopped. *Something I ate.* When was that, really? Eating.

Never mind.

It was closer to morning than not, definitely too late to go back in there and deal with his unwelcome responsibility, too late to do anything, really, but he was out in the open, flailing: do this, do that. Asshole, do something.

Run. Dell ran around the block several times before he came back to 553. He circled the house, running hard along the path he'd worn down over time. Again.

He made a third run, dodging bushes and neatly skirting ornamental urns because he's done this so often that he knows the path by heart. On his fourth circuit, he hesitated under the porte cochère, then ran on. On the fifth, he crouched in the shadow of the jutting bay window, weighing it.

This, he told himself. I will do this.

He snaked up through the hatch into the family dining room and entered the body of the house, careless about where he walked, as though he was almost hoping to get caught. At least it would put an end to this. They'd impound the flash drive and he could sit in his cell over in Raiford and think about something else for a change.

Instead he advanced silently, going through their darkened rooms without hesitation, sneaking up the back stairs from the kitchen and on up the raw plank steps to the attic. The door opened on a dark, cavernous space too cluttered to navigate.

. . .

Not the belly of the whale, Dell thinks, but close. Strung tight and jittering, he runs his Maglite over the generations of discarded furniture and superfluous objects, wondering. There are secrets in their not-a-basement, secrets in the house above, secrets in these people's hearts. He's in their attic looking for answers.

Massed foot lockers and steamer trunks and unopened cartons form the advance guard of the forgotten, flanked by busted furniture that looms like a herd of rotting mastodons— forerunners of legions to come. It would take years to go through all this stuff, so, what?

The beam of Dell's Maglite zigzags; even his guts are quivering. He did whatever he did back there behind the wall of memory and fled the scene. Guilt, he supposes. Then his life got in a wreck. Whoever he used to be, that guy escaped the consequences when his head cracked open, and Dell is not sorry.

He's in stasis. Why else would he have holed up in Jacksonville for months, prepping for this incursion? He just wants to know what's wrong with him.

He is looking for himself in this attic.

Given the amount of Ellis family crap assembled here, where is he supposed to start? A man could spend the rest of his life sorting through the clothes stuffed in all their old wardrobes and jammed into every drawer of their abandoned dressers and chiffoniers. Here are generations of furniture Ellis descendents broke and discarded, portraits and statuary they got tired of, hideous gift items they thanked for and forgot, dozens of shapes massed like limestone blocks carefully lined up inside a pyramid, designed to fall on the first intruder and mash him flat or slide into the exit corridor and snap into place, sealing him in.

Fool, don't do this. Not now. Not today. Get lost up here and they'll hear you bumping into things and call the cops.

He's backed into the wall, feeling his way to the door, when his hand collides with a switch. He flicks it and, son of a bitch!

Look!

No more dithering over what comes next. Up front and waiting for him like an unopened present is a sealed carton marked DAKIN'S THINGS.

It's his To-Do list.

First, hump the box downstairs to his quarters and slit the tape with his knife. Naturally he'll take his time. Open the laptop and list the contents like a good librarian, order them chronologically, whatever works. Get lost in the task. It will keep him busy. Too busy to scour his own past for details, or open the flash drive. Let it lie. He has things to do. Examine the old man's papers, supporting documents, sorting and cataloging like an archivist gone mad.

He brightens. *Hey, maybe that's what I was. Skilled librarian.*

Or not.

Dell flicks off the light and exits with the bulging carton, and if he thinks— *don't even think about it*— if he thinks that at his back, an angry shout just rose, no problem. Nothing to see, nothing to worry about. Everything up here is already dead.

Weird. With no visible means of support, no recognizable trade, no credentials, for the first time, he's OK. He has *this* to do. His future is stashed in this carton; he's sure. He can spin out the days combing the old man's papers, opening envelopes, unfolding and refolding letters like a trained preservationist. He'll make meticulous notes. For as long as it takes to find a link, or establish a claim.

Wherever he is in the ether, the late Dakin Ellis will understand that this newcomer to 553 isn't dredging for their old family secrets.

He's looking for himself inside the box.

It may take weeks. Cheap at the price, he thinks, grinning.

Then he runs his knife through the tape, the flaps fly open and reality smacks him in the face. It's a morocco-bound journal initialed in gold: D.A.E.

Forget the massed ledgers and documents and numbered shoeboxes stuffed with Dakin's mail. It's all right here. In case he was in any doubt, the owner's name is inked on the first page in textbook-perfect handwriting— no, calligraphy:

Dakin Ellis, his book.
Given by his Loving Mother
December 20, 1890

And as if it's preordained, the elegant journal falls open under Dell's hands, exposing a page written long after the owner's script had gone to hell, drafted and rewritten so many times that the spine cracked at this place. As though of the many closely filled pages, this is the important one. It's scored with strike-throughs and filled with word balloons, suggesting that Dakin made dozens of stabs at reorganization, and the finished entry?

Short. Scary as fuck.

January 30, 1895

Our Brucie died inside her. Nobody can know. Not the girls, not my wife, although I wonder. Not Randolph, wherever he is. It was a swift transaction and simple enough. Dr. Woods knew it was a stillbirth, and he saw to it that when the time came, Manette was asleep. He took Brucie out and he kept her asleep for almost days, but when the puffed-up princess of procreation awoke and found my baby in her arms, she stiffened, and I could swear her irises turned black. We never spoke of it, but she refused to feed him. She demanded a wet nurse because, she said, he was tearing her apart.

In time she summoned me: the queen of Jacksonville society commanding her dressmaker to rush a new gown for the grand ball. "We need another baby soon."

Dear God, I tried. "But we have a new baby."

But the woman I thought I knew bared her teeth like a cornered wolf and snarled, "I want a better one," and this time I did see her irises go dark.

Another man would have struck her. I shouted. "Enough!"

So cold, so contemptuous, my wife, the goddess of demand. Hideous, once she dropped the mask. "Nothing is ever enough."

God help me, I gave Little Manette what she wanted. I gave her Everett, her pretty weakling and the only child she ever loved, although we had eight. Eight children, and of the eight, for better or worse, wherever he is tonight, Randolph is all mine.

. . .

"What!" Dell comes back into himself with a jerk. Blindsided by the possibilities.

OK, dude, get the fuck off your butt while you still can. Crawl over to that mattress and crash. No food, less sleep. Figure this out when you're fresh. Then, whatever this is that you turn out to be, like a long-lost descendent? Deal with it.

He won't wake up today. He'll sleep through this day and tonight and most of tomorrow. Drowned in sleep, he will lose all track of time. When he crawls out of his sleeping bag it will be late tomorrow. Then he'll shove the laptop aside and open the Dakin Ellis journal, which he will scour obsessively while life outside his hiding place goes on without him.

CHAPTER 25

ℒane

"Mom, Mom."

Oh, Theo, not now. "Two minutes, OK?"

"You promised!"

"OK." Another day in the life of the Prisoners of 553, and I'm too burned out on waiting to send off one more miserable application for one more crap job that I don't want but know I have to find, reentering the job market is a bitch. Whatever I get, I have to take it no matter how shitty it is because I have to get out of here; I've seen the aunts weaving their fingers with evil pirate grins, mwah ha ha haaa.

"Mom . . ."

As if it's not their fault that their precious house sucked all my money out of the bank, effectively trapping us here, I hate my life.

"I said, Mom!"

I don't mean to snarl, "Theo, stop lurking!"

"I just."

I know, T., I really do. I hate what I'm doing, but I'm stuck to this keyboard, can't move, can't stop. "Hang on, sweetie, I'm almost done."

Done in. Everything inside me groans as I unclench my teeth and try to separate myself from Sister's bentwood chair, pretending that I don't know how long he's been waiting for the hour I promised him. We've been trapped in this house for so long that the kid's run out of things to do. There's nothing left to explore but the attic, which is definitely off limits: *scorpions, rats, cockroaches,* and for all I know, desiccated corpses of the aunts' old flames, their remains gnawed to the bone and their decayed clothing riddled with silverfish. Awful things grow in Florida, and they feed on the contents of these old houses. Ugly things happen under this roof; don't tell him, what with imaginary ghost sightings, the poor kid's already worried enough.

The Internet is a human swamp, but compared to the multiple pasts and bad feelings festering here? It's probably safer. All he wants is something to do! Something harmless, I hope. He says he just needs links and images to post on his Instagram, don't ask. I think he's playing like we aren't marooned, he wants his friends to think we went to Paris or Kathmandu or we're at his dad's penthouse in New York City until after New Year's, and he'll be back in his old school the next day, showing them screen shots of us freezing our asses off in Times Square with lights blazing behind us because as soon as the ball drops, we're leaving for home.

Home? Honey, we don't have one.

Either that or he wants to check out all those singles and divorced dads hookup sites in hopes of locating his father. Maybe he's sneak-connecting to that MMORPG that swallowed him up before Barry bailed on us with, among other things, our electronics in his van. *Oh, Theo, I'm sorry he ditched you, but thank God he walked away. Without you, I would die.*

"Um, Mom?"

"Two seconds, I promise."

"Are you OK?"

"Give me a minute, I'm fine!" In fact, I'm stuck to the chair, or it's sticking to me, I've been planted here for so long. We separate with a pop but I can feel the cane seat fancywork imprint on my thighs.

"You don't look fine."

Shit, do I look that bad? "OK, dude. Your turn."

I back away so he won't see the cane pattern, but he's already doubled over the keyboard, lost in the other world. "OK, bye. Anything you want me to get while I'm out?"

He's not listening.

As it turns out, Rosemary is.

Before I can make it through the hall and down the five steps to the first landing, she pounces. "Going out? Little Elena, is that you?"

Who do you think it is? Sigh. There's no pretending I don't hear her. She's clinging to the newel post like the last leaf. "Aunt Rosemary, it's Lane."

"Don't call me aunt, dear." Quartermaster, chef, whatever, this is not her usual tone of command. Her voice flutters. "It makes me feel old!"

"OK, Rose."

"Did you say you were going out?"

Stop sounding pathetic. Mumble, Lane. Maybe she won't hear you. "Mmm-hmmm."

"Wait!" Then, good grief, her pitched, penetrating whisper closes the distance between us as she drifts down the first five steps to the landing and confronts me. "In the name of God, take me with you."

I try, I do! "You'll miss *General Hospital!*"

Oh, holy crap. There are tears in her eyes. "I know."

"Then maybe."

"No." The whisper turns into a rasp. "It's the only time I can get away without her!"

And I thought you were so close.

So I have to wait on the landing while the old lady scrambles back upstairs to her room for her purse and I have to help her downstairs to the front hall, and I have to wait while she pops on her prehistoric hat with fuzzy dots on the veil, checking her image in the beveled mirror over the side table as she clamps on her red fox fur stole over her best black coat, and I have to engage the hooks so the animals chase each other in the right direction and I have to wait while she checks out her look in the mirror once more before she'll let me open the door on the rest of the world. I have to help her through the door and down the steps and I have to help her into the car because tough as she is, wiry and ordinarily commanding, Rosemary is half herself today, taut and jittery. She won't relax until I've taken the first corner and we're on the cross street, headed away from them all.

She says in that same, taut voice. "Well, where are we going?"

"I was just." I don't know what I was just going to do, I only knew I had to get out of there, and now here we are crawling along River Boulevard, the one road in the ruined neighborhood that hugs the St. Johns River; quiet street, with apartments, small houses and a couple of big hulking relics lining the riverbank, with only a stretch of grass between us and the water. So pretty. Quiet. Until Rose directed me, I had no idea.

"Once Papa rode us downriver in the houseboat, all the way from the landing into downtown Jacksonville, it was so wonderful," she says. "We stopped here," she says, and I brace myself for death by past history.

"Oh" seems like the safest response. Don't want to egg her on, don't want to piss her off, don't mind sitting here in the car, but no way am I ready for another onslaught of not-my-memories. "What if we get out and walk around?"

"No thank you."

"It's the closest I've been to the water."

"Not today."

"That looks like such a nice little park down there at the end."

"That isn't why we came."

Oh, shit. *You came because I couldn't get rid of you.* "Oh please, it isn't far."

"My hat."

"But it's so pretty out."

"Too windy."

"Don't worry, take my scarf. Come on, a little walk would be good for us."

She doesn't say anything. She doesn't relax, even a little bit. She doesn't even take off the hat. She just sits there blinking at me through the fuzzy dots that sit like bugs on that stupid veil.

God this is awful. "I know what. Since we're out together and Theo's on my computer, let's sneak over to San Marco and see a movie."

"Are you insane?"

Probably. Who knows what Internet traps Theo could spring in three hours? "The new James Bond movie is there," I say, thinking, *tell me you remember James Bond.* "It won't be Sean Connery, but there's a terrific new guy."

She snaps to so suddenly that I hear the **click.** "I think Iris is trying to kill me."

"Oh Rosemary, oh, Rosemary!" Bats. That clinches it. Together, the twins are a force of nature, but singly? This one is bats.

Then she says, "The devil didn't die when Mother did. It happened at the funeral, I saw it, and Iris knows that I saw. For a long time we pretended, but with your boy in the house, and that new man . . ."

"What man?"

"It isn't safe."

"What man?"

"The helping one from the other day. You know."

Dell. Pretend you don't. "Not really."

"I think he's still here."

"Why are you whispering?"

The whisper morphs into a rasp. "I don't know who he is or how he got here, I only know that Iris is possessed."

"Oh Rose, I know you girls fight sometimes, but your sister loves you."

"She does not!"

"And you love her."

"You didn't see the way she did poor Everett," she says harshly, breathing so hard that the fuzzy blobs on her veil bob up and down.

"Everett?"

"Or what happened to Alan Deering after Hendersonville."

"Who?"

"Dear Alan. He was my husband for just a little while." Her voice trembles, her whole outline blurs because she's jittering in place so madly that I could swear the car is jiggling too, and if I can't get her out of this car I'll have to throttle her.

I take control, sort of. First step. Reach over and unbuckle her. Run around the car. Open the door, take her by the scrawny wrist and yank her out. "Come on, Rosemary, let's go."

We manage, nightmare that it is.

Separated from the hat, clutching the red foxes as though the breeze will blow them away along with what's left of her hair, Rosemary the general morphs into Rosemary the victim, letting go of those foxes long enough to grip me by both hands and look into my eyes, wheezing. "Oh, Elena, she has the devil in her."

I have to talk her down. "Elena was my mother, Rose. I'm Lane. It's Thursday, now let's us walk out on the pier."

"I heard it in the night."

"Last night?"

"Before. I heard her call out like a thing possessed, and I knew."

"Look at those guys. Sailing, in these waters? They must be crazy!"

"It entered her the night Mama died, and Iris changed."

"In this wind? They almost capsized!"

"I saw it rise up out of the coffin when they lowered Mama into the ground. That night I heard the devil's voice in her."

I can't ground her. I do what I can. "Toxic water, full of industrial waste."

"I heard it through the bedroom wall."

I grab her wrist. "What if they fall in?"

"Last night I heard it again, but it was not with Iris."

"Their kids will come out looking like space aliens."

"It was thumping around in the attic right above my head."

"Nice walk out on the pier, Rosemary. Come on, it isn't far." I tug, but the woman digs in.

"First I heard the footsteps and then I heard it drop on the floor. Right above my head!"

"Do you a world of good." Tug harder.

She won't budge. "And then I heard somebody coming down the back stairs, I knew it was her, I heard her come back into her room and flop down on the brass bed, you know that sound, when it hits against the wall?"

"OK, Rose, we can get back in the car now."

"I heard what she said."

"Heard who." It is not a question. I am beyond asking.

"I heard her cursing me. Mama is dead and buried, but her devil is in this house."

She is beyond answers, and I am over asking. I shovel her into the car. "That's too bad, Rose."

She fights the seat belt. "You don't understand!"

"Settle down. We have to go."

Before I can close the door on her, she leans out, squawking. "She's going to kill me."

"The devil?"

"No, moron. Iris! Don't you know *anything*?"

CHAPTER 26

Mormama

Poor Rose, she was in love with nice Alan Deering and he loved her, I do believe, and perhaps if she'd let him take her to their new home in Annapolis she'd have escaped, but Alan the architect was a perfectionist; the two of them moved into Sister's room— just until their perfect house was done.

As a favor to my daughter, Alan was out in the driveway directing the crane she hired to lift Little Manette's new marble bathtub to the second floor and lower it into the temporary opening she'd had cut for it. The crane malfunctioned and smashed him in the scant week he spent under this roof.

Bad things happen to men in this house, and he was not the first. There was Leah's sweet boy, taken from us before they could marry; there were two who came courting her daughter, the first Elena, nice boys taken from us in accidents before they could propose. Better for them, I suspect, because Manette would have destroyed them with words, willy-nilly, that I know.

By the time Little Manette died, Poor Elena was almost too old to find an acceptable man. Iris had been married to Stan Worzecka and divorced by then and she and Rosemary ruled the roost, as strict and demanding as their mother at her worst. I saw Cinderella played out on this very hearth.

The first Elena managed to meet that nice boy in spite of her jealous aunts. She and Edwin Parkson were in love. I helped the child to elope, never mind how. They honeymooned downtown at the Windsor Hotel, but only for a night. Our Elena brought her sweet young husband home to May Street the very next day— "Just until we find a house," she told us, but of course it dragged on and on. Foolish girl. I tried to warn her, but I was long dead. In a way.

I was . . .

Never mind what I am.

What could I do to protect the lovely boy Leah's daughter finally married, what could I possibly do? Poor Elena's nice man got caught up in some odd way and broke his neck in that fall down the back stairs. He died a week before the baby came, and he was only the newest in this strange, long line of sad lives and untimely deaths brought on by Ellis women who dared to bring new men into this dreadful house.

Poor Elena begat Leila the free, who begat . . . Her descendents' losses are too many and too tiresome to name. Generations march into this house and march on to death, all but we women, who . . .

Oh, look at us. Oh!

CHAPTER 27

$\mathcal{T}heo$

After a while you get sick of Adults-Only chat rooms, even though you can see the weirdos coming and you know which ones are gonna try to set a meet and then you say you're with the government and the feds are coming to their house as we speak. Dad put me onto that gag, he said he was arming me for the future, but it turns out three weeks later he left, the fuckwad, what does he know?

So. If you can't find anybody you care about on *Zonecraft* and picking up new weapons for your skimmer or blowing away scaly monsters gets old, you have to kick back and go down to face real life. Plus, I played all the way past lunch. Yeah, I have to pass through their TV room to reach the fridge, and, fuck. One of those aunts will spring out all pissed off at me, where were you, why don't you, you never, but I have to eat, right? Better run past, grab whatever and split before they make it out of those great big honking chairs.

The tricky part is doing it while they're deep in their TV. It's in the big back room because they think the giant flatscreen and fuzzy tweed Barcaloungers are an insult to our fine old family furniture, at least that's what Aunt Ivy says. Plus, during commercials the twins can skibble into the kitchen for crunchy snacks and another beer and make it back in time. *General Hospital* is over, but without Aunt Rosemary kicked back in her recliner all, blah blah blah, the switch on the Aunt Iris machine clicked OFF. I can hear her snoring from here. I'll go out and *buy* food. Whatever I can get. It's not like Mom shoved a twenty in my pocket when she bailed. She gave me a five and handed over her phone. In case.

Aunt Rosemary latched on to my mom before she hit the top step, and it serves her right for not taking me with but look at it this way, I'm on my own.

I can check out the side streets off the back of the one that runs behind, and see what this five will get me. If I don't find anything else, like a lunchroom or a falafel truck, I'll settle for crap food from the old guy at the yuck corner store.

I know Aunt Ivy's, like, languishing in her room across the hall with the old black-and-white TV, but I don't have the heart to go in. I keep the ten she slipped me under the doorstop in my bedroom, but I'm not going back in there either, no way. Yesterday Mormama showed up in my room in broad daylight, fuck! Couldn't see her, but I knew. I threw my book at her before she could start. She didn't like, yell or anything. She just flickered and went out. In this house even in broad daylight, no one is safe.

Which is why I'm scoping out the backside of this long, messed-up block for the zibledy-hundredth time since we got stuck here, and I'm shit out of luck. I check out all three side streets but there's no neon down there and no plastic banners, just more junk buildings with lame jungle vacant lots and wrecked foundations surrounding and a bunch of FOR SALE signs out front. No food trucks in sight, not even the frozen custard guy, and not a single plastic banner in front of any of those crap buildings signifying food for sale inside so, fuck.

I'm hungry enough to gnaw my arm off, whatever, I'm not going back inside that wooden sarcophagus until Mom does. Fuck, I'll have to go back into that crap corner store and look for food that's under five bucks, tax included. Plus edible. Plus non-toxic. Plus with no bugs in it, God, OK? OK? While that creepy old guy puts his elbows on the counter with that snarky glare, like I'm about to rip him off, waiting like he wants me to drop dead so he can watch.

Anything that passes for ice cream, I decide, turning right on the big cross street that leads back to May Street because there's only industrial park between there and the interstate, fuck that shit.

OK, ice cream. Prepackaged and in his old freezer, so at least the weevils or whatever froze to death. I don't care how old his Good Humors or Drumsticks are if he even has them, anything that got in there will be frozen too, and if I'm right and there's a cockroach stuck to it, cockroaches don't burrow so I can probably scrape it off, no prob. Thinking about food makes me maybe a little braver. If the ice cream looks OK, I'll take a chance on some Ring Dings to go with.

Like those will be bugfree and nontoxic. Dude, stop dragging your feet.

Then when I'm coming up on the backside of the store, this kid skins out of a second-floor window in the yellow brick heap and jumps on the ladder side of the fire escape. It slides down with him on it and, holy crap, he's bang in my face, hair sprouting out of his ears and tomato sauce stuck in the hair around his mouth, grinning like he'd just as soon pull back and smash me in the face.

He goes, "Yo."

So I go, "Hey."

"Who are you?"

"Theo." Grin back at him, asshole, or try to. Quick, before he can mess with you. "From up the street."

"Like you think I don't know that? You're the only other fucking kid on the whole fucking block."

"No shit." I don't really mean that. I mean, "Fuck."

"Fuck," he says. "But don't let Gumpy hear you or he'll smash your face."

"Gumpy?"

"My grandfather."

"That creepy old guy?" Mistake, Hale. Go, "I didn't mean creepy, you know . . ."

"Fuck yeah I do. He's old and he's weird. He's my legal guardian. See, my dad. Fuck, you're scared of him!"

"Not really."

"I seen you in there."

"No way."

"Way. I live upstairs. Gumpy, he's a mean old bastard, but he doesn't hit. He owns the store. We get shitloads of free samples and everything that rots in the bin."

"Cool. What's your name?"

"Douglas Ditlow, but he calls me Dopey. Dopey and Gumpy, get it?"

"Cool!"

"If you say so. I think it sucks."

"Sorry about that." We just turned the corner into May Street.

"Are you going in or what?"

Problem is, the store looks just as creepy as it did before I knew. "I don't need it."

"I can get you a discount, no shit."

"No shit?"

"Shit. Then we can go upstairs and I'll show you my stuff."

"Stuff?"

"Really. I'm the famous nighttime crawler. I can get into places and come out with stuff people never even know they lost."

Their food is awful— freezer burns on the ice cream and weevils in the cake but the old man gives me a discount and I pretend it's fine because Dopey is watching and the weevils are probably dead.

Then we go upstairs so he can show me his stuff.

It doesn't look like much, empty rhinestone cell phone case, girl's scrunchy, a pair of socks with sequined bunnies on the fronts, a pack of file cards with the plastic wrap still tight, a tough-looking sports Swatch, but man, the kid is proud. "Right out from under their noses."

I did what you do. I went, "Wow."

"In broad daylight, some of it." He shows me so much dumb stuff that after a while I zone out and home in on ways to get him to quit without being mean.

I guess he knows. He flaps an old magazine up in my face to get my attention. "I mean it. See this?"

It doesn't look like much to me but I have to say something "Where'd you get it?"

"From the guy that lives underneath your house."

He either did or he didn't, but he knows something nobody's supposed to know. Instead of asking how he found out I go, "Cool!"

"Not really, but it proves I can get away with anything and the victim will never know." He flashes the cover in case I didn't get it the first time.

It's an old copy of *Wired*. Like Dell went out scavenging and came home with a bunch. "You were in there."

"Pretty much. And you want to know the coolest thing?"

"How did you find out he's in there?"

"He was sound asleep, and I took it right off his chest."

"How do you know?"

"In broad daylight, dude."

"I said, *how do you know?*"

"He's in the store all the time, comes before we're even open, pisses Gumpy off but money's money, so he opens up."

"Money?"

"No big, a few bucks, but it all adds up."

"So you followed him?"

"Who, me? No way. I'm dumb but I'm not stupid."

"OK thanks. I have to go." You'd better. All you have to do now is stand up.

"Dude, you think you're in a different world up there on May Street, but everybody knows. Old lady from Marvista told us there's a guy in there, she was in the store the day after they found that body on the fourth floor."

"Body?"

"You know, last Thursday night."

That stops me. "I didn't hear anything."

"We did. The cops were around. Wife did it. He was asking for it, I guess. They found him in bed with the knife sticking straight up in his chest, her fingerprints, the whole nine, and you didn't know?"

"Not so much."

Son of a bitch, he's sorry for me. "Kid, you ought to get out more."

"Like you think I don't try."

Then he picks up like he didn't just drag me around the block by my hair. "Anyway, I thought he would be gone. Broad daylight, and, shit!"

"He didn't, like, kick you out?"

"Fuck no. He was dead asleep. I could of taken his laptop if I wanted. He never even knew that I was there."

Magazine that old can't be worth much. I poked him. "OK Dopey" (we're on a first-name basis now). "Why'd you take the stupid thing?"

He poked me in the gut; I couldn't help it, I giggled. "So he'd wake up knowing that Dopey was there."

I poked him back and we did what you do when you're about the same size and you think you can take him, we wrestled, all knees and elbows thumping the floor every time we rolled. We rolled around cackling until the old man hollered up the stairs and Dopey said, "Beat it. Gumpy never hits but he can hurt you," so I jumped out the window onto the rusty old fire escape, praying to God that the ladder would slide down.

CHAPTER 28

Extract

Dakin Ellis, his book
April, 1920

I should have died in the war. Europe was in flames. God knows I wanted to go. There is nothing for me here. I wanted us to meet in the trenches, just Randolph and me, never father and son. Two grown men, without portfolio, with no shared past and a common aim. With no history between us, we would win that war together, everything possible because nothing went before.

*Lord, how I wanted to hear that shout. I wanted the Greek Recognition scene— **Father! Son!**— the gratifying smack of flesh on flesh. The past erased, everything resolved. Hope sprang up when Dakin Junior enlisted. Ellis men in the trenches, brothers in arms. Guilt gnaws at me as I write. My namesake was never my favorite son. I would have sold my soul for a chance to fight along-side the boy I lost. Dakin and Randolph, comrades in arms.*

That was never possible. There was bad blood between us long before he bolted. I blame Manette.

God knows I wanted to serve, but they wouldn't let me go. Not the doctors. They would have turned their heads and moved along. Ours was the war to end all wars. We were dying in great numbers, our boys bleeding out on foreign soil. The situation was so dire that they sent everybody to the front.

They forbade me. Not the doctors. It was the women. I blame Manette.

My wife draped disdain in false tears, mewling until the bubble over her mouth popped and words fell out.

"Dakin, you're too old."

Never mind what I said. She wasn't listening.

"Think of your children!" She meant Everett. To Manette, the others were ciphers, and Randolph was a stranger to her.

I raged. I begged.

At last she said what she really meant. "Don't turn me into a widow, you inconsiderate old . . ."

"Old what?"

The perfect lady, she would never use the word.

I stamped out of her dressing room, fixed to leave the house.

She left it to her tiresome, superfluous mother to explicate the curse that we both acknowledged but could not name. Old Mrs. Robichaux stopped me at the bottom of the stairs. Frail as she is, she's strong. She drew me into the first sitting room and closed the double doors before she spoke. "You can't go. Think of the children. Without you here to stand between Manette and your children, she . . ."

I never liked her, but she knew. I felt her out. "She what?"

She was beyond speech. I do not like the woman, but unlike her daughter, she is not false. For the first time in her long career here, old Mrs. Robichaux let me see her cry.

"Ma'am!"

"I don't know what she'd do."

My wife would what? I didn't really know, but I knew the old woman was right. Too many unhappy years between us, hundreds

of words hurled and returned, mulled and regurgitated, and Ma-
nette remains a mystery to me. Without me to see to it, she could
take to her bed and leave our youngest to root in the neighbors'
compost heaps for food, or she could just as easily fall into a tem-
per and start beating them.

"Do you understand?" The old lady confronted me, trembling
with the effort. She was waiting for me to go on.

For all I knew, the minute I walked out the door my wife would
put on her finest and go about collecting men to serve her needs,
which have always been a mystery to me. For all I knew, she would
court returning heroes in a fit of patriotic zeal. She could go out
hunting every night and bring home a silken fancy man. In a life-
time filled with getting and spending, using and discarding, my
wife has never revealed what she really needs. With me gone to
the war, she would get whatever she thought she wanted, bent on
replacing me whether or not I came back, because Little Manette
was never happy in this enormous house I built for her, the per-
fect setting she demanded.

Nothing was ever enough. She wasn't satisfied in spite of all the
Persian carpets, the French brocades, the grand furniture and costly
paintings and sculpture that I bought because I thought it would
make her happy, for a time.

Mormama waited. I stood there, pondering.

A woman like Manette could just as easily seize on some brute
because he was rich and socially prominent. And if he wanted to
have his way with our daughters, I have no idea whether she
would protest or stand back, discreetly looking the other way
because it served her purposes.

I saw Mrs. Robichaux wavering in her tracks— exhaustion, I
suppose. I could smell age coming off of her. She was trembling
with the effort. She reeked of grief, and for the first time in all the
years since she landed on our doorstep uninvited and I uninvited
her, I understood.

I admit it was rude. I had our children lined up on the porch that day, and I blocked the door so she would have to listen to what I told them.

"*This is your Mormama. One more mama than we need.*"

That day she defied me. With her gloved hand, she lifted my hand off the front doorknob, holding it daintily between her forefinger and her thumb. She dropped it, and I let it be. Then she lifted her chin and marched on past, into Manette's house.

She entered because she was needed and for years now she has hung on, defying her failing body in a brave, constant act of will. In spite of everything, she's still standing. She is here to keep her daughter in check.

I thought: **I was wrong**.

She repeated. "Do you understand?"

I did.

To her credit, Mrs. Robichaux never spoke of it, but we both lived with the dreadful possibility of another fire in the bowels of the house.

CHAPTER 29

Dell

"Um, Dell?"

"Shit!" Dell jumps up so fast that the journal flies. It lands on its spine and pages fly out. He lunges for the pieces, trying to pick up everything all at once.

"What's that?"

This kid Theo. Here, where he sleeps. "Nothing!"

"Bullshit, that's somebody's diary."

"It's mine." Angry and distracted, Dell lunges here, there in the half-light, retrieving pages, entire hand-stitched signatures, trying to turn the pieces back into what he had.

The kid is swifter than Dell. He grabs the last floating page. "A really old diary . . ."

"Give it!"

". . . like it belongs to the house," he says, studying the jagged script.

"It's mine!" Dell snatches the page out of Theo's hands and clamps it into the book. There.

He awoke with Dakin's journal on the floor next to his head. He was close last night— what night, was it even night? He was too burned out to deal. He slammed the book. OK, he ran away from it. When? The changing light tells him that it's late afternoon, but he has no idea how long he slept. He thinks he quit the attic just before dawn, but. Yesterday, or did he sleep through another night— how long has it been?

Too long. Clutching the journal, he flopped facedown on the plastic mat he took off an old glider, and passed out. He woke up with a long groove in his face. He's been sitting here for at least an hour, but the plastic piping imprint still bisects his cheek. Worse. His brains went out to lunch while he slept, and he can't get them to come back. It's like thinking underwater, trying to organize gelid shapes that shift on him every time he thinks he knows what to put where.

"So, did you steal it or what?"

Do what you can. Counterattack. He turns on Theo Hale, a genuine Ellis by blood, which pisses him off right now. "How did you get in?"

"Same as ever, asshole. Whaddiyou think?"

Dell weaves in place, clamping the journal to his chest. His mouth is clogged with grit, even his eyeballs scrape their sockets when he blinks. What hit him so hard when he first picked up the book? A detail he was too fried to parse.

He woke up wired. Now he just has to, has to, he has to— what? Whatever it is, it's urgent. No time for coffee, no time to eat. He did the necessaries and squatted here. He has to find his place in this book! When he opened the carton, he found Dakin's journal on top. It was like a message from God. Words flew off the page, words pertaining to him, but it was dark and he was too fried to process them. Intense, he thinks, I was *this close,* but then this damn kid . . .

I lost my place!

It all went to hell in the adrenaline rush. "Fuck are you doing here?"

"I came to warn you."

"Say what?" He clamps down on the book so the boy won't see that his hands are shaking.

Smug little bastard. Sanctimonious. "If I can get in, anybody could."

Set your jaw and hang tough. "You think."

"I know."

Dell hocks, thinking to spit on the cement at Theo's feet, but he's all dried out. Everything is hard. Like making words. "If I were you, I wouldn't mess with me."

Theo says, "Did you used to have an old copy of *Wired*?"

"I have a bunch."

"Really old one, with this red rhomboid thing on the front?"

Fuck, he should eat. Drunk on too much sleep and dead empty, Dell will say anything to end this. "Probably."

"Well, you don't have it any more."

His head comes up.

"Dopey took it off you while you were sound asleep."

"Who?"

"Kid I know. I saw it at his house."

"Never happened. Nobody gets in here."

"Except me." Theo drops in a silence like a fifty-pound weight. Then he adds, "You think."

Mouth like a litter box, gritty and rank. End this. Dell slips one hand into his pocket, locating his knife. "You're the only one that knows."

"You wish. If Dopey got in, anybody could. Get it?"

Yep, still there. "Got it. Go."

Instead, he feints for the journal. "Let me see."

"No way."

"It belongs to the house."

Sleep wiped his hard drive. Scowl. Threaten. "I have a knife."

"Like somebody sneaked in and stole it."

Flash the knife. "Beat it!"

"OK, OK." Theo ducks around the partition that separates his private space from the latticed area under the porch and then sticks his head back in. "I'm just sayin' . . ."

Sanctimonious little shit. Dell flips his wrist and the blade snaps to. "Now."

"You gotta be more careful, dude."

Cautionary little fuck. Stupid, what Dell does then. He flips the gravity knife at the weathered partition, aiming a little to the right of Theo's head. "Out!"

His aim is dead on and the knife sticks, vibrating in the wood. Dell is lost in space, mesmerized by the hum. The kid vanishes, leaving him to pull it out of the wood. Oh, holy shit. *That close.*

He drops to his knees by the lattice between his place and the side yard of the Marvista, scratching a hole in the ground. He won't use the knife. Instead he works slowly, clawing up the dirt like a dog. It becomes important to bury the thing— which he does, finally, horrified by what he accidentally almost did.

That close!

It's not the kid's fault that he came at a bad time, Dell knows. It was me. He was riffling through the old man's journal, looking for something he's not sure of when, fuck. Theo walked into the middle of a half-formed idea. Whatever Dell discovered about himself, or thought he had discovered, shattered like ice on a pond he has to cross if he wants to survive, leaving him in over his head. Drowning as fragments of the surface that supported him broke up and floated away.

He should be doing a dozen other things right now. Rehydrating, getting his shit together, nerving himself up for another hurried move— Theo's right, this place is no longer safe for him.

Anybody could come in and find him here. Rob him blind, if that's what they want, take him back to Rhode Island to face whatever he left behind or drag him off to jail or beat him senseless because he can't tell them who he's hiding from and he sure as hell can't tell them what he did.

He doesn't even know what's on the toxic flash drive. Bad, he knows. Why else does it make him puke?

Dell should be packing up his shit and covering his tracks, but he can't. He has to scour the journal until he finds the entry that smoked him. Somewhere in this mess of densely filled pages, there's proof.

He belongs here. He's dead sure of it.

April, 1920

Now, what would Manette do if I had answered the call to war? What would she have done? My own wife, and I didn't know.

I couldn't go.

Instead, the war took my sons, and it never gave them back. It took Dakin Junior, whom I loved but never really liked. That boy died a hero at Château Thierry, and it took Randolph— I think. Furious, my Randolph, child and man, he was born with my temper and his mother's sweet face. He ran away at seventeen; I loved him but we fought each other all our lives together in this house. The last time we fought it was horrendous.

He ran away! My dearest Ran. He was the best and worst of my sons. We fought, and I lost my boy.

He went Over There without my knowledge. I grieve for what I lost. I grieve for him, but to this day, I do not know whether he lived or died.

Dakin Junior came home to rest in Florida soil. We buried my rigid, dutiful, noble namesake in the family plot, next to Teddy, our sad lost child. At least two of my sons are together now, right here in Jacksonville, where I would join them tomorrow, if I could.

But Randolph that I loved so much, who left this house and this city in a tearing rage? I may never know.

He was seen alive after the battle at Belleau Wood, shortly before the Boche surrender. Another boy from Jacksonville, Clay Woodward, brought home an object Randolph handed off to him in the final days of the war. It's the Spanish piece of eight that I gave Ran on his twelfth birthday. He wore it on a chain around his neck and he was proud of it, I know. It made me happy. I could look at him and see the man he would become. He was still wearing it that last night. To my shame, I tried to pull it off his neck during the fight on the houseboat, but he jerked away from me cursing, and jumped over the rail and swam away.

We were both furious. God help me, I shouted into the dark. I **hope you drown.**

Clay Woodward told me that Ran, my dearest runaway, pulled that same chain over his head at Belleau Wood. Clay brought it home to me. I know the jeweler who sold me the chain; I know the dentist who drilled the hole. Clay says Ran told him to give it to me. I take it as a message but dear God, what was he trying to say?

.   .   .

Dell ought to be out in the world right now, caffeinating, for crap's sake, finding decent food. All he's had since the kid left is half a peanut bar and brackish water from the tap that feeds the abandoned laundry tubs. He needs to get out of his enclosure, go running, anything to straighten out his thoughts and put them back where they belong, but he's on to something, he thinks. No. He's sure!

Logic tells him that the entry that haunts him turned up a few pages earlier than this section— or later. He can't be sure. It fell out when the book flew, but where does it go in the chronology of

Dakin Ellis? He can't be sure. Ellis dated his entries, but he didn't number the pages. All he can do is guess.

Unless he's turning research from what it is into what he wants it to be.

Randolph was the best and the worst of my children, and the only one of the lot who is truly mine. The others were born out of Manette's greed and indifference and my ignorance in the matter of certain things and I love them, even though they're hard to like, but Randolph was mine and Sylvia's and God forgive me, he ran away when he was seventeen. Now, I know that Randolph was called to serve and that he went. Clay Woodward saw him at Marigny, so I know he survived, but, beyond that?

He is an Unknown Soldier to us now.

This, Dell thinks, rummaging through the disembodied pages, speed-reading for details. Going forward at a dead run, he sorts them with his eyes fixed on one search entry with few variations: Randolph. Ran. Intent and for the first time sharply focused on proof of existence, he reads until the words blur. He needs evidence.

The entry that links him to this family. He is shaking with passion. When he finds it, he shouts. His voice is so loud that he has to jam his fist into his mouth— anything to muffle the noise, which means, control the surge of joy.

Never mind what went on between myself and the wife after Brucie died in her womb and we put Randolph into her arms. Some days I curse God. On others, I curse myself. Was it a mistake for me to let my wife believe that my most beloved son, the beautiful boy that lovely, lost Sylvia and I created together, was hers? If it had gone otherwise and Randolph and I had met for the first time in the trenches, would he be here with us now? Would we know each other at once, father and son? Would we be different people by the time we met, killer of your father's heart, reckless blood of my blood? If we met now, Randolph, me wiser and kinder than I was, you matured, both of us freed of our shared past history, would you be here?

Dearest boy, we could have been best friends!

Dell is shaken, inside and out. Rattled to the core. Too excited. Can't think. Can't. Wants to. Has to try. Try.

Randolph. This Randolph Ellis would be a hundred years old by now. No, a hundred and change. Nearer a hundred and a quarter, no, closer to fifty cents, he thinks, I could be Dell Duval, née— no, né, he supposes, that would be the masculine, right— now how does he know that? Dell DuVal né God knows what, and if I am Randolph's son. No. Grandson. No. Great-grandson.

He calculates, rummaging.

Great-great grandson. Then I belong, he thinks.

No. This belongs. Me. In this. At one with the house rising above him. As if it's expanding to embrace him. Listening.

Let me in!

It takes him too long to settle. Dakin's entry rushed in to fill all the blank spaces in his life. With guilt running up his heels and his future an open question, in flight from things in his past that he can't bring back and will not name, he has found a place to stand.

The pieces come together with a snap.

So that's who I am. OK! What if this Ran came back? He did, and he had a kid. What if the long-lost son rolled in after his grieving father died? Like, would the angry mother-woman, this Little Manette, be glad to see him or would she slam the door on him? What if he came back and claimed his fortune after both Dakin and the hateful wife were dead? What if this Dakin Ellis Senior rewrote his will before his car ran off the bridge. No time for lawyers or a trip to the family safe-deposit box. He would have hidden it somewhere in the house.

Energized, he rolls up his frazzled mattress with the journal stashed inside, and begins a list.

Note to Self:

1. Get your shit together.
2. Find the will.
3. The one in the wheelchair likes you. Turn on the charm. Take her a present. Candy, or something you can lift off the decrepit corpse of that downtown department store. Kiss her on the cheek, she'll blush and shiver because from the looks of her, nobody's done that to her since she was young, before the chair. Hold her hand while you talk to her, old ladies love that, makes them feel cherished, at least a little bit. Play this right and she'll beg you to let her help.
4. Shave. Change your shirt.

CHAPTER 30

Ivy

Life is so much, much more interesting now. Last month the twins and I were still all alone together, simmering like tainted meat coming to a boil, the last of our generation left alive. The three of us suffered through meals in near-silence because we don't have the energy to fight, but now, now!

I have a gentleman friend, and my wretched sisters don't know. If we count Little Elena's boy, and boys do count, there are not one, but two new men in the house!

Iris and Rose and I have been all alone together for a long, long time. When it's just us, they never talk to me and they certainly don't listen. They get me up in the morning and give me oatmeal. Then they put me places, like a thing.

We have been alone together for so long!

Nobody comes to visit, although they did come when we used to be girls. Now there is the mailman, there are the meter readers, but nobody wants to have a conversation. They just do their jobs and go. Children don't stop here on Halloween. No one has left this house in costume since Poor Elena came home to die in Sister's room. That year she took Little Elena out dressed as a pumpkin in orange crepe paper, with a little green hat, so cute. All the colors ran because that year, it rained on Halloween. We haven't seen Little Elena since she left for boarding school. I'm just so happy that she's back!

It's been terrible. Iris and Rosemary come and go whenever they want, but unless it pleases them to unlock the front door and let Scooter and me roll out, I am relegated to the back porch. The day the men delivered Scooter, Iris plopped me into the seat and washed her hands of me. "There. Now you can stop whining." Rosemary smiled the way she does, saying, "You can go anywhere you want," but that isn't true.

Rose did have Vincent fix the kitchen door so it opens easily, I think to keep me out of the kitchen while she's trying to cook. She won't let me help. She says I get in the way. Lord, I am sick of her boiled dinners and stewed-fruit desserts, but if I hand her the pepper or Poor Elena's jar of dried-out thyme or *The Fanny Farmer Cookbook,* if I even say the word *onion,* she says, "Ivy. Go out and get some fresh air."

Yes, I can roll out the kitchen door and park on the back porch where nobody has to see, but I do believe that she and Iris hope that Scooter will betray me and topple us both down the back porch steps to the ground, outside the old laundry room where Teddy died. Imagine, poor Ivy crushed by her fancy electrical chair. She died alone and unseen behind the house, on the spot where nobody comes. I wonder if there will be a party after the funeral. I don't think so. Who would come? Everybody we used to know has been dead for much, much too long.

Ah, but now we have the young people to brighten our eyes. Fresh faces. Little Elena and little Teddy. And the other one, that my sisters don't know about. It is exciting. All this *life* in the house.

I'm afraid my sisters are too excited, vying for our young niece's attention, switching *this* Elena around just like they did the other ones. They even argue about dessert!

"This is my kitchen, Iris Worzecka. Do not put those prunes in my fruit compote!"

"Stop it! It's Iris *Ellis* now, and don't you forget it. I am five minutes older than you are, and I can do anything I want."

Look at them doing their little Punch and Judy show. When the boy is around they make fools of themselves, all but playing leapfrog to charm him, and when he will not be charmed, they discipline. Well, let them, for in this contest, the prize is already mine. This new, older Teddy is sweet enough, and we have an understanding, with no need to sit down and discuss the terms.

We have a secret in common.

Little Teddy knows what I know, but we will never say so out loud.

Without having to name it, the child and I are agreed.

Our secret, my handsome young friend said the time we intersected in the night, and I thought, *yes.* It was late night or early morning, and he was right here inside the house! We talked, but only for a little bit. I should have been screaming for Iris to rout him with Grandfather's sword, but he and I knew each other from before. We did, and I was not afraid. The day we met, my nice young man turned Scooter and me so that we could face the sun. When he touched my hand in the night, my heart leapt up. Now, it leaps up at the very thought.

Our secret, he said before he moved on, and we agreed. It is, and then— dear God!— I think he added, "Next time."

Iris and Rosemary. Pfaugh!

Our secret glitters in my heart, like a wonderful present that's much too pretty to unwrap. *I have a friend in the house.* That sweet young man is living right down there in the laundry room underneath the back porch, snug as a bear in a cave. Of course the boy knows. As soon as I heard Teddy Two playing in Biggie's laundry room, I made him come back up the steps and into the arms of the house. I told him, "Don't go down there."

I tried to warn without explaining. *It's dangerous!* He thought he could fool me, but I knew he wasn't the only one down there. The day that nice young man first came over the rail to help me, I added two and two.

Lovely man, but I should warn him too!

I like the child, how can I not love a curly-headed boy named for my sad, lost little brother, burned to death when he was only three years old? Oh, new child with the curly hair. Why do you try so hard to slick it down? In another life, I would buy a horse for this new Teddy and we could go out riding in Ellis Park, but this is the only life I have and God forgive me for not warning them because dangerous as it is for them, I don't want this part to end.

Dear hearts, I need to warn you! I need to warn . . .

"Ivy Ward Ellis, did you get out here all by yourself?" Curse you, Iris, you bossy witch.

"Little Elena helped us." Scooter and me.

"You know it's almost suppertime. What are you doing out here?"

"I'm waiting for the mail."

"Idiot. It's already been!"

"Did anything come for me?"

"Has anything ever? Ivy, get a grip!" My, Iris is in a terrible mood. She and Rose have been squabbling ever since the day our Little Elena took Rosemary out in her car.

"Why, my grip is very strong." I often turn off the motor and move Scooter with my bare hands. It's quieter, and my sisters never know.

"It's a neologism, stupid!"

"You and your TV slang." If I wanted to, I could make Scooter push my sister down the front porch steps right now.

Sly Iris, she bends down to ask, "Has Rosemary been talking about me?"

Trapped as I am on Scooter, seated so close to the floor that even children look down on me, old as we are, all three of us, I am still the senior member in this house. A sage. To be consulted in every emergency. "I'm sorry, I'm sworn."

"To secrecy." Iris groans. "Understand, this is a very special case."

The twins used to fight and kill each other daily while Mama was alive, before I lost the use of my legs. They tangled like a fury of tiny tigers, each bent on gaining control. Do I want to take sides? Should I fall into the old pattern and listen, collecting information from each, which is how a woman in a wheelchair gains power? Yes. "Of course," I say, and she does her best to smile. The fool has volunteered nothing, so I prod. "Go on."

My younger (younger!) sister's stern face is a kaleidoscope now, going this way, that way, each feature trying to settle in the right place. Wait long enough, and Iris will find a clever way to make me want to take her side. At last! "She's enlisted Little Elena in this terrible scheme of hers," she says. "To take all of our jewels and set fire to the house!"

Now, how should I respond? It would be tiresome to say, "There there." Currently, our fury of twins is in a rage, so I won't have to say anything— unless I want to. At my sister's back, Rosemary is lurking behind the half-open front door. The girl is blind as a bat, but with ears so finely tuned that she can pick up the sense of any conversation from twice the distance of our long porch. In a minute, Rosemary will storm down on Iris and yank the scene out of her contorted, flying hands. Four. Three. Two.

Rosemary streaks out the front door. "Lies, you duplicitous, vile woman. Ivy, don't listen to her!"

"Rose is a liar, Ivy. Don't believe a word she says!"

Punch and Judy. They've been this way since the day they were born!

Predictably, they tangle, spitting, "Take this, you," "Take that," sawing back and forth, back and forth, two old ladies, *the Ellis girls,* back-and-forthing their way across the porch and into the front door without a thought for me, taking their argument deeper and deeper into the house.

Finally.

Waiting, I scheme.

We have to talk about it some time. I have to warn my new friend that this house is not safe for him, but how can I do that and keep him nearby, so we can keep on having these sweet talks?

If only he'd come! Come talk to me now, dear friend. You are the only bright light in this endless life of poverty and contention, although I am rather fond of the new Teddy too.

If he does come, how can I warn him and still keep him close? How can I tell my nice new friend that I pray will come along and talk to me here in the gathering dark— how can I tell him that he's laid down his bed on the very spot where my little brother died, that he's in danger, and we must go?

I have some money. After I got hurt, Papa brought me a twenty-dollar Liberty Gold Eagle every time he visited my room, and I kept them all. There is my jewelry, some recent, some heirloom, all part of my inheritance after Papa passed away, and I came into a bit of money from Great-Aunt Lydia, so that although this monstrous house keeps us all poor and dependent on the stipend Papa settled on me and whatever is left of Little Elena's bonds, I have something to bring to the feast.

I happen to know that our old houseboat is still moored out there on the banks of the St. Johns River. Vincent told me, and I do believe it would be a safe retreat.

For his own safety, I know we should save the boy, but it would be a shame to steal him away from his mother, and three would be a little . . . I believe in any circumstance, three is a crowd and if Little Elena came with us, that would make four, many too many to live comfortably on Papa's boat, although if he insists, together we will find a way.

Come find me here, dear stranger. I'm waiting in the spot on the porch where you and I first met. Come and sit next to me here in the dark while I find the words to make you see, and the right words to help you believe.

Let me tell you about little Teddy and the circumstances on that terrible day. Let me tell you how my sweet little brother died, and let me tell you about the other men who have lived and died in this house on May Street, and then, my secret friend who is so very important to me, and then . . .

Mormama and Tillie were taking the girls to Ellis Park in the pony cart, and I knew that as soon as we left May Street, Tillie would let me take the reins. I begged to go, but when I came downstairs in my prettiest frock, Mama flew off at me. "You can't go, young lady. Think of poor Everett, staying back all by himself."

I never liked Everett, and all his long life in this house, Everett despised me. He was born sickly, but I am a cripple because God punished me.

I said, "I hate Everett, Mama." *Quiet, Ivy. It's a sin to hate.* "Besides, I have to help Tillie hold the pony." *Nonsense. Come and help me entertain your poor sick brother, you selfish girl.* I started to cry. "I'm not selfish, Mama, I'm not!" The more I sobbed, the more Mama poked my fat belly and pinched my fat cheeks to make me laugh and forget that I had to stay back and help her with that great big baby, it hurt! I screamed. Mama lashed out. *You love horses so much, my girl. Go out to the stables and help Vincent clean up the . . .* I saw my mother wince. She would never say the word.

She spat out the rest like an enduring curse and yes, it has followed me. *That will teach you to beg.* She dispatched me to the carriage house to help Vincent muck out the stalls. When it happened, Vincent and I were out in the alley, near enough to hear the screams but too far away for Vincent to reach him in time. I was holding the lid to the bin while Vincent dumped the manure.

Is it my fault, then, for leaving poor Teddy alone in the house with nothing to do? Did I really think that Mama noticed or cared what he did or where he went? Forgive me, God. I was careless, careless. Is that why You let Dakin Junior's horse rear up and fall over backward on me the night I ran away? Was that my punishment?

If that nice young man does come and I do tell him these things, as well as several others about the fate of men who have moved into the distinguished, deadly home of Manette Ward Robichaux Ellis, will he pat my hand and say it's just my imagination, or will he see the danger and take me out of here?

I want, I yearn for my handsome friend to lift me out of Scooter and carry me off with him, away from this awful place. Then, please God, oh then I will help my young love to find his future in some new town where I can be happy, and he will be perfectly safe.

CHAPTER 31

Theo

So I escaped because old Aunt Ivy accidentally broke a bottle before lunch. She was afraid to tell them because she hates it when
they get mad, so a spear of broken glass pretty much trashed Aunt
Iris's foot. She was so pissed off at Aunt Rosemary for not sweeping up the mess that she didn't even thank her for bringing towels
to stop the blood. It kept bleeding anyway, so Mom had to drive
them both to the ER.

Aunt Iris claimed she needed Rosemary to sit with her in the
back and keep her finger on the pressure point even though by
that time the bleeding had stopped, but Aunt Rosemary said, sort
of by-the-way, "It's better now, I think I'll stay back and watch
General."

Then Aunt Iris got all bent. She said Mom and I could get her
out front and into the car, you know, living crutches, but she
needed Rosemary to walk her in to the ER while Little Elena
parked, and when she squawked Iris added, besides, somebody

had to save her place in line while she went to the toidy— the *toidy?*— because there was zero time for her to limp into the downstairs one here and do what she had to do right now because this was an emergency, but that wasn't the real reason either.

I never saw one of these stringy old ladies leave 553 without the other one, well, except for that one time. Mom says they're both paranoid. Like, scared to leave each other alone in the house, e.g., if twin one left twin two alone in the house, she'd either spill all her secrets or run upstairs where Ivy can't go and grab all the valuables and take off in a taxi for parts unknown. Either that or she'd spend all day setting nasty traps, like planting marbles in the big mahogany staircase or prying up boards on the back steps so her twin would wipe out next time she went downstairs. Or she'd sneak strange men into the house and do God knows what with them. This makes zero sense to Mom or me, but, hey. They're gone, so, great!

I've been to the ER a couple of times in Daytona, and I can tell you, ER trips always take forever, whether you're bleeding from the ears or you can't stop throwing up. They'll all be gone for three hours at least, probably closer to four, and that's if there are no car wrecks and drive-by shootings and nothing blows up in Jacksonville today.

Except for Aunt Ivy, I'm on my own.

The aunts don't worry about Aunt Ivy because she can't exactly leave here, even if she had someplace to go. It would take two guys with a U-Haul and a bucket truck to get her and her clunky scooter off the porch and she's ferocious about that thing. Nobody takes her anywhere without it, and that's final.

I don't worry about her either, because she's nice. She doesn't rant and she never yells at you, no matter what. She pretty much stays where you put her and she's nice about that too, so when Mom shoveled the twins into the car and took off, I was like whew, thank God they're gone. Freedom now.

I went back to the breakfast room to see if Aunt Ivy wanted

anything from the store, my cover story in case they get back sooner, and Mom asks. I am never going back to that creepy store, not with Dopey living upstairs, his teeth are green. One visit and I'm over him.

I still have the peanut bar that he fobbed off on me, in case Aunt Ivy asks what I got for her, but she won't. She'll just forget. They all forget every five minutes, except, of course, Mom.

It's the perfect excuse. I just ran down to the corner to get Aunt Ivy this peanut bar, Mom, OK?

All I wanted to do was get out and run like hell until I couldn't run any more, like, after everything, I'd come back all chill. Then I could go around back and see if Dell is still mad at me and if he is, fuck him. With Mom gone, I could unleash another search engine on my ex-Dad and try out other things until they came back and I had to stop. Smart as she is, it's not like Mom knows from search history, so why not?

Aunt Ivy was still in the kitchen when I went inside to ask. She was trying to clean up the glass but she couldn't do much from the chair, and she looked so glad to see me that I took the broom away from her and swept it up in a couple of seconds which is easy when you're not stuck in a chair; I felt bad for her so I said, "I have to go out for a minute. Can I bring you anything special from the store?"

She smiled and smiled. "No thank you, dear."

This made me feel so guilty that I had to insist. "Are you sure?"

She came back with, "But there's one thing you could do for me," and I thought, oh, fuck. Then she smiled that shaky little smile and asked would I mind helping her and Scooter go out on the front porch, the door is so heavy that she can't . . . she wouldn't bother me with it, but my mother did ask her to keep an eye on me while she was gone, which I knew for a fact that Mom would never do, so would I mind? She looked so anxious to keep us all happy that I said OK.

So I did, although I freaked when she gunned the motor on the downside of the front door mini-ramp and, shit! What if she was fixing to roll straight down the big old front steps and out the gate but the scooter heeled over and dumped her on her head?

It turns out she was backing and filling to park her scooter at the far end of the porch. That was worse. What if the monster got stuck in reverse? The whole mess could roll backward down the front steps with her in it and land on top of her, and what would I do then?

In fact, she was very, very careful. Like she does this a lot. She was also very particular about where she wanted to park. Dead center by the railing on the driveway side, she told me. For reasons. She just didn't tell me what they were.

Then she had me lug over one of the white wicker rockers and park it next to her so we could get to know each other, which I did. Turns out she didn't really want to talk. She just sat there quietly, kind of like a lady in a deck chair in one of those old movies she likes so much, looking out to sea, so I did too. I looked out to sea with her for another while just to be polite, even though it was about to get dark. Finally she sort-of giggled and told me not to give her another thought, and when I didn't take the hint she said I didn't have to keep her company, she was fine and finally she said to me, point-blank, although I'm too fucking old for this, "Why don't you go out and play?"

The other two aunts, I would have snarked, "Play what?" but this is the nice one. I went, "Yes Ma'am," and I did. I didn't jump over the rail and run, it might hurt her feelings, but I was out of that rocker and down those steps before she finished saying, "Have fun."

I hung a left and headed uphill to the far corner, trying to slow down and not look like I was escaping because I felt guilty as fuck. Two suits got out of a slick black car across the street from Marvista as I pretend-strolled past. It looked official, and I went, Hmmm.

Then I thought, no problem.

There's always something going on in that place. If they turn out to be feds or city detectives, that's about like you'd expect. Plus, I'm clean. Shit comes down at Marvista all the time, but I haven't seen or heard much since the night they took the body out. If I have to, I can play so dumb about that one crime that, witness? Forget it. He's too stupid to testify.

So, fine. *This isn't about me.*

I motored on past, heading up May Street to the far corner, all cool and thinking cool thoughts, and, shit!

Maybe it is.

Instead of marching up to Marvista like I thought, banging on the door and waiting for the owner to come, the two guys peeled off and slick as Mylar, these two suits that I thought I'd left behind, that I totally thought had nothing to do with me, were ambling down from the uphill corner with matching smiles. They were coming right at me, so smooth that I was, How did you get up here from back down there?

This happens and even though you have nothing to hide, not even the rest of the weed Dopey planted on you Tuesday that you flushed as soon as you got shut of him, you automatically get all bent and humble, like, cracking your knuckles with this shit-eating grin. *Is it something I did?*

Until the tall one flashes a newspaper photo at me. "Have you seen this man?"

Guess not. They're looking for Dell.

They describe this nice guy that I thought I knew, although they call him by a different name, checking off bullet points like this is a case for *America's Most Wanted.*

I come up empty. Blink blink.

The short one pulls out his phone and flashes a screen shot at me. Yep, it's him.

I'm like, hmmm. Uh-uh, sorry, nope.

The short one widens the image. "Look a little closer, son. He may have grown a beard."

The tall one says, "Or dyed his hair. Son, take another look."

I'm nobody's son. "Sorry, Mr. Now I have to."

The tall one says, "Not yet."

"Go. They're waiting for me."

Short one says, "No they're not."

Tall one says, "They went out. Now, about your friend."

"What friend?"

"He's about to come into some money. You don't have to finger him, just take the message."

Tall throws in a bonus. "Tell him his father forgives him."

What?

Short threatens. "Tell him it's for his own good."

I feed them the line I picked up on TV: "Um, I need to see your badges?"

The short one says, "Oh, badges. Our pay grade is a notch above badges, son."

"So, you're, um." (Shit, I know they aren't, but I gulp and choke it out just to make them shake their heads.) "Company?"

Guy one. "Private concern."

Guy two. "From the State's Attorney's office."

Which, assholes? Don't say assholes. Don't ask. Make this the uncomfortable silence you read about where the other person goes bla-bla-bla. Which I do until the short one goes:

"Tell him it's in his best interests to check in with us."

I'm still hung up on *State's Attorney's office.* By the time I come back with, "Which state?" they're as good as gone and just to prove they didn't scare me, I do two laps around the block, running close to the wall when I pass Dopey's corner store so unless he's hanging out the second-floor window he can't see me, which he wasn't. By the time I passed 553 on the first round their car was gone, so it looks like I'm home free.

Not really. Not now. I'm so fucked up that I don't know. Plus, it's beginning to rain. On my second round I peel off at 553. At this point, even the stupid house looks good to me. No time for second thoughts. I'm up the steps and across the porch, banging on the front door.

"Who's there!" Aunt Ivy's voice floats in at me from the far end of the porch, all thin and sad, like she's been waiting for me all this time. It's already so dark that I didn't see her until she spoke. It hasn't been that long, but still. She's parked exactly where I left her, just a little closer to the rail.

"It's me."

She starts the motor all *rmm-rmm,* like that scooter gives her power, but her voice is shaky. "Why, Teddy, I'm so glad you're back!"

"I'm sorry." Fuck, all alone out here in the dark, my bad.

Me, I'd be pissed off and yelling, but I guess she's used to these things.

She backs and fills the scooter and comes rolling my way, all sweet and hate-to-bother-you. "Honey, will you do me a favor? Go under the doormat and find the keys, and I'll let us both in."

I find the light switch and it's not quite so bad. "There."

She rolls inside, all cheered up. "That's better! Now, let's go out in the kitchen, shall we? You can help me find us something nice to eat."

CHAPTER 32

Extract

Dakin Ellis, his book
Undated

Mother gave me this notebook on the eve of my marriage. We never spoke of it, but I understand it now, and I keep this book for you.

Thank you, Mother. You tried to warn me, and I'm sorry I responded the way I did. I was a grown man, intent on marrying the girl I loved, and I did love her! Long before I knew, although I had begun to doubt her, Mother, you saw Manette for what she was.

I was young and brash, fresh from army duty patrolling the Panama Canal. With your blessing and Father's considerable legacy to manage, I left Syracuse, New York for the raw young city of Jacksonville, Florida. I was my own man in Jacksonville, just starting out in the golden land, bound to honor Father by making his money grow. I journeyed to Charleston to visit the boatyard that first year, thinking to augment Mr. Plant's ambitious steamship

line with a new vessel and be welcomed into his corporation, al-
though that was not to be. On that first visit I stayed with the
younger Calhouns on Church Street, old friends of the family on
Mother's side, it's just as well she didn't live to see what's become
of me.

Although she was not being presented, a matter that galled
Little Manette and her grandmother, old Mrs. Ware, I met Ma-
nette Ware Robichaux at the St. Cecilia Society Ball. By the end
of the evening, I was in love. She loved me. She did!

She was a pretty girl, she couldn't have weighed a hundred
pounds, so delightfully young and sweet. Forgive me, I rushed into
love headlong. I didn't know she was just fifteen. If I'd guessed
how long it would take to win her or what she would demand
before she agreed, would I have been so eager to meet her every
wish, or so willing to wait? But that night my Manette— and in
my mind she was already my Manette— waltzed away from me
with such a promising smile that I had no choice. She threw me a
gardenia from her nosegay.

I started out in this life strong-willed, hopeful and independent,
but over the years my pretty, willful wife chewed me up and spat
out a cipher. This dainty Charleston belle staked out her territory
like a venal prospector, although I didn't know it then. She filed
her claim a full three years before she accepted my proposal. Little
Manette Ware Robichaux married me for what she thought I was
worth to her.

The girl picked me out coolly as she would the ebony armoire
for our bedroom, to be refinished and moved from room to room
at will. Like the china pug she bought when she filled her private
boudoir with chinoiserie, I would be rearranged according to the
condition of my marriage and her rapidly changing sense of de-
cor. She left my bed after Everett was born— to meet her precious
baby's needs, she said. After that she let me approach her on her
terms, at certain times, in her fancy boudoir. And the children?
Here to serve her purposes, which has always puzzled me— not

her purposes, just exactly why she needed them to complete her portrait of herself: a great lady surrounded by loving children, I suppose. The cynosure of all eyes.

Like them, I was just one more coveted object that failed to live up to her expectations, no matter where she positioned me in her cluttered, overdecorated home— if this house has ever been a home. It's the first thing she said she must have before she would accept me.

A suitable house built for her on the best street in the young city of Jacksonville. These were her conditions. How else could she leave historic Charleston and everything she loved for the frontier?

Manette Ware Robichaux was spoiled.

I thought Zeus had tapped me on the shoulder, but I was wrong. The girl settled on me because I had the means to create, furnish, maintain and enhance the great house she desired. Old Mrs. Ware set out the requirements when I asked for Manette's hand. Her darling Little Manette deserved an appropriate setting for the great lady her granddaughter would become.

Yes, Mother, I should have wondered why my bride lived with her grandmother in the historic Ware house, although it gave her mother great grief.

I understand why Mrs. Robichaux is sour about it. "My child, in that woman's house," she said to me the first time we met, and her voice was ragged. "They think I'm not good enough."

How was I to know why or how Little Manette chose that frilly old flibbertigibbet instead of her plain, sensible mother, who lived several blocks away? I should have considered. I should have asked! But my sweetheart was so pretty and so charming, so intent on pleasing me, that I didn't want to see.

I thought she loved me, but that was never the case.

I left my calling card at Mrs. Ware's house the day after we met at the St. Cecilia Ball, and Mrs. Ware agreed to see me that afternoon. Fine boned, like her granddaughter, and in her narrow face, vestiges of the belle she must have been. She interviewed me so thoroughly that I couldn't catch my breath but when I expressed my intentions, she gasped, "But she's just a child!" The love of my life, she told me, had turned fifteen three weeks before.

I apologized and made as if to go, but she said if I liked, I could come calling on her "sweet child" the following Sunday at four, never mind that my business in Charleston was done and I was expected back in Jacksonville for an appointment with Mr. Henry B. Plant.

God help me, I took rooms at the Charleston Hotel and stayed on for too many Sundays after that, while my business with Mr. Plant died of neglect. Mrs. Ware sat with us on the first few Sundays, but in time she kept the maid busy dusting in the next room on these afternoons, visible through the archway that separated us, and on Sundays that followed, chaperonage became less intrusive, until Manette and I were effectively alone together. We were alone together for long enough for the child to let me know what she expected before she could consider parting with her beloved grandmother and, even harder for her to bear, leaving her beloved Charleston for life in a brand new city so lacking in culture and tradition, so . . .

I promised her this house.

Mrs. Robichaux tried to warn me, but by that time it was too late. Two years after I began the long courtship, old Mrs. Ware invited us for tea, "to meet the child's mother," she said in the note delivered to the rooms I kept in Charleston, so in spite of pressing business in Jacksonville, I could be there as often as I needed to court Manette for as long as it took.

"As we will of course have to include her in the wedding party, I must acquaint you with my daughter, Charlotte. Unfortunately, she has little of the old Ware family charm."

The maid came to the gate and ushered me upstairs to the expansive side porch to wait. I sat in the shade, watching the Spanish moss on the great live oak drifting in the breeze. The table was set for four; silver service, little cakes, all that. I was the first to arrive. I watched flies land and take off from the embroidered muslin cover on the platter of tea cakes until finally the maid ushered Mrs. Robichaux out onto the porch and I jumped to my feet. To my eternal shame, I disliked her on sight, but I saw her to her chair.

As I seated her she whispered, "Mother stole that girl away from me and dressed her like a china doll. She trained Little Manette according to her expectations," she said, and that was all she said. She tried to warn me then, but I was deaf to her. Manette had accepted my ring!

We were married three years later at St. Michael's Church, with a reception and four-course dinner at the Carolina Yacht Club, in one of the finest weddings Charleston has ever seen. Manette's mother came to the wedding in black— still in mourning for her late husband, she told me, although after all the years between, most Southern widows would have moved from black to gray, perhaps even lavender, to celebrate the day.

My wife's house took two years to design and three years to build, and on each visit Little Manette showed me endless images of plantation houses. Then, mysteriously, she produced an architect's rendering of the exact design. She decided exactly where and how her house would be sited— near the St. Johns River, she decided, on May Street, she decided, once I came back to her with photographs of available plots, never mind that the lime deposits in this area and the persistence of floods suggest that our beautiful new house sits on uncertain ground.

I tried to warn her. Stroking the inside of my wrist, she said, "Build it on a high foundation like all the best plantation houses, and you'll never have to worry about a thing."

I still worry, but God help me, I did.

I went to the site every day when I was in Jacksonville, and I brought her many photographs as the work progressed. Our encounters were reduced to discussion over which wallpaper, how much stained glass, what furniture in which rooms. She refused to come to Jacksonville to watch her new house grow. "When it's perfect we'll get married," she promised. "Then I'll come."

Never mind the rest of the decisions she made for me, or how long it took or how much it cost me to win her hand, in the end Manette's new house was done and we were married.

Finally, I thought, but with that woman, it never is.

I hired the bridal suite and extravagant space in the hold of Mr. Plant's finest steamboat to bring my new bride and all she held precious from Charleston to Jacksonville. We traveled with her extensive wardrobe and all her jewelry strewn around the suite and everything else stowed below. There were crates filled with the many paintings and bronzes and flossy ornaments Little Manette picked out for me to present to her when I came courting, each one, she told me, would make her "love"— that's her word, not mine— her new home in the rough-and-ready city of Jacksonville, so unlike quiet, genteel Tradd Street on the Battery in Charleston, the city she had claimed as her own.

"I think I'll love it here," she said to me as we docked in Jacksonville, but standing next to her on the foredeck, I felt Manette's disappointment. Her whole body clenched, and I said what I had to as I drew her to the gangplank.

"You will, dearest. When you're in your new home." Her new home. Hers. Never mine.

I had a coachman waiting to take us from the dock to May Street. I ushered Little Manette through the wrought-iron gate and up the flagstone walk to 553, in many respects a replica of the Hopswee Plantation house, and I will admit that she gasped with approval. Delighted, I slipped my arm around my darling's waist. This time she softened as I clamped her to me, and in that instant and only for that instant, I thought, Now.

Then Vincent opened the great front doors for us; good man, he'd polished all the brass and cleaned every crystal prism in the chandelier. It cost the world to install, but we were among the first in the city to have gas lighting in the house, and Vincent had turned on the crystal chandelier. Our mahogany stairwell glistened in the light from Athena's torch. I'd bought the statue at her request when she confided that she must have it for the newel post, and my lovely bride turned cold and rigid, a marble sculpture oddly configured to remain at my side.

*"Oh," she said, and the spirit of this house rose up from the bowels and screamed at me, **Be warned**. This was the true beginning. My new wife struck. "That chandelier will have to go."*

CHAPTER 33

Lane

Another day in the life of this ghastly house, and I'm not a half-inch closer to breaking out. Worse: yesterday I thought I saw daylight. Then the place yanked me back into its maw and slammed the front doors on us like giant teeth. As if this outrageous neo-Victorian trap swallowed Theo and me whole.

Yesterday I had an actual job interview scheduled for 3 P.M. All I had to do was show up at the downtown branch of our bank—no more than a twenty-minute drive from here on a good day, worst-case, forty-five minutes tops. Hey, on the basis of the zillionth resume I'd printed out and snail-mailed, in hopes, the head of personnel had actually picked up an office phone and asked me to come in. By the time we got off the line, we were besties. Somebody in his office had died of a heart attack and they needed a replacement ASAP.

I could be dressing for my first day at work right now. But Iris gored her foot on Ivy's broken beer bottle. Like a fool I thought, walk-in clinic five minutes from here, no problem, I'll get her patched up and back home in plenty of time, but I forgot. I'm trapped in this tight little world with not one but three sweet old ladies who eat time and spit out the bones. In the Ellis miniverse, nothing moves.

It took out the rest of the day, and my interview? It was a write-off from the moment we got into the car. First there was the wedging both of them into the back. Iris insisted on it, even though the bleeding had stopped. "She has to keep pressure on this vein or I'll bleed to death. Get in here, Rose!"

They settled in behind me like twin Miss Daisys. I drove. "Not here," Iris snapped as I pulled up in front of the clinic thinking, Get 'em in there, pat them into their seats to wait, go to the desk and get her on the list and bail, you can do it. Leave them money for the cab home.

"OK," I said, but nobody moved.

Rosemary made her voice quaver to let me know that she hated this even more than I did. *I'm just following orders.* "Elena, this *will not do.*"

Iris leaned forward and tapped me on the shoulder. "St. Luke's Hospital," she snapped, as if she'd just stepped into a taxi.

Rosemary explained. "We were born there. The family name *alone.*"

You bet I was pissed. "Really?"

"No waiting for the Ellis family, Papa built a wing."

"Just ask for Dr. Woods. Rosemary, direct the child. It's right around the corner, dear." Dear, I suppose, to make up for trashing my day.

Don't ask me why she insisted on being treated in their ostensible wayback machine. Back in their day, they claim as I drive on, socially prominent women like Mama never went to the hospital. They pooped out their babies at home. In what era?

When it was time, Ivy told us during our first long, terrible dinner in this house, a very great lady took to her bed at home, with her doctor and the midwife in attendance and a wet nurse standing by to serve, in case. *Theo, cover your ears!* She said of course "Mama" did the way all true ladies do. In the family bed, where nobody but her doctor and the midwife had to see her (mumble mumble), in surroundings appropriate to her social standing, and I'm thinking, fuck, that can't be true.

Theo was mystified.

It depressed the hell out of me. In spite of everything that's happened since, these obscenely old ladies swallowed the Ellis book of family mythology whole; they devoured the sugar coated past, and because Theo and I are trapped here and beholden, they expect the same of me.

Right, the old St. Luke's was only a few blocks away from 553. Note that I said *old* St. Luke's. One look at the columns along the façade, and my heart went to hell and back. "Iris . . ."

"Oh," she said as we pulled up in front, and I swear to God she was happy and excited. "This is where Dr. Woods took out my tonsils, I was ten, and scared to death. Child, just ask for Dr. Woods, he'll know what to do."

By that time I was studying my phone. Ugly scene when I told Iris it was just a museum now. Never mind what she said to me as I pissed and sweated my way through bridge traffic to the real St. Luke's Hospital over on the south side, Siri is not the greatest. Crazy, but I actually thought I could get this ER thing started and take off. Barring a wreck on the highway, I could do this and still make it in time for my interview.

They'd see the bloody towels wrapped around her foot and send for a wheelchair, right? I could leave the injured twin and the hysterical one off at the entrance, no problem. As soon as they wheeled her away, I'd mutter something-something-parking-garage, and bail. Given the nature of emergency rooms in big-city hospitals, I could do all that and get back here before they called her name. Let the aunts duke it out in the waiting room; let Iris order

Rosemary up to the desk a dozen times to ask whether she's next; they'll take care of you, lady, these things take time, and me?

I was going to drive like hell and park illegally in front of the bank, no matter what the cost. If I wrote my opening speech en route and did makeup before I turned off the motor, maybe nobody would notice. I'd cut and run inside before the cops caught me in the act. So what if they tag the car? Cheap at the price. Hey, if I did well with the guy from Personnel and actually got the job, I wouldn't care if they towed it away. I could always cab back to the hospital with plenty of time to grab Iris some get-well candy in the gift shop and make it down to the ER. I'd probably sit there with them for at least another hour before they took her in. This wasn't an urgent-care situation; the sick and the dying come first, ladies. They'd still be sitting there, waiting to be called.

As it turns out, so was I.

Bridge traffic. Congestion around the hospital. The trail of cars lined up at the ER entrance waiting to get their much-worse-off person into the building. Some went in on gurneys, others in wheelchairs. One was bleeding from the ears. By the time the orderlies came for Iris, I was toast. I sat there while the old ladies fumed. I listened as they wrangled, nonstop.

First it was bad. Then it got worse. Then it was over.

I took my sweet time going to the labyrinthine parking garage and bringing the car around. The nurse who stowed Rosemary and the aluminum crutches in the back helped Iris into the shotgun seat with a fixed, professional smile, but I knew. On the way home I ordered takeout for five at the MacDonald's drive-through window, starting with a towering McFlurry with M&M's in it for Ivy. Then I added big Mac-Whatevers for five. Plus sides, heavy on Theo's favorites. I made Iris pay. Easy enough, now that she was sitting in the front. I could extract three twenties from her patent-leather purse and pay up before she noticed, and started flapping at me.

Then I plopped the carton, heavy with food and melting frozen custard and loaded with resentment, on the cranky patient's lap and warned her to be very damn careful or the sauce would tip over and ruin her fancy skirt.

So that was yesterday, and the desperately boring entry-level job that I would have taken, rejoicing, even though I hated it?

The job that I would have given my all to filling for as long as it took to get Theo and me out of here? That job was gone before I phoned in with my lame explanation. As for where I stood in this shitty game that fate and warped genetics rolled out for me, it was back to square one. Plus rain. While we weren't looking, it started to rain.

I took the Mac-carton off Iris's bony knees and left Rosemary to wrangle her evil twin out of the car and up the front steps. At the top I took that deep breath you take before you swim the length of the pool underwater because like it or not, you'll surface inside this house. In the front hall I tried to make my voice sound, I dunno, *happy*. Had to. Theo, you know.

"Theo? Aunt Ivy? We're back. I brought dinner."

I don't remember anybody but Ivy thanking me. Poor Theo sat there looking betrayed. He and his shriveled great-aunt were sitting at the kitchen table in front of congealing bowls of hominy grits, and the look my son gave me then was an odd mixture of excitement and, I think, guilt.

I was too wiped to sit down with him and work on the what or the why behind that expression, and I'm sorry, but I couldn't sit down at that table with them, Theo or no. Not tonight.

Where this miserable house and everybody in it are concerned, I am well and totally done. I gave my boy the best smile I could manage before I fled with, "I'm sorry, T. I have to work."

Then I separated my paper sack full of rapidly cooling dinner from theirs and came back upstairs to check out my rapidly cooling job prospects and plunge back into the search, exhausting the possibilities, one by one by one, until I heard somebody behind me in the room.

"Mom?"

"Theo!"

"You didn't eat your Macshitburger."

"I will, I promise." Careful pause. "So, what happened here today?"

"Nothing. You?"

"The usual."

"How was it?"

I couldn't bring myself to start. I said, "Fine."

"It's all good and everything's fine, right, Mom?" His voice cracks in the middle and breaks.

"T., are you OK?"

"I'm fine, Mom! OK?"

"Sure you are. What really happened?"

"I have to go."

"Oh, T.!"

Where we are right now in our lives in this house, that was all we had to say to each other just then. I got up and put my arms around my boy and hugged him hard and he hugged me back, all anxious mother and miserable son, fresh out of words. By the end we were rocking and thumping each other on the back. It was all we had left and I'm sorry, it just was.

Tomorrow, I'll find something tomorrow, and even if I can't, I have to get us out. We'll just disassemble this workstation and jam all our stuff in the car and leave before Rose comes down to start the coffee, no recriminations, no farewells, the hell with them. If nothing changes I'm taking whatever cash I have and my two credit cards, on which I've been paying $10(ten)dollars a month just to stay eligible to charge gas, food, whatever it takes.

My man T. and I will hit the road with no resources and without a plan and we'll make it to wherever we have to go because we have to.

I'm done.

CHAPTER 34

Ivy

I managed to have an argument with Iris again tonight; when she's really angry, she pretends to forget that it's her turn to put me to bed. Then she and Rosemary have to saw back and forth over whose turn it is because I am— what was it Little Elena calls it? Labor-intensive. I am labor-intensive because on a certain night when I was young, I threw myself on Dakin's horse bareback and rode off into the dark. Yes it was reckless, racing down May Street at a dead gallop. Given Mama's ultimatum, I would have done anything to get away.

We ran into the dark, Blaze and I, and God was waiting. I woke up in St. Luke's after it happened, I had lost the use of my legs, although on certain nights I feel them stirring and I think, *perhaps, so alas for me.* I will never forgive you, Mama, but it relieved one ache in my brain— the fear. When push comes to shove, I'd rather be *this* than marry the lascivious toad that you picked out for me. You had him waiting for me in the parlor the night I fled. "Such a

sweet boy," you told me as we came down to the landing outside
Tillie's room. Then you gave me a little push. I peeked. He was
fifty years old! Of course I ran.

Then, when Dr. Woods threw up his hands because they'd done
all they could, on the day the hospital was done with me, I came
back into your clutches, didn't I? Papa rode in the ambulance with
me, while Vincent followed with the car. He said, "Honey, your
mother." The unspoken words hovered between us; you had not
seen me since that night when I ran out of the house. Papa mut-
tered and rumbled and stopped because in the face of our mother,
he is hopeless. I think he said, *Be warned.* Of course. When you
saw what I had become then and forever, you covered your face
and cried to the heavens, "Ivy, what have you done? Now nobody
will marry you!"

Now it's as if I have always been like this. At bedtime I need
certain things, and one of my sisters must help. She will supply wet
washcloths for the nightly sponge bath, I do not remember the last
time I bathed in the tub. Certainly not since Tillie died. Then, she
and Vincent saw to it.

Now I depend on the twins. One of them must help with the
sponge bath, the salves, the lambskin booties for my useless feet.
These things undo themselves every single day and must be done
at bedtime on every single night. When my sister takes away the
comb and drops my toothbrush back into its glass, she lets out a
sigh big enough for both of us. *Almost done.* Then if life is flow-
ing smoothly, she must slip on my nightshirt one arm at a time
and transfer me from Scooter to the bed. Next she will pat me in
place and shut the door on me with her eternal "Night night. Sleep
tight." Rose says it sweetly. Iris snarls.

Not tonight.

It's been three days since my wonderful young man and I col-
lided in the back hall, three days of yearning for him to return. I
waited all afternoon! Three days almost to the hour, and that boy
still hasn't been. I know he makes his way into the house unseen

and vanishes with the night, and this time, I intend to park Scooter in the back hall, and if necessary, I will wait for him 'til the sun comes up.

I will confess that I bait my sisters and I do it often, now that my handsome young friend and I have met here inside my mother's house. When Rose and Iris fight, they forget to perform their nightly duties, and I spend the night in this chair— a stroke of luck! After Teddy Two left the supper table tonight, the girls fell into their endless argument over whose turn it was, and although it really is her turn, willful Iris reminded Rose that the new doctor at St. Luke's put eight stitches in the ball of her foot and the last thing you want, Rosemary, is for my wound to open up all over again!

Then Rose told Iris that she personally lost a whole day to that tiny cut and medical incompetence inside our dreadful new hospital, so it was time for Iris to carry some of the load. She meant me, and didn't the lid come off their cauldron of stored slights and indignities then!

While they were arguing over obligation(Rose)versus common charity(Iris), I wheeled out of the kitchen silent as a millipede, and parked in the shadows to await my new man. Naturally, I kept the attic stairway at my back. If either of them thinks of me at all, if one comes out in the hall to ask, I'm on my way into the lavatory, one of the few things I can, in fact, do without help. Tonight my spiny twin sisters are too deep in their recital of fancied slights and real indignities to notice or care what became of me, and I thank them for that.

"Let Little Elena do it," Iris shouts. "It's her turn."

Now, I know Little Elena and the new Teddy are decent children— she brought ice cream, my favorite kind! And, in spite of my sisters' expectations, I know that they are transients in this house. I know, without betraying any confidences, that they are contriving to leave and I wish them Godspeed, although Iris, Rosemary and I, the last three Ellis children of our generation, keep the keys.

We three.

We three. Even Everett died a few years back, I forget when and I don't know how he managed it, but I do remember thinking, *Why not me?* Rose and Iris don't care about me, not one whit. I am an inconvenience. No one does. Except, perhaps, the handsome stranger who is so kind.

Oh Lord, please, please dear Lord. Let him come again tonight!

CHAPTER 35

Dell

Words thud into his head, 1-2-3, setting up a vibration. He snaps awake. *What?*

Give it back.

"What!" Idiot, don't shout. They'll hear you. Dell is too messed up to know what this means, or to care right now. He has priorities. Sometime while he was out cold, it started to rain.

Fuck yes he is vulnerable here.

First, Theo wakes him up to tell him that some neighborhood punk sneaks into his squat while he sleeps. Only yesterday, he thinks, outraged.

Turns out some stranger waltzes in and takes Dell's stuff off him and gets away without his knowing. So much for the obstacle course and makeshift alarm systems he depended on. So much for security. He said OK, Theo, bye, but the kid hung in, all lonely and lurking, until Dell lost it and flipped the knife. Residual shock, he supposes, and he's sorry.

It was too close.

Whatever he thought he had here, it's done.

He should collect his gear and clear out before he does anything worse, before . . . What? Before Theo tells and his feisty mom comes down on him? Before the cops, feds, outraged employer, ruined lover, before whoever or whatever is hounding him crashes into his last safe place and drags him out into the light.

Security here is shot. It went to hell faster than the rotting lattice underneath this porch. He might as well throw a Marvista block party in here, or torch the place or blow it up and walk out with his head high and his arms wide, open to whatever comes, but he can't. Not yet.

Dell whatever-my-last-name-is used to be a normal, ordinary guy— at least he thinks he was, but push just came to shove. Normal, ordinary people confront their problems head-on. Normal people identify their issues and attack them one by one.

OK. The note that brought him to this address: done. He's here. Reason? Too soon to tell.

The flash drive: God knows he tried.

The matter of the nameless suits out there hunting him: not so much. Is it really that hard to face whatever he did back there? He doesn't know.

Listen, this is not avoidance!

Dakin's book comes first. He plunged into his ancestor's notebook and got lost in the revelations— how long ago? He's in so deep that he can't find his way out. When Dell no-last-name is done here on his bed at the far end of the undercroft, he will damn well have a name, he thinks, no matter how long it takes. He will read and reread the Dakin Ellis journal, dropping notes on scrap paper to mark the trail.

He thinks he's framing questions for poor old Ivy, leading up to the matter of the Dakin Ellis will. That's worth every hour it takes. No matter what's going on upstairs right now or in the real world outside, no matter what comes down on his head because he is no longer safe here, he needs to know.

Dell reads and dozes, wakes up and reads some more, deep in the Ellis family past. Some of our ancestor's entries are obviously considered, as if the writer drafted them before entering them in the classic copperplate that collectors love, others are scrawled in haste and hard to read. *Our* ancestor? Really?

He's lost track of time. He's lost track of everything but the need to hang on in this volatile situation in a place that until today, he thought was safe.

Dell is looking for proof of the existence of, well.

Himself, starting with his real name. His real name and everything that comes with. *It's about this Randolph,* he tells himself, and can't stop what comes into his head. *What if I?* You bet he is obsessing.

He obsessed all yesterday while in the house overhead, life went on. At least he thinks it was yesterday. He's in so deep now that time blurs. Something big happened up there. Whatever it was, whenever it was, things got weird. There was a crash. One of them screamed and overhead, the others ran back and forth, bringing this, taking that, for at least an hour. Then they all ran out of the house and went off somewhere. Well, all but one, and the kid? He doesn't know. On any other day, Dell whatever-my-real-name-is would have been right on it, rushing upstairs to help. Earnest, useful, ingratiating Dell Duval. He's good at that, but while he was buried in their past, yesterday turned into tonight, and he's not sorry.

He has fixed on certain entries. e.g.

> *If Manette had been interested in more than acquisition, if she had been an iota more in her heart than the dutiful martyr wife resignedly submitting, there would have been no Sylvia and I would not miss my love so terribly . . .*

And, written years later,

> . . . *Then my beloved lost son would exist in life or in*
> *death, not in his uncharted No Man's Land where I*
> *can't go and nobody can reach him . . . I still write to*
> *him, but like a castaway putting a note in a bottle and*
> *hurling it out to sea.*

And,

> *If they found a body we could identify.*
> *If someone I trust came back and told me he was*
> *dead.*
> *If one of my notes reached my lost son and he wrote*
> *back. Then the nature of my grief would be quite*
> *different.*

This brings Dell to his feet. Did he really tell old Ivy, "Catch
you next time," like a little kid? When was that? Around four in
whichever morning, when he bumped into her in the kitchen. Right,
he was heading for the attic but found her there; they talked, he
moved on, and in the Ellis family's third-floor land of the lost and
the forgotten, he found this.

He checks his watch. *Catch you next time.* That would be
around now. OK, ablutions. And I know this word, why? English
professor, he tells himself, still shopping for past lives. Plausible
or not, it makes him feel better.

Start with her.

First, clean up for the incursion. He should have gone out and
found a free shower before those places shut down last night:
YMCA or one of the homeless shelters down town, but it would
mean sloshing around out there in the rain. Looking the way he
does after all this time inside old Dakin's head, he'd fit right in,
but it's too late. He'll clean up under the spigot here, shave in front

of his cracked mirror, put on a shirt that looks fresh and walk in on her looking like a real person.

Like, what was that entity they had in the old days?

A gentleman caller. Don't go crazy, Dell, scrub and shave, so she won't run away screaming. Dude, the old lady can't walk. Plus, when she remembers that he is not this guy Vincent, Ivy thinks he's her best friend. Maybe they really are friends, unless she thinks he's some long-lost love of hers, fresh off the battlefield, here to take her into his arms.

Not clear.

Chances are, the old girl will be waiting for him, at least he thinks she will: her face when she agreed, "Our secret." The bubble that forms over her lips as soon as she recognizes him— that hopeful smile. Like the faithful dog that sits in the same spot because you gave it a bone last time, this lady lives for the next. Use it. Get in there like you really are that dream boyfriend. Old and crippled or not, she still believes. Play the part while you probe what's left of her mind in hopes that some parts of her brain are still working.

Washing up at the corroded iron laundry tubs, exposed and shivering in the December night, Dell is strongly reminded of his body. Like an alarm went off: *what have you done for me lately.* He isn't really cleaning up for Ivy. The weakest part of his mind is fixed on feisty, troubled Lane Hale who also lives upstairs, that lovely woman just about his age. As though she, and not Ivy, may happen into the kitchen at the right time tonight, and she'll let him take her hand.

We wouldn't need to talk, we'd know.

Together, they would swarm up to the attic, settle in on the decayed sofa under the eaves and talk their brains out, spilling their guts in the reflected glow of his Maglite. *In your dreams.*

The best thing about Lane Hale aside from the obvious is that unlike poor Ivy, she's tough. In a good way. Her voice is so clear, compared to the old ladies' phlegmy tones and incessant clucking that at times, he stops under the window and listens. Lane, who was so friendly the day Theo covered for him at Staples; he wonders if he's the only one who felt the tug. On a better day at a better time, he'd make a proper date. Ask Lane Hale to meet him somewhere for coffee, plenty of people around, nothing to see here, no threat. He'd ask her to bring the kid along, proof that he's not a con man or a predator, just an ordinary nice guy who hopes to know her better, not a scene you can play in the dark at 4 A.M.

He wants to be in love with Lane, but this is not the time.

If she's even awake at this hour, she will be working. He'd like to ask her out, but his sense of time is that he doesn't have much. He should have used his time in this house a hell of a lot better than he has so far. Muddled as he is, sleep deprived and jittering, high on possibilities, Dell is not stupid.

Brace up, man. Get in there and do what you have to, to get what you need.

He'll take his preferred route into the house, up the hatch into the dining room and on in through the back hall to the kitchen, putting next steps in order as he goes. If Ivy's here, dozing in her scooter, make her some tea before you start the conversation. If she isn't, the attic waits. Mulling and discarding speeches, he pads along the Persian runner and on into the back hall.

"I knew you'd come." It's so dark in here, her voice is so small that he can't be sure he heard her, but he knows the tune. Ivy isn't in the kitchen. She's parked that scooter in front of the door to the back stairs. Lying in wait? Apparently. She waits a beat. Then in a husky contralto, she reels him in. "Our secret."

I was right. "Yes Ma'am."

"Miss Ivy."

"Yes Ma'am!" No tea needed to start her engines. The lady is bang. Awake. Think fast, dude. Close your fingers on her wrist. "But we can't talk here. Let's."

No need to finish that speech, either. She's already released the brake on her scooter and without a hint of fear, she lets him wheel her through the back hall and into the kitchen, her own monument to trust. She sits placidly while he opens the back door and propels her out on the long back porch, where he'll try to romance her into telling him everything he needs to know while they watch the rain. He sees himself taking mental notes like a good reporter—reporter?

Another feasible past life for Mr. no-real-name, who will follow up on Ivy's garbled answers with kindness and more gentle prodding, trying to extract something he can use.

The exchange will unspool for so long that when they're done, he won't have time to do anything but roll her inside to the spot in the back hall where he found her, and what he does after that is an open question.

He parks her next to the rail and sets down one of the rusted lawn chairs next to hers so they can talk while they watch as rain crosshatches the receding night. Then he bends close to her ear and whispers, "Don't worry, I'll get you back inside in plenty of time."

"Oooh," Ivy says. "Plenty of time." The next noise that comes out of her is a stifled giggle. As though he is a suitor.

"You must be proud of your family," he says, to put her on the right page.

Her tone changes. "Not all of them."

Right, he thinks. We're in this thing together.

When she's quiet for too long, he prompts. "A long line of Florida pioneers."

She startles him by patting his arm. "Don't be afraid."

"What?"

"The little slithering you hear."

"Ma'am?"

"That's just a house lizard, they're harmless. Nasty little Everett used to sneak after them with fireplace matches, the long ones." In her head, she's a little girl again. "I told on him, and Mama slapped my hand."

"That's terrible." Think fast, she's, like, ten years old right now. Try that. "Honey, did your mama ever tell you about the diary that your great-grandfather left behind?"

She lifts her shoulder, flirting. "Who?"

"You know, the man who built this house?"

"It's Mama's house. Everybody knows that." Old Ivy's not ten any more. Inside her head she's a girl of seventeen, before the accident took her down.

Chill, Dell. Thoughtful pause. Ask without letting her know it's a question. "I wonder what else he left behind."

"Papa?"

"More likely your great-great grandfather, Miss Ivy, you're much too young."

"We were all young then."

OK, maybe this will bring her back. "The city fathers named Ellis Park after him? Very important man."

"Oh, men. Men. Believe me, honey." Ivy turns his hand over and lays two fingers across his wrist. Seductive or frightened—how old is she now? He doesn't know. She rasps, "This is no place for men."

"This beautiful house?"

"We were never happy here."

"Ma'am?" Then, before he can get her attention or forestall the flood of information, Ivy just starts.

"Now, my sisters try to keep it secret because they still think they can meet someone and marry out, but." She launches her story like a log on a flooded river, talking so fast that all he can do is grab hold and hang on. "You might as well know, dear, it's for your own good, and this is the least of it. Our Papa was never happy here. Nobody is."

"But the first Dakin Ellis must . . ."

"Hush! Everett was the only one who was ever happy in this house, he was Mama's precious and she won't hear a word against him, but my poor, lost brothers . . ."

What? "Randolph?"

"Mama hated all those handsome dead boys, and she hated Papa as we learned when she died, that poor, sweet man! He lost his boys, he lost everything, but he lived on and on . . . He lived on and things happened to all the other boys who came under this roof, terrible things . . ."

They were hurtling into rough waters, but by this time there was no interrupting. All Dell could do was grit his teeth and hang on tight as the words rushed on.

"That first fire, of course, and worse things happened to them after that, one of them after another, my dear brothers and all the other men . . . everybody suffered, poor Leah and that sweet Laurence, who tried to elope with her. Mama wanted to put him in jail, and . . ."

Rain. *Is it always like this?*

"The only one who got away whole was big old Stan Worzecka, but he didn't *belong.* He was a day laborer but Iris married him anyway, for a while. Mama didn't want him and the house didn't either. After all, he worked with his hands, and gentlemen don't do that. He lasted a week. Akron, Ohio. My word! Naturally Iris went with him, but it turned out he didn't want Iris after all. Mama was mortified. Our first divorce! I wonder what happened to Stanley, we never hear from him."

How crazy is she anyway. Bring her back to the point. "We were talking about Randolph."

"Now, Rosemary's nice husband was killed at the porte cochère, it was that awful crane, it mashed him against the column, a terrible thing . . ." And she's off, rushing him through rough waters, "Then Poor Elena— she was Leah's orphan child, but we're not supposed to know— Poor Elena brought her new husband home to live until they found a house. Oh, that sweet boy! It was that awful accident on the stairs. When he fell he broke everything, but it was the rusty nail that killed him, festering inside of the cast. He got blood poisoning, but nobody knew until terrible red streaks came running up his arm and by the time they cut it off it was too late. It was all through his system and it just went on and on, through his heart and up into his brain, and he died the week Leila was born . . ."

"Who?"

Don't even try. They're in the rapids now. Rocks ahead, probably the falls. Don't fight it, just go with, Dell tells himself, surfacing long enough to hear, "Every man who enters this house ends badly," while Ivy floods him with details.

Until she stops, coming back into herself with a little cry. "We have to get away! Oh dear, I didn't mean to frighten you, sweetheart. I just wanted you to know."

Then she collapses into sleep with a little sigh, leaving Dell alone with the words that woke him up a lifetime ago.

Set down like stones inside his head. **Give. It. Back.**

He rolls the sleeping Ivy into the kitchen and parks her next to the stove to hide the opening he uses to drop out of this life and into the dubious safety of his quarters below, where, once again, he addresses all that's left of the first Dakin Ellis: his journal. The box. There are things he needs and things he hasn't found yet, and now that Ivy's brains have blown out her ears, at least for the time being, there's this.

He thinks he squeezed all the good out of DAKIN ELLIS: HIS BOOK before he quit, but the old man's handwriting deteriorated about the time Dell crashed, the writer rushing into death, his reader wrecked by hours studying copperplate that became illegible.

At the end, Dakin gouged thoughts into his cream-laid pages with tremendous force, scratching his heart out with a deteriorating pen. For whatever reasons, the old man never noticed that the point had split. He just dipped that pen back into his inkwell and scratched on. The last entries look like cabalists, illegible to outsiders.

Like him.

The journal was the only useful document in the carton. The

rest is detritus from the old man's office, the contents of an orderly mind: meticulously kept ledgers, none on 553; receipts from hundreds of transactions, what seem like thousands of bills rendered and dutifully marked PAID, along with reams of unused letterhead and decades' worth of neglected pocket calendars, every one of them stamped with the name of a local merchant, nothing that Dell needs, but he plows on until, on overload, he shoves the journal, the carton and all its contents inside the protective garbage bag. He sleeps hard in spite of the rain, and when he wakes up, he will have no idea what day it is, or how long he slept.

CHAPTER 36

Mormama

Wake up, you idiot.

Wake up, new Teddy. This is your last chance. Or mine. Once, I had the power to move people I love, or I thought I did. I must have, I don't remember, I've been this way too long.

Wake up!

Everything pending, and this Teddy sleeps like the dead. Oh dear, don't say that, don't scare the child tod— Never mind.

Damn my daughter's atrocious house and damn my useless, vaporous body and damn this voice that even you can hear only at certain times. Boy, I am talking to you! But in this house in this year of my third century of existence, I have thinned out. Voice, when I most need to scream you awake. Substance, when I want to pick you up by the ears and shout.

Wake up. You have to go.

It's stirring in **undercroft.** *You won't see it; even I can't. I can't* name the evil, but I know it's coming and I know that it will be terrible. I can feel it in my useless bones, and when it does, it will extinguish you, if you are still inside this house.

The hell of life in this world is that you never know who will hurt you or what's coming into your cage of living flesh. You won't know why these things attack you or how much you will suffer unless God intervenes and you are told . . .

I used to be a person in this world, just like you. I should have marshaled all my powers to prevent this, but forgive me, I didn't know!

I thought I knew my firstborn child, but she was never mine. When I found out otherwise I thought I could manage it, but I could not have guessed what she would do or, oh my God, how awful it would be.

Or what she would become.

What could I have done if I had known?

Wake up, wake up Theodore Ellis Hale. Go warn your mother. Run! Make her pack up and leave this house before it's too late. As you still defy me, consorting with your white trash friend in the **undercroft**, by all means, warn that dirty boy. And while you're at it, son of five forlorn daughters of my dainty daughter, retrieve Dakin's special book!

When you leave this doomed house, take the book. **But do not open it until you're safe.** Hurry, Theodore of second chances. Tell the world about Little Manette.

The force in this house scattered after that woman died. It has become many, and this is dreadful. The it that informed Manette is peripatetic. There's no knowing which of her remaining daughters will become what their mother was, or on which day, or for how long.

The evil spirit comes and goes, but its agents are heartless, so careless with lives that not one of you is safe.

I should have known!

That screech as she tore out of me! I thought she was re-

sponding to my pain! I should have known this was no ordinary child.

My daughter was a leaden vessel of hate.

Mother burst in on me, crying, "What are you doing to my baby!" I should have been warned. She swooped down like the bad fairy and snatched my child out of my arms, and the baby I could not bring myself to name stopped screaming and settled into her like the last puzzle piece, completing a worrisome scene. I heard William calling me from the hall but Mother pushed me down on the pillows and ordered the nurse, "Tell him not yet. Not until she's presentable."

I should have known.

Eleven months later my sweet Billy came into my arms like a gift, flexing and snuggling as though we were still one body. For the first time I felt real love, and Little Manette? By the time I saw what she was becoming, it was too late.

I had no idea that my daughter never belonged to me. From the day my grudging mother, the first Manette, seized her, she was her grandmother's property.

I had thought I'd name her Anne.

The day of her christening, Mother came into my room in a mass of silks and plumes. Margaret followed, carrying an elaborately wrapped gift— a christening present, I thought. How nice. I should have known.

Before I could gather my wits she pounced. "Here I am, my dainty Little Manette. My pretty, pretty girl." Then she swept my baby up and in my presence, ripped off the Robichaux christening gown and with one toe, tucked it under the bed. "Godmother's prerogative."

I had asked William's Aunt Mary. I wanted someone in William's family in this baby's life, but Mother would not be denied. She brought forth a ruffled gown straight from Paris, marquisette, I think, trimmed in Belgian lace, with undergarments to match, and as I watched, she transformed Little Manette.

"Now!" She held the child up like a trophy, trilling, "Doesn't Baby look pretty in her lovely dress? My sweet, sweet little baby doll."

Yes, Manette was pretty, with her cupid's-bow mouth, her long eyelashes, her china-doll face, and when it pleased her to be gracious, she was. She was sweet and lovely to everyone she didn't despise. Pretty, although beneath the surface lay a fire-breathing instrument of rage.

Pretty was Little Manette's first word, and it defined her. Like cologne splashed on an unwashed body it was so sweet, and covered up so much.

"Isn't it pretty," Mother said on Little Manette's first birthday. We were on her second-floor veranda at a little party for four . . . after all, the Robichaux house couldn't possibly measure up. She thought William's house was shabby; we both knew.

Mother gushed, "Baby will love having her party outside."

She meant that this was where the Negro seamstress who made it would deliver her birthday gift. It was a quilt.

"It took her a year to finish," she told me. Then she giggled and covered her mouth. She whispered through her fingers, "I won't tell you how much it cost."

The quilt was white, appliquéd in a diamond pattern, with a pink border and pink diamonds inlaid and cleverly curved to create the delicate script that slanted across it from corner to corner. When I saw the legend my heart sank, but I steeled myself and managed the tight, uninflected voice that I will manage when I can't bear the gift or the giver but must thank her, even though I know too well that Mother never liked me.

"Oh thank you."

"Aren't you excited?" Mother took it from my stiff hands, trying to turn me around with her voice. "Isn't it pretty?"

I could not for the life of me say yes! "Very," I said at last.

She would not let it go at that. "Read it aloud, so Little Manette can hear. It's perfect for her."

I stifled a groan and read the legend aloud. It was,

PRETTY IS AS PRETTY DOES

William slipped his arm around my waist and pulled me close, trying to ease my pain, but my skirts were too many and it was never enough. My precocious one-year-old lunged at him, hissing, "stop it, stop," and when William refused to let me go, she kicked her father's ankle. Then she hurled herself down on the rush grass carpet in one of those tantrums I had learned to fear, wailing until Mother lifted the quilt in a kind of benediction and dropped it over her like a cape, at which point my uncontrollable daughter rose out of its folds like Venus and gave her grandmother her most beautiful smile.

I should have stifled her in her crib.

William died before Billy was born. We were never in love, but my William was a sober, responsible gentleman. He was always kind to me and I grieved for him, but I had his son to lift my heart.

Manette never did anything to my Billy when I was watching, but at the outset, there were signs. Pinches. Little accidents. When I was there, she was unbearably sweet to her baby brother, and every drop of it was false. Billy never said anything against her but there were too many times when he winced under my touch, too many scrapes and bruises that he refused to explain. He was a wonderful little man.

But the years wore on and soon Little Manette would be four, and my Billy was almost three.

Naturally Mother insisted on holding Manette's party at her house. It was particularly hot that day but she despised messes, so at 3 P.M. we were to celebrate on the upper veranda, she said grandly. In the blazing heat. She had Margaret set out marzipan cakes decorated with pink candy roses embedded in the pink frosted M on the top of each, and Lapsang souchong tea for the two of us, with pink lemonade for Billy and Little Manette.

"*On the veranda*," *she said grandly, opening the door. We were to sit in receding shade as the sun started its slant and merciless sunlight drenched the upper porch. "Isn't this lovely?" Mother said.*

We ate with perspiration rolling down our faces. Billy was quiet, even for Billy, while Little Manette postured and struck poses in the special birthday dress her grandmother ordered hand-made to her exact measurements by the talented Negress who made the quilt. It was pink. After thirty minutes in that harsh sunlight, even Mother was beginning to fade. Please God, I thought, please let this be over so we can all go back indoors and mirabile, we did.

*"And now." She staggered a little as she rose, but she managed a grand gesture. "And now for your **big** present, my darling girl," and didn't Little Manette stand up and preen? And Margaret appeared as if from nowhere, along with a colored girl I didn't know— a big, earnest girl with a hopeful smile— she was taller than any of us and, I saw by her ragged dress and torn knuckles, she came from a family that needed every penny Mother bothered to pay.*

The two maids came out the side door and with a flourish, pulled the canvas off a big, unwieldy object that I had been too blinded by anxiety to see.

Mother was so proud!

She'd bought her precious Little Manette a child's bouncing horse of her very own. Oh, Billy. Billy my love, you wanted it so! I would have bought it for you, perhaps when you turned five, but here it was.

The horse was made from an iron strip that the maker had heated and hammered into a curve, creating a giant spring. It was firmly bolted to a solid base, and at the top of the curve there was— gracious! A beautifully carved wooden horse's head with glass eyes and a real horsehair mane, and hanging from the child-sized genuine leather English saddle on its little platform, a real horsehair tail. It was lovely, really, although I thought a Western saddle would be safer for any child. I said, "Mother, what a grand gift."

"Now," she said, "you and I must go inside and chat a bit while the children play. Quickly, before one of us faints!"

She saw me glance at the horse, glance at the rail, calculating, as any mother would. I judged it at a safe distance, the horse just low enough, the rail at the right height. What difference would it have made? Little Manette issued orders to Margaret and the big, awkward girl Mother had introduced into the party— the poor thing couldn't have been more than twelve. "Lift me up!"

"Don't worry, I hired that one to look after the children, and of course Margaret's here." Mother took my arm like a woman possessed. "Now come inside, and let them play!" Then she said over her shoulder, with false concern, "Now, birthday girl Manette the Second and the most wonderful, don't let Billy near that thing!"

I should have known!

Margaret followed us inside with the tray. She offered to set it down on the table but Mother waved her off. "Thank you, Margaret. That's all for now." Then she turned to me. "She tells me what's-her-name out there is a strong, reliable girl. She says," and she did a humiliating imitation, "'That girl be's solid as a rock.' Now, sit down. I insist."

I doubted that, because Margaret's mastery of the language was flawless, but I answered like a dutiful servant. "Yes Ma'am." Naturally, I positioned my chair next to the screen door because I needed to keep them safe. When I peeked, Little Manette was bouncing, bouncing, with the colored girl's strong hands around her waist. The child was slight enough to keep her new horse going, but not heavy enough to bounce very high; she bounced on and on, furious at her horse for not going faster, while Billy watched. I saw from the set of his shoulders that he knew his sister wouldn't let him get near her horse that day.

I thought, it's all right, Margaret's there. She loves that boy.
I should have known!

Tomorrow I would see to it that Mother's man Richard moved the thing downstairs and out into the courtyard below before my children saw it again. Or better yet, to William's house. Perhaps by the end of tomorrow, Little Manette would be so jaded that I'd go into the garden while she was napping and give my Billy a gentle ride.

Then he screamed.

My four-year-old looked up at me from her seat on the woven rug. She was alone on the porch. And the colored girl? I found out later that Little Manette had commanded this child Odetta to find Margaret and fetch more cake, and when she refused? Just four years old, but Little Manette was inexorable. A living monument to will. She may have threatened whipping; she may have threatened prison. Or something worse. I don't know what she said, but they were both in the kitchen when Billy screamed.

My two were only alone for a minute. The girl and I rushed out on the porch through different doors, terrified.

Then Little Manette turned to us with that beautiful, blank face. She was alone on the porch, with at her back the bouncy horse, alarmingly close to the rail and my Billy smashed on the pavement below. She faced me without blinking, mystified.

"Billy fell."

We were never certain how it happened, but I should have known that day. I should have known!

I should have put an end to her the day she was born. I should have taken that fall down our steep stairs and dashed her brains out, and what did it matter if I died too? None of this would have happened.

All the— monstrosity that brought this family down would have died with her.

Theodore, Teddy Two, whatever you call yourself, listen! Listen and be warned!

In the name of God, Theodore, new Teddy, what does your mother call you? Theo? In the name of God, go!

God forgive me. I should have stamped the life out of her while I still had the power.

CHAPTER 37

Dell

Dell's shelter underneath the Ellis house is getting swampy. He woke up to raindrops pock-pocking on his head. Some time in the night the porch above him sprang a leak: nature's way of telling him to get up and move out. The mud surrounding the cement floor where he slept looks squishy, like quicksand in a jungle movie. The kind that sucks you in and swallows you whole.

If it invades the cement margins it will wipe him out, along with crucial evidence he's collected to prove that he belongs in the house overhead. He ought to bundle the stuff and move out, but he has things to do.

He takes care wrapping the journal, the carton and the laptop in extra garbage bags scored on his last Dumpster run. He backs his makeshift table up to the foundation and sets the packages on top. It looks like the safest place. He wraps the flash drive in plastic and seals it in an old Altoids tin to muffle the vibe, and centers it on Dakin's journal. *There.*

He puts on his baseball cap and slips into his last garbage bag and goes out. He'll wait this out at the all-night diner, stalling over coffee-and until it gets light.

• • •

He's been camped out in the downtown branch of the public library since the doors opened. He was the first one inside, and— surprise— he smiled so nicely that the head librarian has done everything in her power to help. He's been here all day.

There isn't much on Randolph Ellis of 553 May Street, born in this city January 30, 1895. Yes, he's tracking down his ancestor, if Randolph is his ancestor. Given what he's read in the old man's journal, it makes perfect sense. All he needs is proof.

Hey, it beats spinning his wheels in his dank quarters back there underneath Tara, while the leak gets worse and the rain smacks into the dirt outside like celestial piss. Now that he knows there are guys out looking for him, now that they've tracked him to the ancestral home, he'd rather wait out the rain in a safer place.

He should have moved his stuff when the kid crashed in with his half-assed warning yesterday. He should be halfway to Savannah or Newport— *Newport? Dude!*— by now. He should be long gone from here, but he has this to do.

He's looking for the missing link.

For a guy with his skills, and he can't tell you why he has them, a Web search never takes long. But Dell Whoever is thorough. Libraries like this one have more to offer than anything bouncing around the Internets, and he's been through most of it. In the past few hours he's searched a hundred years' worth of microfiche. He's skimmed a dozen town histories and moved on to the few bound volumes of the *Florida Metropolitan,* which morphed into the *Jacksonville Journal* long after this Randolph Ellis left town. He has looked for Randolph in a heap of primitive high school yearbooks, but except for one mention in the Day School archives, it's almost as though the guy simply vanished. Like, *zot!*

How could a kid who meant so much to his father leave no trace? If he can find out where Dakin Senior's favorite son ended up after that incredibly old, long-dead war, he knows he can do the rest. He can follow this Randolph's descendents and their descendents and find out who he really is and where he belongs.

Here. I belong here.

He can feel it. Now, prove it. Prove it and his life will change. Dell no-last-name can walk out of whatever he did and whoever he used to be, and into this new person.

Then he'll come in that front door in broad daylight and tell them, hey, I'm your long-lost, and they'll have to take him in. Naturally the old girls will welcome their— cousin? Great-nephew? Descendent of the long-lost prodigal son, home at last, and whoever these suits are that the kid says came looking for him?

He's over them.

And, whatever they thought he did?

He's not that person any more.

Hell with the suits, plainclothes cops or feds or knuckle-dragging thugs who came to town bent on making him pay up on some forgotten debt. Hell with the guilt and anxiety that kept him sleeping badly on the hard cement, wondering what the fuck he did before the taxi bashed him out of his life. Fuck waking up in the hospital with his memory smashed to hell.

He can stop being that guy.

Once he proves that he's this Randolph's great-great grandson or, OK, his bastard descendent, he'll have a nice new family, and he can forget the rest.

And to hell with his leaky squat under the mother ship. The old girls will settle him in a comfortable guest room upstairs, and then? Let them knock themselves out curing what ails him with a warm bed and hot food and family that cares about him, freeing him to discover the rest of himself in peace.

Of course he'll amuse the ladies and do chores for them, moving heavy objects and running errands like a nice great-whatever while he does what he has to do to get what he wants.

Everything he needs is somewhere inside that house. Deeds, he thinks. Site plans. Notes. Personal letters. The will. The old man would have remembered his secret beloved, the real mother of his bastard son. Given what Dakin writes about Randolph in that journal, given the messes that he, Dell no-last-name, has made, he's pretty sure Randolph was the old man's favorite. Even if he wasn't, Dakin would have made provisions for both of them in a secret will **To be opened in the event of my death.** Of course there is one. All he has to do is find it. Then he'll step up with the paperwork and claim what's rightfully his.

How much longer can these women live, anyway? They're at least a hundred and twelve. Hang in, dude, and eventually you'll inherit, no matter how long you have to wait.

At the moment, he's leafing through the crumbling pages of the few bound volumes of the *Metropolitan* that are too fragile to scan. He made nice with the librarian and she was thrilled to help a researcher who cares as much as she does. He's rummaged through index cards and pulled multiple histories of the city out of the stacks but there's nothing on Dakin's runaway son except for this one item, which may be all he ever wanted. To look for his likeness in Randolph Ellis's face.

Now!

The last volume yields a blurred news photo of a birthday party that Mr. and Mrs. Dakin Ellis of 553 May Street threw for one *Master Everett Ellis, Five Years Old*, in 1901, OK, Randolph would be six. The photographer posed all twenty guests on the top three steps of the big front porch at Tara there, with the stringy birthday boy perched on the top step, the capstone on the pyramid. He's positioned dead center, scowling in his dapper white linen suit even though they've put a cardboard crown on their angry little king. Dell stares into the black-and-white photo until his eyes cross; this newsprint was flaky and yellowed with age for decades before it came into his hands. Another few years and it will vanish, like the past.

The other guests are arranged on the two steps below this Everett, polite courtiers. Dell thinks he knows which ones belong to the late Dakin Ellis Senior, and the late Mrs. Dakin Ellis— they have their father's anxious squint. They have their mother's high forehead, the sharp chin, even the littlest ones. Handsome woman in the many, many society photographs in the *Metropolitan,* but nobody you'd like. And the bastard son of Dakin's beloved? He leans closer. The photo is grainy, the faces hard to make out.

Wait. Here's a passionate, dark-haired boy positioned at the far right end of the bottom step, several removes from the king for the day. He looks nothing like the others. The photographer has him halfway out of the frame. Like he doesn't count. Unlike the others, who fidget and lounge in degrees of protest, this boy is at ease, giving the camera a great big what-the-hell grin.

That one, he decides. That's him.

He leans in so close that his nose grazes the page, memorizing the face of the child who belongs to him. That he belongs to.

At closing time.

Dell's tempted to slit the margin and pull this page out of the volume, but only a fool would touch paper this old. It won't come out in one piece. Besides, who defaces an archival volume? Not him. *Oh shit, why do I know about archives. Chill, you don't. Unless you were one. Stop.* Only a fool would jam what's left of the page into his shirt and walk out with it, not in this rain. He can't take care of anything even when the sun's out, not living the way he does. Let the archivist look after it until he comes back with Ivy to confirm the ID. If she knows. He thinks she does. She's that old.

Fool, you'd need a forklift to move her and her scooter any- where. And a van. Rethink. Maybe the truth of his ancestor is buried deep in Ivy's memory, and he can exhume it— with a little help. If not, there's always the attic. Go home.

Home? He thinks so. There are signs. That confirmation he found in Dakin's journal. The bastard son. Dell belongs.

He knows it.

All he has to do is complete the proof.

It's a long way from a guess to documentation, but he'll find it, he thinks, going along with his head bent against the driving rain. It's somewhere inside that house. He'll skin up through the dining room hatch and find it. Given the rain, he may not have to wait until night. Hell, he can even sleep up there, and if it takes days, weeks to get what he needs?

He can wait.

CHAPTER 38

Theo

A bunch of messed-up dreams rolled in on me when I went to bed and they don't quit. It's like I'm trapped inside a giant goldfish bowl, bed and all. It won't matter how fast I run, I can't get out of the bowl, and the worst part is, some lady is yelling at me, but I don't know why, no way can it be her, it's too *loud*. I made a head sandwich to shut her out but there aren't enough pillows in the world.

Holy crap, she's out there, banging on my . . . **Go away, lady, you're a nighttime thing.** Then she yells.

"Theo? I said, Theo!"

"Mom?"

"Theo, get up!"

Holy crap, why do I feel like shit?

"Do you know what time it is?"

How long has she been knocking? I think, *Don't piss me off.* I say, "Not really. Look at your phone!"

"Lunchtime!"

"No way!"

Fail. She's already pissed. "Way. It's almost noon!"

I take the pillow off my face and yell, "I'm coming, OK?"

It sure as hell doesn't look like noon. The gray light in my dumb-old-lady's idea of a ship's cabin is all wet and corrupted by rain. It's raining so hard out there that the glass in my porthole is fogged, like we're in the ocean and the house just submerged.

There's a different smell coming up from the kitchen too. Like Mom's been down there making her corned-beef hash and scrambled eggs for me. Like she's trying to make up for something I don't know about, but I'm not hungry, I just feel bad.

At lunchtimes Aunt Rosemary usually dishes up PB&J, baloney, that stuff. Today it smells like real food cooking. I woke up feeling like crap. All weird and fletchy, like there's something I'm supposed do, but I don't know what it is. Facing lunch with the aunts sucks, but it beats dealing with bad dreams, so I grab my hoodie and bonk-bonk-bonk down the back stairs, in case Mom thought I wasn't pissed.

It turns out she's made her corned-beef hash and scrambled eggs for me, along with cocoa and Poppin' Fresh. Like she's trying to make up to me for something I don't know about.

Whatever, I'm not all that hungry anyway.

Brunch or whatever Mom wants to call it goes OK, probably because it's just her and me at the table with zero aunts on deck, a major plus. Maybe they all went back to bed because of the rain or else they're stacked in their recliners in front of the dark flatscreen with Aunt Ivy parked on the end, all lined up and waiting for *General,* at which time Aunt Iris finally turns on the set. It's like church for them.

So Mom and I are alone in the ark, like, waiting out the flood. I'm not what you would call hungry. I feel bad. I look up and Mom isn't eating either. She's pushing it around her plate. Oh shit, is it something I did?

I go, "You're not eating."

"Neither are you. Theo, is there a problem?"

"Not that I know of. Ungreat sleeping. Bad dreams."

She serves up an oh-is-that-all smile and the Hale family punch-line for whiners. "Take two aspirin and call me in the morning."

Damn Dad, I mean, damn you Barry, every family has its own language, and you wrote part of ours. You left us with a fucking playbook for every occasion, and this one is W.C. Fields getting stuck in the middle of the blizzard. They're in this drafty log cabin and he's putting the family to bed, we saw that DVD a hundred dozen times. I hand Mom the setup line we use to reassure each other. "You open your window a little bit, Ma."

And Mom snaps off the good old comeback, the way she always does when we're letting each other know that we're OK. "Good night, son. You open your window a little bit too."

The problem is, we're not OK. It isn't. We just finished lunch, but it's fucking dark outside. We're sitting in other people's kitchen messing with food we usually like, nothing to say and nothing we want to do. OK, we're both depressed. Because rain. Because rain, and that's just part of it. There's me. Plus, Mom really is acting like she's guilty, or she's about to be. Something's wrong, and she can't figure out how to tell me what it is.

I go, "Mom?"

It comes out in a terrible rush. "Barry wants us to meet him in Biloxi."

"Agh." I piss and sweat over what to say to her. I want to do it, I don't want to do it, I want everything to go back to the way it was before Barry threw us in the trash but I'm really pissed off at him, I don't know what Mom wants right now and she looks at me like she knows what I want but there's nothing we can do about it, at least not today. I want to do it, I don't want to do it, I don't know what Mom wants and I go, "Is that so bad?"

Her mouth is zigzagging, like she doesn't know which face to make. "What do you think?"

She isn't exactly explaining, so I stick it to her because what went on in my head last night is too hard to explain. "What do you think?"

The zigzag flattens out into a straight line and she comes back all hardball. "I said, what. Do. You. Think?"

"OK, it would suck." Then this thing that chased me all night catches up and mows me down. "But we've got to get the fuck out of this fucking house!"

"I'm *working* on it!"

"Oh shit, Mom, I'm not trying to guilt you, I just."

"Theo, what's the matter with you?"

"Nothing, I'm *fine*!"

"Don't. Don't even try."

That squint. You can see through me, Mom, but what's up with you? "OK. Somebody told me something about this house that creeps me out."

Her head whips around. "Who?"

Shrug. Make that face.

I'm a hard ticket today, starting with the sleeping so late plus not eating her special brunch, and now this. "OK, Theo. What did they *say*?"

I don't fucking know! Think fast, dude, switch topics. Now. I'm not about to tell her what I thought this *whatever* yelled at me, and I sure as hell can't tell her who I think it was. Worse. If I tell her, she'll blow me off like she did that day in the parking lot when she went all there-there on me. Can't let her snap into full-on mom, like I'm freaking out like a little kid. Lie. "It was Dell."

"That nice guy from Staples?" She brightens up.

"Yeah."

"That helped me with the box?"

Work it, dude. "That one."

"What did he say?"

Now it's my face going eight ways to Sunday. "I don't know!"

She sighs. Relief, I guess. She's got that look, like she's about to go all there-there anyway, which she kind of does. "Don't worry, T. Whatever you heard, it's just another story. Old, old houses like this one? Stuff gets around. Sleepy Hollow kind of things, OK?"

Damn if I can tell her it's OK. I sort-of nod.

"Don't give it another thought. Think legends. And if you run into what's-his-name— Dell again, ask him who sold him that one. And tell him Lane says hey."

Ding! "OK."

She actually smiles. Like that settled anything. At least she's happy. "Well, back to the drawing board."

I say what you say when your mom is going back upstairs to go on not getting a job. "Go forth and knock 'em dead."

But she smiled. It was about Dell, I think, and in spite of him throwing his knife at me, I think in some weird way he could be our last hope. Like, he doesn't have a car, at least not one that I know of, but Mom does. She and I could run away tonight, we could sleep in the car, but we have zero money to get any further than the Publix up the way. What I don't know is, does Dell?

Maybe he has money stashed somewhere that kid Dopey was too scared to look or too dumb to know. What if he really did break into Dell's place that one time, and he really stole this magazine off his chest while he was asleep? Either it's a lie or Dell was faking because he was not about to get stupid and bring the cops down on him because he flashed the knife. Woah. Dell owes me one.

Look, he rose up and attacked me just for coming in! I told no one, so he owes me, right?

He probably does have money somewhere, right?

It's raining buckets, right?

It's gotta be damp as fuck down there, and if I go back into Dell's hideout with Rosemary's umbrella and some— right, left-over hash— on a paper plate covered in foil, he might even be OK with me coming back to visit after all. And *if the back porch is leaking* the way I think it is, he'll at least thank me for the umbrella, right?

Look, Dell's gotta be as sick of this place as me. If I say so and he says so, maybe we can talk. I'll tell him what I think, and if he has money and we have the car, maybe we can get the hell out of here. He's strong, I'm smart, all we have to do is break it to Mom. Then we can load up the car and bail on this nightmare scene before the rain lets up, and if Dell is, like, hard to convince?

All I have to do is give him that weird message the two guys in the totally *Men in Black* outfits fobbed off on me, so, cool! Whatever he thinks I did to him the other day, he'll have to forgive me, right?

By the time I think this through and go back to the cabin— er, bedroom— on the landing for a couple of things, good old *General* has started up, so I'm good to go out through the kitchen and down the back steps and into his squat, hideout, whatever; it's cool, and being as I'm in high planning mode right now and it's a terrific plan, for the first time since I woke up freaking, I'm cool.

The problem being that wherever he is right now, in spite of the raining-buckets part, Dell is nowhere around. At least it isn't raining inside, although whatever I'm walking on under here squelches at every step so whatever I think I'm doing, it won't be sneaking up.

No problem. His stuff is still here all right, no water leaking in overhead, it's still dry except for the part where the cement apron drops off, which is totally turning to squelch. The old wood room or whatever where Dell sleeps is perfectly dry except around the edges, but I went in up to my ankles just getting around the partition.

Shit. He's not here. My only friend in this crap universe is totally gone. Like, who in his right mind would want to go out in stuff like this without rain gear? Oright. Garbage bags. Everybody in their right mind uses garbage bags. So, what? Look for the money?

Bad idea.

Sit here and wait?

Nope. They'll be hunting me. Mom would freak if she found out that her Mr. Nice Guy lives underneath this fucking house. If Dell came in and found me sitting here, he'd freak. OK, stupid. Leave a note. Then he has time to think about it and get back to me before I show up and he flips the knife. Fine. Done deal.

All I have to do is go into the crap on his not-exactly desk and find something I can write on. Done. Blank inside of the laptop carton. Sharpie. I print large, so there's no mistaking it:

URGENT ISSUES
1. WE HAVE TO GO
2. WE NEED TO TALK
3. PING ME. SOMEHOW

I hope to hell he gets back to me. Somehow. I lean it on a book dead centered on his sleeping bag, so he'll see it first thing. Then I rethink and add the last item, which either is or is not a good thing.

4. THE GUYS HUNTING YOU LEFT A MESSAGE.
THEY SAID TELL HIM THAT HIS FATHER
FORGIVES HIM.
WHATEVER.
T.

CHAPTER 39

EXTRACT

Dakin Ellis
Undated—

Dearest,
If only I knew where and how to send this letter to you I would hand carry it to your front door wherever you are. I would fall on my knees and beg you to let me in. If only, if only. Dreadful, not knowing anything and for so long, but after we embraced and completed the transaction, you vanished and I still don't know why or how. I wanted Manette to plummet to her death so I could marry you. Entrapped or miraculously single, I will always want to marry you.

Sylvia Elliott Marden, I miss you every day of my life, and I grieve for what I did to yours. You deserved so much more, and with a much, much better man than I. I never should have stopped to help you on that first day of our secret life. I should have let my rage drive me on along the river walk until it was spent, past the city limits and all the way to Mayport and beyond. But I saw you

striding along the riverbank with your hair down and you were
alone, so angry and so wild that whatever the cause, your mood
matched mine. Yes, I fell in step with you. I was in a rage with
no other means of expressing itself and so without speaking, we
walked on and on.

    It was another one of those days when my wife drove me out
of the house. Diminutive, demanding Little Manette.

    I endured years of deep discussion of Manette's lust for the next
pretty thing. Recitals of my flaws. Oh, Sylvie, lover, my dearest,
my wife was intent on perfecting me, even as she lavished thou-
sands upon thousands of dollars on the parade of objects she
brought into this loathsome, insatiable house. She must have this
particular tapestry to complete the picture. That urn. The perfect
gilded triangular chair.

    Every few days she needed another precious This to complete
her life, then a That and another That and another and another,
until her costly, unending Thats crowded me out of her boudoir
and out of her bed, which they did except at certain utilitarian
times. Eight or nine more, I suppose. You see, the goddess of ac-
quisition had decided that her next essential That would be our
second child. It seems Dakin Junior was too stolid. She wanted a
girl. Manette was very specific in this case. She wanted a pretty
daughter that she could fuss over and dress up in pretty things
from Charleston and New York and even Paris to complete the
scene. Another child, I thought. It's certainly time. She can dedi-
cate herself to motherhood instead of her insatiable need for more
things. That's all they were. Things.

    She said, "Our matched set. A boy and a girl. Just think how
darling they'll be when Nurse puts them in their matching outfits
and takes them out in the pony cart."

    Like a fool I thought: Now. Our real lives together will begin
now, but weeks before we knew that I'd planted her next baby
inside her, Manette had carpenters paneling the second-class bou-

doir because with her new daughter, and she was sure it would be a daughter, there was no room for me in hers.

Her next baby, mind you, not ours. The other children were never ours and certainly not mine. Until Manette tired of them, they were hers. Then Tillie took care of them.

"Walnut paneling for you," she said, planning my exile for the second time, the first being as soon as she had Dakin Junior safely in the world. "I'm having the men stain it black, of course, ebony's brittle and much too hard to work with over a certain size." Generous girl, she added that as soon as Dr. Woods told her she was expecting, I was welcome to return to the chaise longue in her dressing room for as long as it took to perfect the décor because of course the help needn't know what we did behind closed doors. "Maroon velvet portieres for you, I think," she said, and she was practically singing as she laid out the details. "So manly. And I'll find the perfect Persian rug to match. And a leather easy chair. The ideal setting for my handsome husband! And," she added, "when it's done, perhaps I'll let the girls at the club add our house to the tour of stately homes."

To keep the peace, I agreed to this. Then this. Then more. There was always more.

It was a Saturday when we finally came down to it, Manette and I, so I couldn't pretend I had business at the office, my usual mode of escape. On weekdays the office routine keeps me safe for the while, but never for long enough. There would always be dinner, the two of us. Her lust for the perfect thing.

That Saturday morning she used me hard. I did this errand, then that. Fortunate, I suppose, because most of them took me out of the house. After our lunch Tillie brought little Dakin down from the nursery and I took him to the park to spin out the afternoon, but eventually the children's hour ended and it was dinnertime again.

Tillie would feed Dakin Junior in the nursery, but Manette and I?

Until the boys were old enough to sit up at the long mahogany table and that would be years later, we dined alone. I would persist in my manly duties until she had the daughter-to-be firmly planted and then we would be done. Everything else in her life proceeded in order. Was I not giving her everything she asked?

Still, I was trapped at that table until the last dish was served. And what drove me out of the house on that Saturday? It was the pony cart. The day I saw you on the river walk, I had walked out on the special pony cart my wife conjured out of a few pictures and thousands of words. We'd need it to carry Dakin Junior and our pretty daughter into the park, which came as news to me. Of course she'd be pretty. Of course it would be a girl. "They'll be darling in the pony cart. Idiot, how could you forget?" Manette drove me to it, and she rode me hard, as though it was fait accompli. *She dithered over whether we should have the cart custom made in Paris, what kind of fittings we needed, what color pony, black would be very nice, would a red patent-leather harness with little bells be vulgar, would it be appropriate to have a matching coat for Nurse to wear on chilly days and what would the children wear, would we need to expand the stables to accommodate it, perhaps we needed to hire a groom. I kept my temper. I always do. I told my wife exactly what she told me whenever I tried to draw her to me for any show of warmth, "We'll see."*

Then I escaped. I left the house in a walk, but once I passed the Cummers' house near the river, I exploded. Sylvie, I was forbidden to shout. Manette would say, "Dakin, hush! What will people think?" Instead, I pounded along in miserable silence, brutalizing the pavement with every step until I rounded the last corner and saw the river.

And I saw you, stalking along the path. You were pitched forward at an angle no respectable Southern lady would ever take, head down, shoulders hunched. I saw that you were even angrier than I. We didn't talk about it that day or ever, really. You never told me much. You strode along and I strode along until we reached the end of the pier just off the point. Then we stopped and without speaking, we watched the river together, letting our rage follow the current until the last of it flowed away.

Enough. I told you everything! You never told me that your situation was tenuous. I knew that you cared for your mother in the rooms she took after she moved out of her home in Massachusetts and came here for the sake of her health, but you never told me that the funding would evaporate the day she died. We both know how and why we fell in love. I cherish the desperate arrangements we made to be together once everything between us was understood and I know that it was glorious, oh my darling, oh, God!

You never told me when your mother passed away. Or that you were pregnant when you hugged me close and confided that you needed to leave Jacksonville to move your mother to Asheville for the mineral springs; you said you loved me, you said you hoped you wouldn't be gone for too long. By that time Manette was overwhelmingly pregnant, although her date was months away.

Overbearing, too. She expected me to be available at all times. "In case," she said, never guessing that her newest acquisition would be stillborn. She still doesn't know.

And you! My dearest Sylvie, thank God the hospital called me in time. Thank God you had the wits to give them my name because you were so certain that our baby would kill you and you wanted him to be safe. I think you expected to die: your just punishment for lying with me, close for a while, so happy in our love. Oh, Sylvie, you broke my heart. They took me for your employer, but Dr. Woods knew.

He told me what he knew that Manette never would. She was carrying death. Her baby died in the womb too close to the end of term for him to interfere; she was due to deliver within the week. He understood our situation, yours and mine, and it was he who decided what came next. He showed me the paperwork, and I had him move you from the ward into a private room

*where I could love my new son and we could be happy in what
little time we had.*

*I went to you as soon as you and our son were settled in the
private room. And for the first few hours, we were together, loving
mother, devoted father, beautiful infant son. Together, we named
him. Then we embraced, holding on for as long as we could before
Dr. Woods a-hemmed outside the door and negotiations began.*

*That day you and I sealed the bargain. You let me think that I
could divorce Manette, and as soon as I made the necessary arrangements, we would marry and raise Randolph together, we
named him for your father, and you? Oh, my dearest dear, I thought
I was helping you!*

Instead, you gave me the saddest, finest gift of my life!

*Manette's Brucie would be born dead the next day, thanks to
Dr. Woods. He introduced the magic of twilight sleep, and my
voracious Manette slept for two days and woke up with Randolph
in her arms. Our beautiful boy. Because I feared the woman as
much as I used to imagine that I loved her, I stayed the night with
them: her face when she woke up and saw that it was a boy. Her
face! She studied him as though examining an antique that had
come to her without her trusted dealer's pedigree: the appraiser's
skeptical squint.*

*My dear, that night turned into many nights because I was
afraid to leave him alone with her. More than anything, I wanted
to be with you, but I had to stay with the woman day and night as
long as our baby slept in a cradle handcrafted to match her frilly
bedroom. Her newest acquisition was a disappointment. She
wanted a girl.*

And, Randolph? Dear God, I was protecting him!

*For too many days I brought Manette this, handed her that: the
silver-backed hairbrush and the silver-backed hand mirror, fetch-
ing Tillie to do certain things for her, because I had to stand watch.
I spent too many nights in Manette's hand-carved rocker with
ruffled cushions, fearful and half-awake, and that was my mistake.*

It was almost two weeks before my wife tired of her new toy and handed him off to Tillie and banished our Randolph to the wet nurse's room just off the stairs.

I should have taken you out of St. Luke's that very day, doctor's orders notwithstanding. I should have booked a stateroom on the steamer leaving Mayport that very night. I would have come back to Jacksonville to do the necessary paperwork, ceding the house to Manette, with everything else set by with provisions for Dakin Junior to inherit, for I'm a responsible man, and if maintaining them cost me every penny I would ever make, so be it.

We would still be together, you and Randolph and I.

By the time I came back to St. Luke's and the private room I had arranged for you, there was a new patient lying in your bed. Dr. Woods, the floor manager said, was operating and must not be disturbed. I confronted the nurses, the orderlies, even the women who cleaned the rooms. Where was he, where were you, why wasn't I told? By the time I stormed down to confront the people in the office, he was at the bottom of the stairs. He backed me up the steps, one at a time, so that we had the conversation, as it were, hanging in space.

"I tried to keep Mrs. Marden," he said. He said "Mrs." to protect your reputation. "I tried to keep Mrs. Marden at least until she had stopped bleeding, but she insisted on being allowed to convalesce in her own bed. I begged her to stay long enough to let our nurse bind her breasts, but she said her mother was a trained midwife, and knew all about such things."

I left before he could pretend that I needed him to give me your address. I knew where you and your mother lived, at least for a while, I knew which rooming house on which street in the poorer section of Jacksonville, and when you refused to let me move the two of you to something better— for your mother's sake, I told you, for all the good it did me. I argued. I pleaded. I grieved.

I went to the place where you used to live, but your rooms were empty and the landlady told me that you had cleared out months ago, soon after your mother died, no, no forwarding address, no point in leaving a message. For years I combed Jacksonville, thinking you had found lodging here. I hoped, I studied the death notices, and during the terrible spring after we lost Teddy I looked for you in Savannah and in Charleston, going on foot from door to door, and under orders, I did my duty, for Manette was obsessed.

In a fit of acquisition, she demanded her pretty, perfect daughter. "The image of her mother," she said. "Then you can stop." No, Teddy would not do, not even Everett, although he came closer than any of the daughters that followed.

In the end I euchred Manette into visiting Asheville to take the waters for her health— too many babies, none of them good enough, until the surgery after Leah's birth ended it. She needed a spa! I put her to bed in the family guesthouse at Biltmore— of course she leapt at the chance. Cachet!

In Asheville I walked the streets day and night, desperately looking for you, oh, Sylvie, I miss you so much, and you aren't anywhere! I search, I hope and I grieve, because you are well and truly gone from my life and now, in the wake of his rage and my folly, our handsome, angry boy is just as gone.

I will not see you again in this lifetime, my dear, but, sweet love! If God is kind, I'll join you in eternity sooner, rather than later. I am sick of waiting.

CHAPTER 40

*L*ane

Day three of the deluge, I think, but the way things are going, I can't be sure. I can't be sure of anything except the hard, flat rain. It's gone on for so long that the whole house groans like a hippo in labor, and everything about today scares the crap out of me.

It's the entrapment thing.

T. and I are trapped with these people, at least until it stops, and the tension is rising. So's the water. May Street is its own river, with my getaway car standing in water up to the hubcaps under sheets of rain, with more to come. Even if it stops this minute, T. and I are stuck until the brakes dry out, and pretty much surrounded by the aunts. They come at me with: am I sure I shut all the upstairs windows, would I check again, for safety's sake, will I please run upstairs one more time and lock them like they told me to the first time, and which I did, although there's no convincing them.

All right, Elena, just double-check for your crippled Aunt Iris, won't you, dear? I'm in too much pain to go up and down stairs once a day, you know. Oh, and while I'm up, why don't I run down to the corner for some fresh candles, three new flashlights, a shortwave radio and by the way our flashlights all need new batteries, we have absolutely *no way* to find out what's happening when the lights go out, they always do when it rains this hard, thank God Father built us high off the ground like the Hopswee plantation house, so 553 isn't privy to flood, dear Mama demanded it, all three of them are mired up to the hubcaps in their shared ancestral fantasy, poor old things! The air is filled with the rattle of fretful Iris and Rose nattering in counterpoint, while Ivy, who's the real cripple here, murmurs, "Leave the poor child alone," while they jabber on and on and on after that, tipping me and Theo into their Möbius strip, trapping us in the loop.

Stranded.

As of today, I'm technically screwed. Don't have enough money to leave 553, can't get a job even on sunny days, can't even get an interview, and given that Barry left Deland with everything of value packed in his U-Haul, I don't have anything left to sell.

You bet I'm pissed off and anxious, but I'm not desperate. I survive on variations of Plan B.

If the rain keeps up I can always riffle through the few books the aunts keep in the house, trolling for abandoned bills, or, worst-case, I'll go up in that hellish attic and rummage through generations' worth of junk, looking for loose change. I was up there once when I was thirteen, but it was so spooky that I never made it past the first wave of monumental crap. It's scary. Terrifying, really. As though the house is plotting to trap us under an avalanche of junk or, oh, shit!

Fixing to swallow us whole.

We have to go! All I need is cash. If we raid Rose's larder before we take off, we can eat what we take and sleep in the car and pray to God that the car doesn't crap out on us before we make it to the next gas station. Wait too long and archaeologists will dig us up a thousand years from now. Ossified, like the bodies at Pompeii.

Theo is wilting too. My big boy is so depressed that he slouches away whenever he sees me coming, and if I catch up and ask him a question, for God's sake all I want is a little conversation, he'll answer, but he won't look at me.

And the aunts, the aunts. They're so sad and, I don't know, so sort of perpetual, as though this is how it's always been, and they think this is the way it should be until the end.

I can't stand one more of Rosemary's awful lunches, her lame leftovers and their crap table talk over stale beer, and I'm too depressed to sit through another of her dinners, which are always worse. At night we have to sit down in that big old dining room, with generations' worth of china facing us down in the corner cabinets. The twins start up even before we sit down: how lovely it was when Cook was still here and William brought hot biscuits to the table and there were finger bowls and people who waited on you always said, Yes Ma'am. They threnodize about the days when Mama, their sacred, holy Mama coached her darlings on etiquette, "Take your oar out of your boat, dear," and "Ladies never, *ever* talk with their mouths full," and then Iris tells us how Mama told them that her dear *Mother,* and she doesn't mean their living grandmother, even though she's sitting right there at the table, oh holy shit, that would be Mormama, who *are* these people?

Don't ask, you already know. Take care, lady, or you and your tough kid Theo will be trapped, like them. Iris, ranting on about how *Mama* used to lift the elbow of the offending child and put a hot biscuit under it like a sweet little pillow. Object, humiliation. Unspoken message embedded. Polite children never, ever put their elbows on the table, Rosemary explains, hung up on lore that's come down through, ack! Generations.

As though Mormama really *is* still here, more or less as I told

Theo because you have to come up with *something* when your kid freaks. You just do.

OK, at first he and I loved to mock the aunts and laugh a little bit, but we're over it. We're over them. Until or unless I can find us a way out of this, these dinners will go on forever, with the rain coming down in a dismal counterpoint that is, to me . . . Never mind what it is. I'm afraid to name it.

When Theo escapes those dinners ("Now, say, 'May I please be excused, Aunt Iris?'" which he must do to her satisfaction) Iris and Rosemary grill me about my expectations, now that I've let myself go ("Elena, your *hair*," "Elena, you can't go out wearing *that*," and, "Elena, those awful purple shoes of yours, Elena, a lady's naked toes are her personal business").

They mean: since I let myself go and lost my handsome man because I look like something that the cat dragged in. As I lost my handsome man, what am I going to do about it? When am I going to *take care of* myself? They mean: pluck, shave and perfume and get a beauty parlor perm like theirs. Pull myself together and shop for some decent clothes so I can dress up and go out and get him back, or at least start hunting for *a suitable replacement*?

As if I accidentally dropped Barry while I was stepping into my purple slides and he rolled under the dresser. They yammer on at me while Ivy goes back inside her head and pulls down all the shades because for once I and not Ivy, the foolish girl who lost control of her horse and the use of her lower body, am the target of the nightly Inquisition.

I hope Ivy dreams, although it's possible that she just shuts down, conserving energy. I never know, but today I seize on her and lay my path to escape, at least until dinnertime.

It's mid-afternoon, and we're still sitting at the lunch table. I start with how peaky Ivy looks, how hard it must be for her, stuck in the house for days, can't go anywhere without our help, poor old lady at our mercy, she needs a little fresh air.

The aunts bridle at "old" but I lift my shoulders in the definitive fuck you and grasp the handles on Scooter and wheel her out of the room before they can protest, buying off Rosemary with, "Leave the dishes on the table, Aunt Rosemary. With Iris laid up in that cast, you're cooking for us and doing all the cleanup too. I'll take care of it, I promise. As soon as I take poor Ivy out on the porch for a little fresh air."

Bitching and protestation, what do you expect from these shriveled old wrecks, cranky from too much rain, convicted lifers doing hard time in the ancestral prison, doing a stretch unbroken only by our rush trip to the hospital before the unending drizzle segued into flood warnings and the storm.

Ivy let out a sigh as I opened the front door, in effect, springing her. Yes, it's a desperation move, it's as dank out here as it is inside; 3 P.M. in December and it's already getting dark but, hey, out here, we expand in the silence. The rain is so thick that I can't see much past the porch rail so I fix on the mist created by the water coming down off the eaves as it smashes to bits on the front steps. Mmmm, I think. Hypnotic.

Pretty much. Ivy sits there thinking whatever Ivy thinks while I segue into a mind-video of Barry and me at Niagara Falls back when I thought he loved me.

The smoke, one of the old-timers said when I asked about the cloud of mist. From the sky, you can see it from miles around, he said, and this is making me uncomfortably nostalgic. I'm about to spill my guts to Ivy, the way you do in bad times, when she shifts Scooter a little bit, to get my attention. Then she just starts.

"I think Mama almost loved me until I got disfigured, which is what she called it, and to this day I don't know if she hated me most for that, or for killing Teddy, which she screamed on my worst day. Dakie says she had to have somebody to blame. All I know is that she shooed me out because she was all wrapped up in Everett, that's what Papa calls how she is with him, and the last time he came home, Dakie said the same thing. He said it wasn't my fault. Then he said, 'But you know Mama. We're all to blame.'"

Don't ask, Lane. Let it happen.

"So Teddy was gone, and he was only the first. Dakie and Ran both got lost in the war and Teddy is in the grave, but Everett stayed and stayed. He was Mama's sweet baby every day of his mortal life, and she didn't care a fig about the rest of us. All my best brothers are gone but Everett lived to be eighty-seven years old.

"Mama said we were just jealous, but we had him for too long! When the Hillman brothers finally carried him away, we were glad.

"Everybody knew he was plenty old enough to be in the war, but Mama insisted that poor Everett had a Condition, so she kept him close to her, she said, Girls, don't you bother him, and don't you dare bother me. He stayed safe inside this house almost his whole life long, except for that one time . . ." She just trailed off and I didn't mind.

I sat there getting lost in the rain while Ivy went rummaging somewhere else inside her head and for the first time in my life I thought, This isn't so bad.

Then she started up again, and it was. "He wasn't really sick. He was spoiled to death. Mama kept him close because he had pretty blond hair and cupid-bow lips and he looked like her, and, oh, she said, 'He has a perfect nose,' and, you know what? He was just like her. He only ever cared about himself. Oh dear!" Ivy covered her mouth like a bad little girl.

"As for the rest of us, we couldn't satisfy her, no matter what we did. We tried so hard, but we only made her mad. Randolph ran away and she was glad. Dakie got killed in the war, but she didn't even cry. She had Evvie. She had the tailor make him a fresh white linen suit for the funeral, and she walked into church with Everett on her arm like her new beau. They went to every concert and afternoon party at the club. She doted on that boy!"

Right. That gauzy watercolor in the floral nightmare they still call Mama's Room, that's Everett, posed like the Gainsborough *Blue Boy,* although he's all in white and way too skinny to be real.

The painter positioned him by the pier table in the sitting room, with his, I guess it was a Buster Brown haircut, neatly reflected in the mirror at his back. Snotty kid that you hate on sight.

She sighs. "Everett was disagreeable. He whined because we took him out to play, and Mama was furious! She didn't give a hoot for us, it was all Everett. Well, Everett was a great big sissy. Once she brought him down to the houseboat with the rest of us and Papa was so glad. We almost got him to play. Then Randolph put him in the water and he bawled to heaven. Ran had him by the pants so he was perfectly safe, but he hollered like a stuck pig, 'Let go,' so Randolph did. Ran pushed him at Dakie and Dakie grabbed him by the collar and pushed him back. Ran said, 'Look, he's swimming' and everybody laughed. Mama was furious. She made Papa bend Randolph over his knee and whip him with his belt. She lined us up on deck to watch. Papa whipped Randolph in front of us all and everyone but Randolph cried.

"Everett was a great big sissy, and that's that. They died and we had to take care of him," she says. "I hated him."

I never met the old bastard, but I felt it. "Me too."

Ivy looks at me with her crumpled mouth set and her eyes on fire and asks, "Oh, Elena, is that a sin?"

What could I say? "I don't know, I don't *know*!"

"We had him all his life, except for one month after the war. Papa set him up with those new jewelers in Palatka, but it didn't take. He was back on our doorstep in three weeks, and we had to take him in and keep care of him for the rest of his mortal life."

What to say, what to say? I manage. No inflection, I'm that done with this conversation, this eternity in the rain, deep in Ivy's abiding sorrow. "I'm sorry."

Sweet Ivy goes tart. "We're not."

Wow! "He was that big a pain in the ass."

Her voice shoots up. "Language!"

"Oh Ivy. Oh, Ivy." I can't just leave her here. "Let's go back inside."

"But of course Mama was gone by that time, she never would have let her precious Everett off the leash. Palatka. Indeed!"

We observe a moment of silence— for Everett, I suppose.

And then she says, "You know, after Leah died, Mama started getting bigger, and she brought up Leah's baby Elena as her own."

Scary, this. This story, in our world of rain. "My great-great . . ."

"Yes. She never spoke of it, but we knew. Whatever she had growing inside her didn't go away like babies do, it just grew and grew until she took to her bed. My twin sisters had to carry her meals upstairs to her on silver trays that Christmas, not the maid. Mama insisted, and it was her last Christmas . . ."

Stop.

"And after Christmas dinner . . ."

Don't stop.

"Now, I wasn't there to see it, Rose and Iris had the honor of taking Mama's turkey dinner up to her bed that day, but Rose-mary swears, my sister Rose tells me, Rose tells me!!!"

Don't break whatever spell this is, Lane, don't ask, don't say, just let her talk until it's over.

"Iris saw a black cloud coming out of Mama along with her last breath and oh, Elena, it's trapped somewhere in this house and sometimes it goes in and out of my sisters, I know it does! Child, I know I've almost seen it, but I can't swear . . ."

Then she stops. As though that's more than enough.

Oh God. Oh, God. "It's getting dark, Aunt Ivy, let's us go inside, OK?"

"You go, sweetheart, I love being alone out here in the fresh air." She reaches for my hand.

"Are you sure it's all right?"

"Of course, dear." Her fingers land on my wrist like a dying bird. "You can always come back for me later."

CHAPTER 41

Iris Ellis and Rosemary Worzecka, Née Ellis

The Ellis twins began their lives in their mother's architectural monument within minutes of each other, stolid Rose and willful Iris fighting for supremacy, Iris and Rose, forever at loggerheads, when in fact, their mother still calls the shots.

Little Manette wasn't satisfied with any of her daughters, but she was enchanted by the idea of a matched set. She had her twins done up in identical organdie dresses, with taffeta sashes and matching hair bows to set off their bouncing finger curls. Iris always wore yellow, Rosemary, pink, so if she happened to speak to them, Mama could tell which was which.

The *grande dame*'s twin ornaments are a little dusty now, their porcelain surfaces crazed by time and their features sharpened by use. The old girls switch moods faster than they swapped sashes and hair ribbons as children, making sure that Mama never found out which one to blame. These days they come out of their rooms in different attitudes like rotating figures on a weather house, the witch for foul weather, the princess for fair. The sun/thundercloud indicators show up in Iris/Rosemary or Rosemary/Iris in no predictable order, depending on where the gray vapor in the house settles that day, and the hell of it is, you never know which is which.

They disagree, but not in any way you could predict, so it's a new ballgame every day, for as long as they don't die. Bored? Fine. Do what people who have lived together too long usually do. Fight.

Which the twins do, wrangling over which lipstick, which breakfast cereal, whose turn it is to change Ivy's unmentionable or deliver her morning Pop-Tart. These days they fight over everything. Except matters pertaining to their sainted mother. In the matter of the late Manette Ware Robichaux Ellis, they think as one. It won't matter which of them speaks first, moodily sitting out the rain on the second-floor screen porch that juts out over the front porch roof. They pass the time doing what custodians do, for they are indeed custodians of this creaking tribute to Manette Ware Robichaux Ellis and her vanity: worrying.

The house is so big! Mama's works of art and costly artifacts are so many! They're responsible for too many things! It's been this way since they were six, when Mama presented them with little feather dusters and two bits of chamois bordered in pink and yellow respectively. "Now girls," she said, "you are Mama's *very special* housekeepers. You follow Emma around and wipe up after her, maids just don't *do* like real ladies do. After all, they're just maids! Now, it's up to you to make sure those colored girls take care of everything, I want you to pick up anything Emma misses, and check all the surfaces to make sure that Mattie wipes them clean."

Later, and later went on all their lives until Mama took to her bed, there would be regular white-glove inspections, with reprimands if they overlooked anything, spankings if any of her cherished Staffordshire figurines showed so much as a chip, and if anything *broke* on their watch . . . Well.

The responsibility was tremendous. Even more so after Little Manette called them to her bedside and swore them to the task. "And you, my precious beauties. When I am gone, all this . . ." She tried for a sweeping gesture but failed. Her hands drifted to the peacock quilt like butterflies, quivering in place. With her next-to-last breath, she finished, ". . . is yours," which should have been enough, but Mama was as driven as she was commanding. She finished, "To take care of until the death."

Only Iris heard what she said next because Rose was scurrying to fetch a priest, and only Rose has ever repeated it, as she did to Little Elena on the waterfront because even she recognized it as ugly, ugly! *Leah was a tramp.*

When Leah died, the twins did what one does in these circumstances, they grieved for her, even as their hearts expanded like balloons about to pop. *Ours. All this will be ours.*

That was before. Love came and went: Mama looked down her nose at Stanislaus Worzecka when he first came to the house: NOCD, she declared. The marriage didn't last long, and poor Alan Deering perished after a week of married bliss. When Poor Elena died a timely death, they worried. Who would take over her chores?

The twins' excitement waned as their responsibilities grew. Today, the task is staggering. All this rain. All that *stuff!*

What will we do if the river rises so high that it lifts our grand house off its foundation in the impending flood? What if the currents carry us downriver to God knows where?

Even on stormy days like this one, when the house beneath them shifts in new, alarming ways, Iris and Rosemary think ahead. They have to. Always did. Always will. Who knew how long the house and all Mama's treasures would endure in a flood?

Who knew that Mama was dooming them to live so long?

If the current lifts beloved 553 right up off its lot on May Street, how can they best protect and preserve dear Mama's precious things? If the water breaks up the fabric of the house: studs, beams, lath and plaster, disconnecting all the planks and the clapboards of 553 and it floats away, pieces of their past scattered and landing in new and unexpected places, what then?

Fretful, anxious— no, terrified!— the old girls chatter, shoring up their ruins with words.

"I was her favorite, she put her Tiffany flower brooch in my sash when we were eleven and she said, 'With power comes responsibility.' "

"No, I was her favorite, when she gave me the diamond pendant she said, 'Rose, we are the custodians,' and she meant me!"

"She gave me her silver-backed hairbrush, Rose."

"That doesn't mean you are her favorite."

"It does too! I'm the oldest, and I come first. She gave *me* the silver-backed hand mirror and the silver comb."

"Oh, Iris. How are we going to take care of all her beautiful things?"

"Well, we *are* the custodians."

"And her favorites."

"Yes, we were always her favorites."

"No. Everett."

"Oh, Everett, Everett! That ninny. He doesn't count."

The past, the past, their past is longer than any future the rest of us running around in the world will ever have. If the house that contains and supports them is rocking in the wind, they are too preoccupied with the past to realize, or comprehend the threat.

"But he was her favorite."

"It isn't fair!"

"He couldn't take care of himself!"

"Everett left his special bear from Uncle Johnny out in the rain, and it had *real panda fur*."

"His electric tricycle rusted to death."

"Were there electric tricycles back then?"

"Who cares? He left it out back and when it got ruined, Mama made Vincent whip Randolph for not bringing it in."

"That was a pretend whipping. Vincent wouldn't hurt anyone."

"But he had to pretend. He had to pretend it was his fault that Teddy . . ."

"Never mind."

"She had to blame somebody, didn't she?"

"And it couldn't be Everett."

"And Dakie was too old to blame."

"She blamed Randolph for everything."

"Poor Ran. No wonder he ran away."

"The war."

"He never came back."

"Poor us! I still miss him."

"Me too. He was our Unknown Soldier."

"It's sad."

They are hunched in their braided cane rockers, weighed down by responsibility. Their porch is like the wheelhouse of a giant ship, and when it's raining this hard, the twins always come out here to keep watch. The eaves are steep, but the screen picks up refracted spray. It's damp out here, but they can see all the way up and down May Street and it gives them the comforting sense of control. From here, they watch for enemies approaching, calmly waiting for the rain to stop and the waters to recede.

Ivy is downstairs somewhere, she can't do anything, so she won't go far; Little Elena will have parked her somewhere safe, and the irresponsible girl had better make that brat of hers watch his aunt while she goes back to her endless busywork on her expensive computer thing.

All right then, that's taken care of, and if those fool children get hungry they can certainly feed themselves, although it wouldn't occur to them to check on their poor old aunties, sitting out here in the dark, heroically standing watch or whatever men do out there at sea on their great big ships.

Thoughtless brats. They won't starve. Didn't that uppity girl cook a great big breakfast for her precious Little Teddy at 11:30, positively ruining their appetite for lunch? She spoils that child!

Why, the two of them up and walked out on Rose's fine cooking with petty excuses. God knows where the boy went. Only God cares. Then Little Elena turned on poor Ivy's motor and they motored out of the kitchen, leaving the two of us to worry all alone, deserting us in this terrible time when frankly, we could use a little help!

We bear all the responsibility. Rose and Iris, Iris and Rose. Well, we truly are Mama's favorites, not counting Everett. At least Everett's dead, what a load off our minds!

With power comes responsibility. We try, we try!

When all the tumult and the shouting die, we will be here in 553 May Street, taking care of everything that Mama entrusted to us. Together, we take care of Mama's house and all Mama's precious things, and we do it all by ourselves because these days you can't get decent help. They cost the world! So not counting Ivy, who isn't fit to look after a potted violet, we carry all this on our backs.

And Mama's house contains such treasures! How could Little Elena push all dear Mama's chinoiserie into a corner like that, how could she deface it with that hideous cardboard desk? She's turned Sister's beautiful room into a garbage heap, so whatever happens, it serves her right. We won't go in there to check for leaks tomorrow after the rain dies, we won't go in even after the sun comes out and every drop of flood water evaporates. We don't want to see our Leah's room defaced. The file cabinet. That ugly desk! It's like finding a hoptoad in the heart of a rose.

It's sad, what happened to Leah though. Everett was Mama's favorite, he was even more favorite than us, that nasty little dirty word, and we tried so hard! She rebuffed Dakie, and our handsome big brother tried even harder than us, and Leah *was the one that broke the camel's back.* The more Mama turned against the others, the more she took to us.

She was nice to Ivy before she ran off and got hurt, which, frankly, ruined her looks. When that poor thing came home from the hospital, Mama fixed her up with rouge and pink Max Factor so she wouldn't look so pale, and when time passed and Papa brought in the wheelchair, she wailed with grief.

Every night we had to kneel down and pray for Ivy to stand up and start walking, and every day that Ivy tried and failed, Mama hardened her heart. And, Leah? Poor Sister, Mama was so done with babies that she didn't even name her after a flower. She let Tillie name her, that's how little she cared, and sweet Tillie saw to it that Leah got a pretty name, even though it made her different from the rest.

So Leah was the last, and by the time God took her away from us, she was also the least, because of certain things that Mama refused to talk about. Then, it was like a miracle! God gave her sweet little baby Elena, our own cute little playtoy that we could dress up and fuss over and play with, like a living doll.

Mama pretended Elena was our baby sister and we let her pretend. Pretend she did. She held that baby's story tight inside her until that terrible last day. And yes, we were both present, at least until the last minute. Rosemary and Iris, Mama's two flowers, Iris and Rose, but Rosemary saw death coming and ran downstairs to telephone for a priest.

So Iris alone saw what happened and she heard what Mama said right before her mouth opened and the murky spirit inside came out. Iris saw it, and what Rosemary says about it is exactly what Iris says.

We saw the spirit leave her, whatever it was, and now some days Rosemary speaks in Mama's voice like Mama did in her sudden furies, and other days Iris does, because the spirit is still inside the house. It stays with us because, yes, of this we are both certain. In the end, Mama loved us best.

Better than Papa?

Especially Papa, because he defied her in ways we're not allowed to talk about.

She didn't even like Papa. She never loved him at all.

Oh, but she loved this house.

She loves this house!

And this house and everything in it is ours to protect and defend for Mama, for as long as Mama keeps us here.

CHAPTER 42

Dell

She's sitting up there on the broad front porch in spite of rain and descending darkness: Miss Ivy Ellis, so carefully composed that only an empath would know that every muscle in her is taut with waiting. Maybe it's the rain diffusing what little light there is left in Jacksonville, Florida this afternoon, maybe Dell is worn out and freaking. Whatever it is, the old thing's face gleams like the head of a goddess on a coin, living emblem of a household disrupted.

She cranes. "Who's there?"

"It's me."

"Oh, sweetheart. I thought you'd never come!"

Dell rocks back on his heels, but only a little bit. Keeps his voice even, asking, "Who do you think I am?"

She frowns as though he's a fool to ask; his identity is a given. "Where were you? Where were you all this time?"

"At the library," he says, advancing. Proceed cautiously, man.

You don't know what year she's in. He waits for her to process the information.

Whatever's going on inside her head, Ivy's voice is close to breaking. "Where were you all this time?"

"In your family archives down at the library, Ma'am." As though that will satisfy her.

"Don't call me Ma'am. You make me feel old!"

"Yes Ma'am!"

"I waited so long."

"I'm sorry. I got held up." Dell has no idea where in time Ivy Ellis is drifting right now or what she wants from him, but homeless and nameless as he is, used up by days of research and driven by possibilities raised by the ancestral journal, he is bent on one thing, and at the moment, this ancient, bedazzled old girl sits before him like a gift waiting to be unwrapped.

She wails, "I waited and waited."

He lingers in the shadows, framing his next response. It takes him a beat longer than it should, two beats, three to come up with it, but Ivy has been waiting for so many years now that she is patient. Finally he says, "I'm so very sorry, dear."

Her voice melts. "Oh. Oh, thank you."

Get to the point, asshole. Whatever it is. "What are you waiting for?"

With a blissful smile Ivy answers, "Why, for you, of course."

"Me?"

"Mama won't let me out of the house the way I am, she doesn't want anybody to see me like this, all useless and crippled, so count your blessings, dear. Bad pennies never stay in Mama's pockets, as you know. You are so very lucky. She used to love me, but she never liked you."

He has nothing to say to this. Waits.

"Why didn't you take me with you when you went away?"

Careful, careful. "Who do you think I am?"

"Why, you're my best, bad brother, and you know it."

Bingo. Dell can't help it; he laughs. "I thought you'd never guess."

"Oh, Randolph!"

"Oh, Ivy!" He seizes her hands.

"Don't!" Just as suddenly, the clumps of skinny old fingers turn into Silly Putty, slithering away. *RmmRmm.* As if on its own, Scooter revs up and backs her away from him. "Good Lord, child. Whoever you are, you certainly aren't Randolph Ellis."

"No, I'm not."

"Hold still!" She squints and squints. "You don't even look like him!"

"No Ma'am, I'm not him, but I could be . . ."

"My best bad brother is long dead."

". . . related to him."

Then she wails so loud that he moves to shush her, but there's no way to stop what comes next. "He came home too damaged to have any children at all!"

Thud. Whatever he thought brought him here, he was wrong.

"All that agony, and I'm the only one he told."

"I'm sorry." He is, but he's not ready to take this apart and study it right now. He's sorrier than he knows.

"Don't apologize," Ivy says, "I knew you weren't Randolph on the very first day, but you're good company, and . . ."

Careful, Nameless. Wait.

"I needed a sweet boy I could tell. I get so *lonely,* being the only one who knows."

After a while, you just run out of things to say. They sit there listening to the rain.

Finally she says, "See, the war maimed him; the Boche artillery took his foot. He came home with gangrene, and the worse injury. It would break Papa's heart. And Mama despised him. He loved Papa but he didn't want to show himself until he got his wooden leg. He was ashamed."

He can't help it, he echoes, "Ashamed." *Like me.*

It takes Ivy a long time to complete this thought. "Because he was a cripple, just like me."

"I'm sorry!"

"Oh, please stop saying that! It was lovely, seeing Randolph again. The two of us hugging, knowing I'm the only person he told." She almost smiles. "He sent Vincent with the message. I was so glad! On that Sunday, Vincent waited until they all went out to church. Then he brought my brother to the house and we were so glad that we hugged and laughed, oh, we laughed. I didn't know it was our last. He held me close so I wouldn't see how bad it was, and we talked about all the Sunday parties we'd have together while they were at church, laughing and, oh, it makes no never mind, because I never saw him again."

A long sigh. Another painful wait.

"Next Sunday Vincent went for him, and he came back with the note. The influenza took him, along with half of south Jacksonville. I kept the note." She fishes around in her skinny bosom and comes up empty. "Never mind. We were so happy that one time, and now he's dead."

Dead, and Dell is dead empty. No ancestors left on his plate. He's just whoever the hell he really is.

She adds, "I'm sorry, dear."

Days wasted on his stupid search for affirmation. Documents, the missing will, if there ever was one, that's all he was looking for, anything that would locate him at this exact point in time and space for a real reason. Proof! "Me too."

He turns to go, but her voice nails his feet to the deck. "Please!"

"I." Manners kick in. "I'm sorry."

"Stop saying that!"

"I'm . . . I have to go."

"You can't leave now, son. I need."

"Really, Miss Ivy. I have to . . ." What? Get it together. Draft your to-do list. Pack. Shut up shop. Move on.

She's not exactly clawing at the air, but she is. She's that desperate. "I *need*!"

"Ma'am, do you need to go to the . . ." *Don't go there.* "Oh, you mean inside. Let's get you inside, it's too wet out here for a special lady like you." Yes he is wasted. Spent and wobbling in his tracks.

"I'm sorry," she says, as Dell turns the chair and opens the front doors and starts her down the long front hall, back into her crappy life. "I'm sorry, I'm sorry, I'm sorry."

Then Ivy turns the scooter smartly and faces him, and the light inside her switches on. Once again she is that bright, patrician figure on a medal, gleaming. "And when you're finished packing . . ."

Did I tell her? He doesn't think so. He turns politely. "Ma'am?"

"Come back for me. It isn't safe."

Wuow.

"I'll try." There's nothing left for him here. He needs to get down there and deep-six all his useless evidence. Destroy the index card and ditch the jacket. *They stiffed me.* What was he really wearing when he got hit? *That was never my coat.*

Then, why . . .

Ivy calls after him. "Promise!"

Split. Get out while you can. Leave or you'll get stuck in the mud, and that's not a metaphor.

There's no telling how much deeper it will get.

"Please!" Her voice curls about him and clings. "Don't leave me trapped in this terrible house!"

"Yes Ma'am."

$\mathcal{M}$ormama

Lord, did you not hear me pray? I have been praying ever since the first drop fell. Did I not pray hard enough or loud enough to be heard wherever You are? What do You want from me? So much wind, all that water, could You not lift this old ark off its foundations and release the poor souls still trapped within?

It rained so hard and for so long this time that I hoped! I thought, this time, oh Lord, this time.

Hurricane winds, days of rain sheeting down, rain that goes on and on, there is no end to it. There's water running in the streets, water overflowing the curbstones, rain drenching our sidewalks and creeping up to cover the lawn, it's the worst I've ever seen. Forgive me for presuming, I thought, Thank God, the flood.

Let the waters rip this tomb of iniquity off its moorings and carry Manette's house, our prison, out into the St. Johns River, let it rush us downstream to death; I thought God would crack this ark wide open, I saw it smashed to bits in the rapids, and I thought, Fine.

Then the current would carry the rest of my daughter's temple to possessions downstream and out to sea, and every soul still trapped in here would be freed. I thought the winds and waters would tear bits and pieces of my daughter's folly off our floating prison and I gave thanks to God. But it's still here.

I feel the house rocking on its foundation, I hear it groaning under the strain and yet, and yet . . .

Oh Lord, let the St. Johns River take us; let Manette's house smash against the jetty and rebound on every rock it strikes, let it lose planks and plaster and supporting members on its way downriver, let the storm blow all her windows to perdition, releasing all my daughter's lares and penates to the wind. Lord, scatter Little Manette's cherished objects on the ocean floor, send all her porcelains and furs and pretentious costumes flying willy-nilly as her shrine to avarice settles in the sand and breaks to pieces on the rocks, and let all the souls trapped within this house fly up to you.

Oh Lord, accept us. I begged you take me instead of him, but it was too late, and here we stayed, the soul of Teddy trapped in the earth below, I promised Teddy, Lord. We've waited for so long!

I have prayed for fire, flood, hurricane or lightning every day since he burned up. I prayed for invasion by Seminole Indians or hordes from all those heathen countries to converge on us and put an end to this, but the life in Manette's house goes on and on. I used to pray that an earthquake would shake her monument to greed off its foundations and smash her pretty ornaments to shards, and last night I had hopes.

Oh, I hoped. But the sun is rising and the rain has stopped. The storm is gone and the house that Little Manette Ellis demanded is intact, even to the front porch rockers, and we're still here.

When we lost Teddy I died a thousand deaths, and over time I have died a million more, because a part of him is still down there in the earth under the cement. By the time we got back from Ellis Park the screaming had stopped, but I could still smell the fire.

I know how it happened. It came into my head that very night. God brought me down the back stairs after midnight, long after the doctor came and the undertakers took what they could find of my darling boy. Nobody told me that it was the last possible moment, but I knew. In fact, Dakin and Vincent leveled the ground at six the next morning, and the workmen came in and poured cement at noon. He had his reasons, and I understand.

I went down underneath the kitchen porch to the laundry room and I knelt on the charred ground where my boy shrieked in agony and I cried and cried. Then I felt him. I didn't hear Teddy, I felt him, and I knew at once what this terrible day had been like for him, all but the last big. No! God spared me the pain. Or Teddy did.

He spared me the moment at which. At which! I can't bear to think of it. It wasn't a recital, there was no apparition. It was pure Teddy in my head.

Manette was testy that morning. She'd called Tillie and me to her boudoir, and I saw. She sat in her embroidered wing chair with Everett cradled on her lap and she snarled at me. Her little sweetheart had a cold. He was four years old! The older children scattered; they knew what she was like, but Teddy was a loving spaniel, curled up close to her feet, in hopes. My hardy, neglected boy wanted love, but with the toe of her beaded slipper, she nudged him aside.

"Hush. Evvie is feverish."

She handed off the smallest to Tillie and me and dispatched us on that idiot outing to the park, trilling, "When Nurse takes my girls out in the pony cart, people always say, I know you belong to Manette Ellis. I can tell by the eyes." Girls, because that was the picture she composed. Frilly white dresses and white kid sandals, pink silk bow ribbons in their hair. No boys.

If only I'd refused!

But my selfish daughter was balancing her needs on that Saturday when all the children who were old enough had gone out to play because even for the best-managed families, the schools were closed. Manette dispatched Ivy to the stables and Vincent came with the pony cart long before Tillie finished making the last of the twins' silly finger curls.

Teddy begged to go. Manette laughed. "They make pictures for the Metropolitan *on Saturdays, silly. No boys allowed!"*

The Sunday Metropolitan *included pictures of society's prettiest children photographed in Ellis Park, and she insisted that I go with Tillie, to make sure that the twins' curls and bow ribbons were perfect and they were properly posed. "And Mormama," she said, because* **she could not bring herself to call me Mother,** *"don't let him click the camera until they smile!"*

Only Teddy knows what happened after we left the house, and he let me know.

They were together in her boudoir, Manette and her cherished Everett along with dear Teddy, always so amiable and anxious to please. Then Everett gave a little cough— eh-ah, and she lifted him up like a baby prince and cried, "Oh my darling, you've caught a cold!" and Everett cuddled and whispered into her neck, "I don't feel so good," at which point my daughter saw poor Teddy stretching his arms up to her with such yearning that she cried, "Your brother is ill, Teddy, don't bother me!"

And Everett, whom God condemned to a long, unhappy life as a malingerer, whined, "Make him go away!"

And she did.

My sweet boy said something to his mother that it would break my heart to repeat. So loving. So hurt. So sad. He tugged at her skirt, "Oh, Mama. I just."

"Go out and play," she told him, although he knew it was forbidden, and when he hesitated, she lied. "Biggie will take care of you," she said, although Saturday was the day that Biggie boiled water for Manette's whites— her precious towels, her fine sheets.

"I can't." He swallowed his tears and tried to explain, but no words came out, just noise.

Then Little Manette shouted in a big, ugly voice, "Stop that, Theodore Ward Ellis. Just go." Then she added, almost as an afterthought, "Your brothers will play with you." This is how well Manette knew her sons.

The big boys were already halfway up May Street, running after the pony cart. When they caught up they stuck willow whips into the wheels, laughing at the noise they made smacking between the spokes, and I laughed with them all the way to the park. At the gates, Tillie threatened to whale the tar out of them and they turned back, but by that time Teddy was making his way downstairs and into the great parlor, excited by how wrong it was, and how good it felt.

It was wrong but it was wonderful. Three years old, and on his own! He was all alone in Mama's house, free to do as he wished. Manette would say it was all Dakin's fault because of the matches, but she'd never say it out loud. First she blamed Vincent, she blamed Biggie, after all, they were undependable by nature, the colored help. Then she blamed Teddy's big brothers for neglecting him, she advanced on the strength of her reproaches, her hideous Dies Irae: **It was all their fault.** After all, it couldn't possibly be hers.

In fact, Dakin was the only one in the house who smoked; men do, ladies would never think of it, and that day Dakin died a thousand deaths, although Manette never spoke of it. Cigars, he chose. Nasty cigars to make his point, and don't you think Manette's houseboy John liked his master insisting on that bowl of kitchen matches in the first-class parlor because he was too busy to go to the kitchen to get a light? Lord knows John knew better than to *leave matches within reach of the children, but when you get to be eighty, you just get tired. He did Manette's bidding until he started dropping things, and she let him go. He kept the kitchen matches in a tin on a shelf so high above the stove that no child could reach, but Dakin's silver matchbox lived in that cut-glass bowl on the pier table, and then . . .*

It was Saturday, and my little Teddy . . . Oh, dear God, my dear God, where were you that day?

I don't know what he stood on to reach the top of the pier table or how he got down without breaking the bowl, but he sneaked out the back door with Dakin's matches while John's back was turned, and by the time we came home the screaming had died and then . . . and then . . .

"No!"

What's that? The boy cries out in his sleep. "Oh, lady, you don't have to say it!" *As though the first Teddy inhabits him.*

Oh, yes. I do. You know full well that I do.

Dakin had them rake the spot and pour cement over it the very next day, as though anything could protect Teddy now. We stood down there with the servants, Dakin and I and his remaining children, everybody but Everett and, of course, Manette, to see it done. We stood and watched as the men edged the cement and scored it, and we had to stand there and wait for the cement to dry so nobody would try to carve initials into it, do you understand?

"Yes Ma'am."

Teddy is here among us. I know. In my grief I knew, and that night I knelt down on the ground and I made him a promise. I will take care of you.

"What?"

Take care of you, child.

Oh Teddy, oh child, I thought that when I died, I would lift you up and we could fly up to God's kingdom together, free at last, but that was more than a hundred years ago. I left my body a long time ago, but I'm still here. There are too many souls trapped here in Manette's monstrosity, along with scraps of my lost boy, the last bits of hair and bones and the soul of my poor, dear Teddy, sealed into the cement. All those years, and I must stay for as long as I am needed. No. For as long as this loathsome house still stands.

CHAPTER 44

$\mathcal{T}heo$

Mormama was all up in my face again last night, she dumped a shitload of words on me, like a stealth bomber zoomed down and trashed me in my sleep. It never stopped, she wouldn't go away, talk about death sitting on your face. I still don't know what it was about, but I think I yelled at her at the end and I know she barked at me. Whatever, old lady. I'm over you.

Plus, it's early as fuck, her barking woke me up. At least the rain is gone. Half past sunup and I'm bang awake, which totally sucks.

I'd rather sleep, because in my not-a-ship's-cabin in this dusty house that smells like death and mildew, this is how you keep your crap life from killing you.

I lie there halfway between sleep and real life, and I pretend that I'm anywhere better than this, like I'm in my bed back in our real house that the bank took, or I could be up in Atlantic City with Dad, I mean Barry.

As long as I stay in this half-life called *somewhere better,* he didn't leave us, it was government orders and he had to go. They sent him on a secret mission, he just came back from Special Ops and everything is fine and tomorrow I'll wake up back home in my own bed, just like before.

But I won't. It's the fucking crack of morning and I'm bang awake in their shitty old house, with my guts screeching and no way home.

OK, Mormama, did you really yell at me on purpose or did all that stuff come out of you accidentally, like vomit or shit? No idea what she was telling me, no idea what it meant, I just know that we're trapped, and she says . . .

She says we have to get out. Like, how?

Get up, stupid. Plan.

Gotta warn Mom. Help her pack up her stuff pronto, and make her hurry. Go ahead and tell her what Mormama said. She said get out of this fucking house before the Big Bad comes down, and do it fast, and if Mom thinks I'm crazy? Tough. We have to go. If we have to sleep in the car and live on rainwater and crap food out of machine cities in crap gas stations to make it, OK, fine.

It isn't safe.

"Damn straight!"

The house rocked and creaked all night and I twitched every time I heard another crash, all, *what's that?* It was probably shutters banging in the wind or junk flying around, but the worst part is, the rain stopped some time last night but the noise is still going on. Stuff cracking, like the foundation just heaved.

The storm moved on and the sun came up like it's supposed to, but I can hear their house shifting and groaning like an old, old person that got sick of carrying us and now its joints are so bad that it can't sit down.

Child, stop dithering!

"OK, OK!"

She's a fucking ghost, asshole, get a grip. Go downstairs and shove food in your mouth, you're not dead and everything is fine.

It's so early that I can probably snag a box of Pop-Tarts and the milk carton and get away clean before the aunts bushwhack me with fried Spam on oatmeal, or old Rosemary dishes up something even worse.

Take it out front and eat while you scope the terrain. Which shutters fell off. Whether any of the junk that the wind threw around last night landed on our car. Go on down to the street and pull it off before Mom sees it. Then go wake her up. Be cool about it, so she won't think you panicked. *Get up and get ready, Mom. We can't stay here.*

Weird.

The first part is easier than I thought. You know, grabbing food. No aunts on the main floor, not a sign of them, not even Aunt Ivy whimpering like she does on days when they forget. You can hear her through her bedroom door down here but you're not supposed to go in and check on her because she doesn't want you to see her like that, but if she was in there crying and I walked on past, I would just feel bad.

Today she's not anywhere, so, cool! Plus, there's an unopened box of raspberry Pop-Tarts sitting out here on the pantry counter, just asking for it. There's milk in the fridge, but, yuck. Sour. No water either, as it turns out, at least nothing you'd drink, just thick brown used-to-be water with gunk floating in it. Good thing this is our last day in this heap. So I'm thirsty, but it's OK. I do what you do when dumb things happen. I open a hundred-year-old can of pineapple slices and throw out everything but the juice and take the can and the carton out front.

So I'm cool, it's all cool, the house is still rocking like the wind never died but I'm cool with that until I open the front door. Everything looks OK, but it isn't. Flood water's mostly gone, nothing bad fell on our car but, holy crap, there's mud all over the street and mud filling up the gutters and creeping over the curb, and this isn't just an annoyance, it's more like a disaster.

Mom's hatchback is up to its fucking knees in mud.

Don't panic, Hale. Sit down and eat. Think. Shovels, you need to find out where they keep the shovels and if they don't have any, steal Mom's running-away money and buy them at that creepy corner store. Then get Dell out here to help us dig out the car.

If that sun comes up the rest of the way like it usually does, by the time we're done packing, it turns half that mud into dirt. Sun dries up a foot or more mud before we start to dig, and that makes it easier, right?

So, what if it takes all day? With three of us on it, we're cool. Yeah, I said three. Dell owes me. I left the damn note for him. He owes me, and he will damn well help us dig. Shit, we're his ride out of Jacksonville hell. There are suits on his tail. Those feds or whatever came around twice that I know of, and they'll be back as soon as the city's Zambonis or whatever vacuum the streets. That means, run. It's all in the note.

Plus, his father forgives him for that thing he did.

Whatever it is. I underlined that part in the note. Fuck yes he'll dig us out. Then he and I will throw our backs into it and push until Mom gets traction. Then we catch up with the car at the corner and jump in.

If he saw the note.

If he came back last night.

If he came back last night and saw the note.

Part of me wants to go down there right now and check on him but it's too early, and you can't just walk in on a guy like Dell. Piss him off and he flips the knife, which he did so fast that you don't even know if you're still friends. Last time it was just a warning.

At least I think it was.

This is bad.

Wait, Theobald, Theophane, Theophilus, Theodorus, Theodasshole, shit!

Chill. The dude didn't come back last night, why would he. Dell is not stupid. He would have waited it out in a warm, dry place. He'll get coffee before he heads home. Just sit here and wait. Your man Dell will be coming back from wherever soon. Give him a minute to go into his place and find that note. Then you can, like, wander down and knock because last time, you didn't, and that was your mistake. Your *big mistake*. Give him five minutes to read your note and forgive you. Then . . .

Wait!

What's that?

CRACK. Holy fuck! The trees! That whole row of trees at the far end of the porch, the tall ones that hide the truckers' parking lot? They're fucking shaking!

CRACK. The surface of the earth breaks. Shit, no way! Then, shit, shit!

The trees just, they just . . . *WHAM!*

Drop. Bang out of sight.

"Mom."

The whole freaking house shudders, but the noise coming out of the hole where those trees stood a minute ago? The sound that the mess of sliding rocks and gravel makes following the trees into deep nothing? Just. Stops.

Like God electrocuted us.

Except I'm not dead.

Run to the end of the porch, asshole.

Asshole, look.

I'm afraid to look.

CRACK!

"Mom!"

Everything on the far side of the driveway is gone.

"Mom!"

CHAPTER 45

Lane

A scream knifes through hours of work and anxiety. It penetrates my thin layer of bad sleep. *Theo!* It lodges in my heart, quivering, and I jump up.

"Theo!" *Is he all right?*

But I hear my boy shouting all the way up the front stairs, "*Mom*," on every step. "*Mom*," "*Mom*," "*Mom!*" He comes pounding along the hall, trailing words that I can't make out. We smash into each other and stand, shaking, shaking.

"T!" *Not dead. Not hurt, thank God.*

"Ow!"

"What's the matter?" I run my hands down his arms, testing. "Hold still!"

"Outside!"

"What is?"

"Everything, Mom. It's gone!"

"Theo, let go!"

But he throws his back into it, tugging me along. "I can't!"

He has me thudding down the front stairs behind him. On the bottom landing, I dig in. "I said, let go!"

Then my boy turns on me with a glare that I will never understand. He grabs my shoulders like a crazy person, all spit and fury.

"You don't get it. Half the planet is gone!"

He leaps the last two steps and runs outside. OK, kid, OK. I don't know what to be afraid of but I run after him, although from here, it doesn't look that bad. The front yard is trashed about the way it always is after a Florida storm, more or less situation normal, except for.

"Oh, shit. The car!"

"It isn't just the car."

Weeks of anxiety on no sleep, followed by this insane wakeup call, OK, I turn on him, screaming, "You woke me up for this?"

I don't know when it happened. My boy is taller than me. He stands over me, glaring, with his hinged jaw hanging like a furnace door. With both hands he turns me and points, roaring loud enough to wake up the world. "Not that, Mom. OVER THERE. Half the planet is gone!"

My God. My God!

Where there used to be a tall green line of Florida cypress trees rising between 553 and the cyclone fence, the tin shed and the truckers' parking lot next door, there's nothing. Correction. The trees are gone. The fence between us is gone. Half the parking lot next door is gone. The columns that support our old porte cochère are standing on the verge of a gaping hole.

On the far side of the rim, what remains of the trucking company's property lies on a gradual slant, which means that whatever chunk next falls off the earth will probably drop off the Ellis property, porte cochère, driveway, hedges, then . . .

How fast do these things move?

"What is it, Mom?" Theo is a live wire, borderline panicky.

Deep breath, Lane. Be matter-of-fact. "Sinkhole. Like on TV."

"Mom, Mom! What the fuck?"

Calm, lady. Calm. "Theo, you didn't get this in school?" Yeah, I overexplain. "See, this is at sea level. The whole state of Florida is layered. Layers of topsoil over a layer of dirt over a layer of I forget, oh, crap, they built a lot of Florida on fill, like, they dredged up . . ."

He grabs my arm. "Stop."

But I'm going all kindergarten teacher on him. "Anyway there's a limestone layer at the bottom, that holds everything else in place . . ." *Oh God.* "Look. Has anything else moved since it fell?"

"How the hell am I supposed to know!"

"Shh, honey, it's cool. You're cool, it's just." It takes all my strength to keep him in place. I use factoids to calm him down. "See, whenever it floods, which it does a lot around here, a little more of that limestone washes away, until . . ."

"Mom!"

Hang on, don't let him know how scared you are. "It's OK, These things don't happen overnight," I tell him, although sometimes they do. "You've seen it on TV, like that one that swallowed up all the cars? Lots of times these sinkholes take days to finish. It could even take weeks, nobody knows how fast this one will go."

"Mom, shut up. We have to get out." T. says the obvious. "We have to get *it* out."

And I don't get it. "What *it*? You mean the aunts?" The aunts I was supposed to love and never liked. Hateful Iris, in her wretched walking cast. Rose and Ivy. Ivy. "I suppose we do."

And my son turns on me. "Not them, asshole. The car! I'll get shovels." Then my boy surprises me. "And Dell."

The car is a lost cause, but I say, "Dell? How?"

"Not sure." T.'s face changes colors: ashen to red. "He might be in his place."

Play dumb. I know. I've always known. Before I can say, "Don't bother," he's on the run.

By the time I reach the back door he's halfway down the steps, yelling, "Emergency, emergency!"

Then, from the far right, I hear, "Tell the child not to bother."

"Ivy!"

She's down at the end of the back porch where naked sky replaced the line of trees, serenely watching the progress of the void. She turns to me, smiling. "His lovely friend isn't down there any more . . ."

"Shitshitshitshit": Theo, pounding back upstairs.

Ivy is sweet, so very sweet. "But he nicely rolled me out here before he went." That smile!

T.'s face does that thing that breaks my heart. "He took everything except my note."

I do what I can. "He'll be in touch."

Ivy lights up. "He will, he will!"

"Fuck no he won't."

She says kindly, "He will, dear. He hasn't gone far."

"Let's go back inside and get started," I say, trying to figure out what to do next.

All of a sudden my big boy looks smaller. "OK."

"It's cool, we'll be fine. Give me a hand with Aunt Ivy, OK?"

He's trying. He says, "Sure."

Then Ivy looks up at us with that smile that makes her so different from her dread sisters and says, "No thank you, I'm perfectly fine right where I am."

I look at her, at the no-trees, at the yawning earth where the property ends. Does she know what this is? Does she know what it means? I think she does know, sitting there with a mass of knotted scarves and ribbons and, I think, clothesline in her lap, cradled between her knees. "Are you sure?"

"Lovely morning, children," Ivy says, and it is, except for the yawning sinkhole. Is that thing bigger? I don't know. To be honest, I don't want to know but Ivy knows, I think, and for the first time since I came back to May Street, she looks perfectly happy. "I'll just wait for him here."

T. says darkly, "But he's gone."

"Why, no, Teddy. Your friend is right here." Ivy makes a beautiful smile. "He's upstairs in the attic, dear."

"OK, Theo. That's it. Let's do this." I buck him up the way his father would, all man-to-man, pulling him to my side because we are the corporation now. Mother and son against the world. Do what we have to do, and the rest will come later. *I love you, kid.* "Let's go."

But in the doorway, he turns on me. "I can't."

I grab his wrist before he can pull away. "Where do you think you're . . ."

He tugs, but I cling. We are up against it now. "Attic, OK?

"It's *not* OK."

Then he jerks free. My son Theo, in command. "You get your stuff. I'm getting Dell!"

CHAPTER 46

Dell

Crazy, but it's steamy up here: direct sunlight on the sodden roof, he supposes. Deep inside the attic at the top of the creaking house, Dell crouches in front of the heap of objects he rescued from the rising sludge in his hideout at ground level. He's here under orders. She. It? **I am a presence.** It said, **Put it back.**

He's been here all night.

Thinking, if you could call it that.

He won't need any of this stuff. He won't take Dakin's journal with him when he leaves this place because given what he knows now, it is useless to him. He'll put it here for her. He won't take his stolen laptop or any of the other items he wrapped so carefully and taped inside layered garbage bags to keep them safe. They're foreign objects now.

He neither needs nor wants the mysterious flash drive the so-called suits were so crazy to retrieve; they're just his father's tools, dispatched to collect his property, which his father thinks Dell is. He will spare the old man the most important item stored on that memory stick, which is not incriminating financial records that he pulled off the senior Calvin Leighton's hard drive before he wiped the machine. He was never Dell, he is Cal Leighton, in flight from that life.

Figures are nothing to him.

There is only the file that he stored at the last minute. Cal took it off the neat little tablet his sister Carla used to take everywhere with her. It's the heartbreaking document that she left for him, with instructions to mail a printout to their father's office, for reasons. He won't need the flash drive to retrieve Carla's last message to him.

He has it by heart. They were that close. It's Carla Leighton's testimony, unless it is her living will. She entered it the day she died, so he would know.

Carla was doing the only thing she could do, she wrote, knowing exactly what would happen next. She made this document for Cal because she loves him too much to let him blame himself. He loves his sister more, and this fragment is all there is of Carla Leighton left in the world.

Damn Theo for bringing the forgotten grief back to life. Mindless, carefree Dell Duval went out the window as soon as he read the note. Memory flattened him, and when he got up, his real self was back. That fucking note. Damn kid planted it in a spot that would arrest a gorilla in mid-charge. Damn the pushy red block letters and damn the blunt black lines underneath.

It was the first thing he saw, coming in. It sat there like a ticking bomb. The kid's careful list of particulars, numbered 1 to 4.

4. THEY SAID TELL HIM THAT HIS FATHER FORGIVES HIM.

And in that second his throat dried up and his belly trembled. Memory roared in on Cal Leighton like an express train, and it smashed him flat.

Before he left his father's house for good, Cal stored everything he needed on the flash drive he despised and could not lose. He made it for protection, he thinks, although at this point he forgets why. Finality, he thinks. So we both know that I'm never going back. The memory stick holds: details of all of Dad's transactions, numbers and passwords for the millions hidden in vaults in Geneva and Hong Kong, and the holdings stashed in a half-dozen offshore accounts. Before he fled his old life, the second Calvin Leighton . . .

My name is Cal Leighton.

Cal Leighton stored all the whos and the whats on Calvin Leighton LLC that, put together, would convict his father in any court in the universe. They're loaded on the USB stick he kept as insurance long after the hearings in the matter of the death of Carla Leighton were done, along with the document that reduced him to tears, composed to exonerate him.

What Carla wrote grieved him every day of his life until the taxi hit him and he forgot. Including the detail that caused such grief, even though she wrote it to guarantee that in spite of what she planned, her brother would walk free, and the forgetting? It was like a gift from God.

After the taxi hit him, the guy he was yesterday woke up happy and free from all anxieties, well, sort of. He woke up nameless and homeless, free, except for the card with this Florida address and the flash drive that couldn't possibly belong to him. That newly minted man, that bootless, carefree Dell Duval ran ahead of the guilt until last night, when he finally came home to his squat and found the note.

Four items numbered. The first three, he could handle. The kid's warning. The kid's needs. The suits.

This.

THEY SAID TELL HIM THAT HIS FATHER FORGIVES HIM.
WHATEVER.
T.H.

Calvin Austin Leighton, brother of Carla Leighton, the dying girl who left the world in an act that threatened his freedom. Yes. He got through that summer on denial, although a fool could have guessed, and his sister never let on. She knew she was dying long before she did what she did. At the hearing, the senior Calvin Leighton's high-end lawyers argued the case on his son's behalf, after which Cal took what he needed and walked out on the rest.

It was not assisted suicide, he tells himself now, although he knows. It was an accident. She couldn't have murdered herself. Doubt and guilt plagued him from that day until the speeding car plunged him into oblivion. It was hard, not knowing who he was, or what or why, but it was better that way.

Now here he is.

He knew Carla was sick when he left for Cambridge in January of the year he finished his MBA; she was too sick to come visit over spring break; she was too sick to come to his commencement that June, and Dad? Business abroad. The day he flew home with his Harvard diploma, Calvin Leighton sent his driver to meet his son at the plane; he'd cut Cal a check in honor of the occasion, but, Carla?

When he came home, she was waiting at the door. He was shocked by the change. Lovely Carla Leighton, diminished. His kid sister was gaunt and tremulous, thinner than he'd ever seen her, even during her anorectic phase. She was in a wheelchair but when he walked in she stood up and threw her arms wide. They hugged and she fell against him, hanging on because they both knew what would happen if he let go, she was that weak, but he had hope.

His joyful kid sister was ashen and trembling when he eased her back into her chair, but he hoped.

And his father? Never mind. Congratulations and nice to see you. Leaving for Switzerland. Business, you know. He said, "Good man, Cal. Good job."

He supposed it was. He had nothing to say.

Calvin Senior did. He said the usual. "You came home just in time. Now, take good care of your sister," he said, and he left for three months in Bern. Carla laughed just the way she did before the other surgeries, the radiation, all those doomed experimental therapies that kept hope alive. Cal fell silent. She kept her voice bright, "Don't worry, Dad. He will."

"Business," Calvin Senior said, and it usually was, although his son thinks it was the bastard's clean getaway. Well, the hell with him. Cal took Carla everywhere that summer: family camp in the Poconos in June, down to Sanibel, Florida in July for a month at the spa, as though the waters would cure fourth-stage ovarian cancer; to their summer cottage in Maine. Carla wanted to make this a summer of last good times, but Cal kept going on the only drug left in his arsenal: hope. In September, he'd drag her back to the Mayo Clinic; they'd find some way to fix her. They'd do something.

She wanted to see their favorite promontory at the top of the rocks on Mount Desert; it was hard, but Cal made it happen for her. On the overlook at the point, he set the brake and begged her not to get out of the chair; reluctantly, she acceded, and together they looked out on the world for a while, not talking, just letting it be. He steadied the chair with his hand on its back as the wind came up over the water.

"Oh Calvin, look!" Carla's hand lifted his eyes to a great blue heron, pointing as the bird took off and soared; Cal raised his right hand to the sky, following hers.

Together, they traced the bird's path and in that last second, at the peak of the heron's arc, his sister soared; wheelchair, lovely woman, everything in stasis in midair until she plunged to her death.

Of course he killed her. No. He set the brake on that thing. He did! Kill her? He couldn't have. No wonder he laughed when the cab sent him flying into the snow; he flew, just like Carla, and his heart lifted, *What a relief,* but he didn't die. Why couldn't he die?

Now he is up here on the steamy top floor of the Ellis sarcophagus, why? That urgent voice needled into him from somewhere in the belly of the house for— yes— it was for the second time last night. The same three words dropped into the dark. Woman's voice, he thinks, although he can't be certain; he will never be certain of anything, but he thinks he heard. **Give it back.** Dakin's testimony. Carla's? They will never have Carla's, but he brought the journal here.

Mysteriously, the objects and cartons around him are at a slight angle and beginning to slide; the contents of the attic are sliding, as though the house itself is crippled and walking cranksided, and, what?

New words come in, somebody, a woman, some woman, *old woman,* cries from the depths of the house. **Look Out.**

"What?"

The kid, that first day: *This house is under a curse.*

Look out, my darlings. You.

He shudders. *Mormama.*

Then the kid's shout rises from somewhere below. "Dell. Yo, Dell!"

"Mormama?"

Yes, you!

Kid's voice is closer now. "Yo, Dell!"

Look out for them.

"OK!" Released, Calvin shouts, "OK!"

As Theo opens the door at the bottom of the stairs.

Running, Cal finds himself bouncing off walls because every step down is on a slant. With Theo in tow, the freshly minted Calvin Leighton rushes to alert the others, and get them out of the

Ellis house. Together, they run to collect Lane and her belongings from Sister's room: laptop, printer, a small canvas bag.

As the three of them explode into the hall outside the big front room, a door to their left flies open, exposing the two old ladies camped out on the second-floor porch. *Those twins!* Don't alarm them, Leighton. Don't piss them off. "Ma'am, Ma'am!"

Lane says, "Get up. We're leaving!"

"Hurry." The house lurches. As the matched Adirondack chairs begin their slide across the slanting screen porch, Calvin shouts, "I'm trying to help you. The house is going down!"

Annoyed, the old women wave him off with identical snarls. *"Don't bother us."*

The sound as the layered mass of sand, shale, whatever the house sits on, crumbles and begins its slide into the void drowns out whatever he says next, but he thinks he can hear Mormama saying, **So much for them.**

By this time it's all Calvin can do to get his two charges down the slanting staircase and into the street before the driveway and the porte cochère drop off the façade on the side and go crashing into the void, and beginning tremors threaten the outer wall as the first clapboards snap. At the curb, Theo digs in his heels. "Wait!" He wants to watch.

Cal turns Theo with one hand, gripping his shoulder to hold him in place. He looks to Lane. They don't need to speak. He abandons the printer, Lane, her bag; they exchange nods. She starts across the street while he unwinds Theo's fingers from the laptop. They're only things. "Let's go." They move fast. Without looking back, he propels the kid through the muddy gutter and across the road to the relative safety of the walk on the far side of May Street where Lane waits on solid ground.

He plants Theo next to his mother. That smile!

Grinning, she pulls Theo to her. Planting him in front of her, she crosses her arms across his midsection, holding him in place while across the street, the earth has stopped sliding, at least for now.

"Mom, the car!"

She is radiant; *we survived.* She says, "Forget the car. Let's go."

Cal is poised, listening as bits of asphalt and stone drop into the pit. The house is listing now. Foundation's still sound, he thinks, but when that goes . . . Deep breath. Think. He asks. "Where?"

"Good question." They are together in this. She grins. "Just say when."

There is a crack as the ground supporting the porte cochère goes and driveway, pillars and all, drop into the void.

"Soon," he says, and it is a promise. The bank where the main house hangs could go any minute now. Still . . .

When he left her there, he set the brake. He's sure he did, he thinks, and he could not tell you whether he means his sister Carla or the old woman on the back porch.

Ivy. Those hopeful eyes. Deep breath. OK!

"I have one more thing to do."

One more thing, Calvin tells himself, calculating the building's rate of collapse. The film of mud on the street has more or less dried, and he kicks cakes of dirt aside as he heads back into the dying house and hurries through the long front hall, aware that he is running on a slant. Everything's on a slant. That back porch. If the rail holds, she's still safe, he tells himself, crashing through the kitchen and out the back door. Forget the chair. I'll carry her, and at some level he is wondering if this is what brought him here.

The underpinnings of the porch: the back steps, studs and beams and fragile lattice, pop and crack as they separate and fall away, but he reaches Ivy just in time.

Her arms fly up. "Oh, Randolph. You came back!"

"We have to hurry."

She is enraptured, singing. "I knew you'd come!"

"Look at you," he murmurs, studying the intricate knotwork

of scarves, sashes, clothesline and monofilament that Ivy made to hold herself in place, like a clever spider securing her position in the design.

She beams. "It wasn't hard."

"That's great, but we have to work on this," he tells her. Cal tugs on the knots, strongly aware that the foundation on their side of the house is crumbling as, block by block, bits of the house that has become Manette Robichaux Ellis drop into oblivion. Ivy's chair won't budge. The brakes are locked. Ivy's knots shrank until they froze. He shouts over the increasing racket, "When this is over, we'll have to get you a nice new chair."

Then Ivy shouts, loud enough to be heard over cascading rubble, "No!"

"Oh, lady." His heart rushes out.

But she already knows what Calvin, Dell, whoever he thought he was before this happened, is just discovering, as the porch floor pitches man, Ivy, mechanized chair against the rail. In their pain and confusion, they lock hands and she cries, "Oh please, Randolph. Don't leave me!"

"I won't, I promise. I love you and I'm sorry," he says to Carla, to Ivy, to the pretty, anxious girl waiting for him out there on the street and to her son, as the layer of earth beneath the house gives way in a tremendous explosion of the physical, and Little Manette's creation slides into oblivion. It will vanish seconds before the news trucks plow through the mud in front and the first helicopter circles overhead.

Lane locks Theo into her hug as Little Manette's failed mansion plunges into the void, wood and stone, plumbing and pretentious marble, all the designer's good things and cheap ones disassembled. Despite all her best efforts, the woman's legacy is lost to the world, along with all the envy and resentment, the hatred and the accidental follies of the repressed children she tried to train, and moved around like ornamental shrubs. All her silk wallpaper and draperies unfurl as the walls fly apart, disassembling what remained of Little Manette Ellis in this world. In seconds, her monstrous house dies, consigning all her gifts and purchases, her years of bribes and her warnings, the thousand fabrications of vanity and folly, to the earth. The evil that created this cries out from the depths as its brittle carapace smashes to bits.

Then it plunges, and all the souls trapped within it fly up.

ACKNOWLEDGMENTS

I was going to begin by thanking John Silbersack and David Hart-well for everything they did to bring *Mormama* as far as they have, but between the beginning and now, David exited the planet without giving us a chance to say goodbye. It's been fun, David. I'm sorry it was over so soon.

Special thanks to John for telling David, "say she's a national treasure," and to Jen Gunnels for pointing out that in its shaggy, slouching-toward-Bethlehem way, *Mormama* is "a woman's novel," all this well before David's unexpected departure. His last email to me ". . . but I've finished *Mormama* . . ." is time-stamped the Sunday night before he died. I mailed back, but I wish I'd said, "What do you think?" but I am way too polite.

We picked up the pieces in your absence, dude.

With astute readings from daughter and amazing first reader Kate Maruyama and Associate Editor Jennifer Gunnels, who is picking up the pieces for David's many orphans with grace and tremendous skill, *Mormama* shaped up, and I can't thank you enough. And as always, many thanks to Joe.

And Ko, Ko, the fucking candelabra made it into the book. Now it's a pair. I wonder if there actually used to be two.